[signature]

PHOENIX NOIR

EDITED BY PATRICK MILLIKIN

[signatures]

This collection is comprised of works of fiction. All names, characters, places, and incidents are the product of the authors' imaginations. Any resemblance to real events or persons, living or dead, is entirely coincidental.

Published by Akashic Books
©2009 Akashic Books

Series concept by Tim McLoughlin and Johnny Temple
Phoenix map by Sohrab Habibion

ISBN-13: 978-1-933354-85-9
Library of Congress Control Number: 2009922933
All rights reserved

Second printing

Akashic Books
PO Box 1456
New York, NY 10009
info@akashicbooks.com
www.akashicbooks.com

ALSO IN THE AKASHIC NOIR SERIES:

FORTHCOMING:

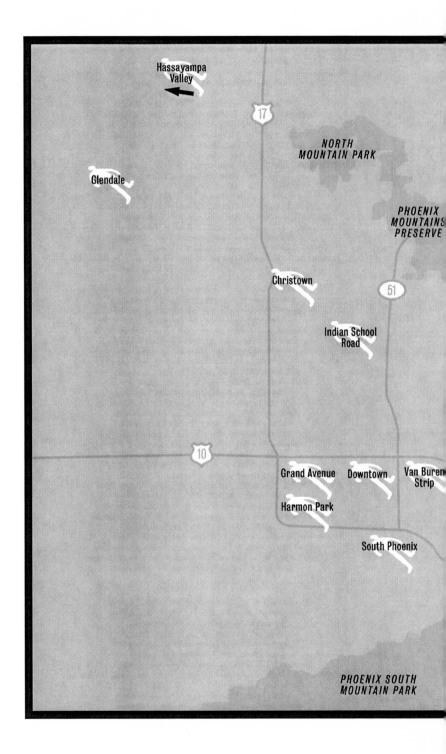

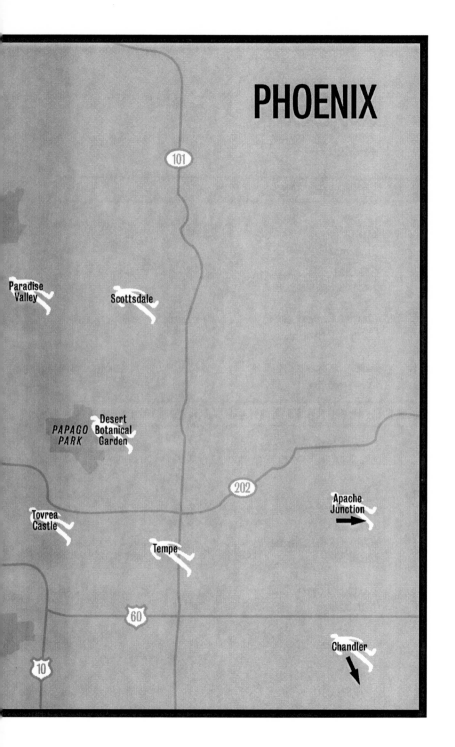

PHOENIX

101

Paradise Valley

Scottsdale

Desert Botanical Garden

PAPAGO PARK

202

Apache Junction

Tovrea Castle

Tempe

60

Chandler

10

TABLE OF CONTENTS

PART III: A TOWN WITHOUT PITY

PART IV: THE CRY OF THE CITY

INTRODUCTION
Sunshine Is the New Noir

P hoenix is a young city, even by Arizona standards. The desert metropolis, easily the largest in the Southwest today, wasn't established until 1867, much later than Tucson, Prescott, and other Arizona towns. As the legend goes, fortune-seeker and former Confederate soldier Jack Swilling noticed the ruins of the extensive Hohokam canal system while passing through the Salt River Valley and recognized the economic potential in getting the irrigation ditches up and running again. Centuries earlier, the Hohokam Indians had disappeared, no one really knows why, but the elaborate canal system they left behind provided the foundation upon which a new city would arise. Swilling battled alcoholism and opiate addiction and would later die in Yuma Territorial Prison under suspicion of highway robbery (he was posthumously cleared of the charge).

Although historians debate whether Swilling or fellow pioneer Darrell Duppa first named the town "Phoenix," the idea it evoked, a new civilization rising out of the ashes of a previous culture, is revealing. It implied new beginnings, a place where hard-working young families from the East could start over anew. Of course, it wasn't always such a great deal for the nearby Pima and Maricopa Indians.

Early boosters promoted Phoenix as a desert paradise, a lush resort town where health-seekers could enjoy the benefits of clean dry air and warm winter weather. The burgeoning city was quickly so infested with "lungers"—people suffering from tuberculosis and other respiratory ailments—that alarmed citizens pressured advertisers to downplay the palliative effects of the environment. Magazine ads from the '40s and '50s show squeaky clean white families enjoying the "relaxed pace" of desert living: children playing in the sunshine, Dad practicing his golf swing or sipping a highball by the swimming pool.

From the very beginning, Phoenix has always had a darker side. It is a city founded upon shady development deals, good ol' boy politics, police corruption, organized crime, and exploitation of natural resources. Close proximity to the Mexican border makes the city a natural destination spot for illegal trafficking of all kinds—narcotics, weapons, humans. These days, "America's Toughest Sheriff" Joe Arpaio routinely makes headlines for his vigilante-style hunting of illegal aliens and his casual disregard of human rights. And he keeps getting reelected.

Modern-day Phoenix is a textbook case of suburban sprawl gone unchecked. Endless cookie-cutter housing developments, slapped up on the cheap, metastasize outward into the desert, soaking up energy and water that we don't really have. All of that concrete and asphalt traps the heat, raising temperatures to apocalyptic extremes. During the summer, these "heat bubbles" can be lethal (during one record-breaking month in 2004, fourteen people died from heat exposure, most of them homeless).

The city recently overtook Philadelphia to become the fifth largest city in the country, and the Phoenix metro area now rivals Los Angeles County in size. As in all major cities, the gulf between Phoenix's haves and have-nots continues to widen with the steady decline of the middle class. The affluent northeast valley— Scottsdale, Paradise Valley, Carefree—has little in common with the sunburned working-class neighborhoods of South Phoenix and much of the west valley, though the developers are trying to change that with gentrification. The population of the city continues to grow and morph, but the legacy of the early ward system, in which much of the political representation resided in the wealthier— and whiter—first and second wards, lives on to this day.

What does all this mean? Crime, and lots of it. The stories collected in this anthology provide a revealing glimpse of a dark underbelly that the tourists rarely see. Novelist and veteran journalist Jon Talton provides a masterly portrayal of WWII-era Phoenix, back when The Deuce, our old skid row, was in its heyday and the city's corrupt power structure already firmly entrenched. Edgar Award–winning author Megan Abbott offers a stylish interpretation of the notorious Bob Crane murder, and brilliantly captures the mellow, sun-baked vibe of Scottsdale during the 1970s. Diana Gabaldon takes the lid off contemporary Scottsdale with a dark and sordid tale combining such disparate elements as squirrel genocide, an illegal orchid smuggling operation, and a murdered Welsh botanist. Investigative reporter Robert Anglen gives us a tour de force of noir depravity about a career loser from East Mesa who is forced to live his miserable life . . . backwards. Up-and-coming Phoenix scribe Kurt Reichenbaugh delivers the goods with a lean and nasty tale of betrayal along downtown's storied Grand Avenue. Longtime Phoenicians will dig Gary Phillips's contribution, in which L.A. detective Ivan Monk comes to town to investigate some loose ends surrounding the early-'70s murder of a local soul singer. The story was inspired by the real-life slaying of Arlester "Dyke" Christian of funk/R&B group Dyke and the Blazers, whose big hit "Funky Broadway" few realized was based on the main drag in South Phoenix. And then there's Navajo writer Laura Tohe's bad-ass riff on the femme fatale convention when her womanizing protagonist meets his match with a lady who just ain't human. This is but a sampling of the dark and diverse tales you'll find in *Phoenix Noir*.

I hope you enjoy this collection. The stories represent our city in all of its contradictory glory, the good and the bad, urban blight and stark natural beauty, everything jumbled together and served up smokin' hot, just the way we like it.

Patrick Millikin
Phoenix, AZ
July 2009

PART I

The Big Heat

BULL

BY JON TALTON

Downtown

Union Station

I should have been suspicious when Logan said it was a routine job. It wasn't that there were no routine jobs, only that Logan lied routinely. He was a short man with toad lips and a head that was bald and blotched except for a small tuft of dark hair just above his forehead. Always sitting behind his desk made him appear even shorter.

"Get out to Twenty-seventh Avenue, know where it is?"

He knew I did. I was one of the few people who had actually been born in Phoenix. I tamped out my Lucky Strike in the big ashtray on his desk. "It's just fields out there."

"Yeah, well, they found a foot at milepost 903."

That sounded pretty routine. People fell under trains and lost things. It had been a lot worse a few years ago, during the Depression, with all the bums and alkie stiffs.

"The Golden State will drop you off."

My suspicion made me light up another cigarette. "The Golden State Limited is going to slow down to let a bull get off two miles from here?"

He pulled the cigar from his mouth. A string of saliva kept it tethered to his fat lips.

"*Bull*. I hate that shit. You're a special agent for the Southern Pacific Railroad. Have some pride."

I took a drag and drew it down to my shoelaces. I walked to my desk, opened the drawer, and pulled out my Colt .45 automatic, taking my time about slipping on the shoulder holster and replacing the jacket.

"Go, you son of a bitch!" he hollered, spitting tiny tobacco leaves across the room. At the door, I heard his voice again: "And be on good behavior for a change. Got it?"

I got it, all right. I took the back stairs out of Union Station, avoiding the mob of young guys in uniform in the waiting room. I crossed the brickwork of the platform and made it to one of the dark green Pullmans on the Golden State just as the whistle screamed highball and the big wheels under the cars started moving. I flashed my badge at the conductor and he let me on, giving me a vinegar look. He didn't want to be slowing down for any damned bull. I let him brush past me and I stayed in the vestibule. It wouldn't be a long ride. The town passed by out the door. Over the red tile roof of the Spanish-style station, the Luhrs Tower marked downtown. If I turned the other way I could have seen the shacks and outhouses south of the tracks. Warehouses and freight cars gradually gave way to open track.

Five minutes later, I dropped off the train into the rocky ballast and found my footing. The air tasted like dust and locomotive oil. There wasn't much out here: the single main line that ran through the desert to Yuma and Los Angeles, a few Mexican houses, the Jewish cemetery. Then there were the fields, regimented rows of green with lettuce, cabbage, and alfalfa running out along the table-flat ground until it met the mountains and the sky. Stands of cottonwood bordered the irrigation canals where I used to swim on the oveny summer days. Now, in January, the air was dry and cool and familiar. I couldn't believe it was already 1943.

The town was changing. It had slept through the Depression like a kid in a fever dream, but the new war had brought Air Corps training bases, a new aluminum plant a ways from town, a camp for Kraut POWs, and endless streams of troop trains. Patton had trained his tank corps down by Hyder. The paper said Phoenix's population was now an unbelievable 65,000. Out here Van Buren petered down into a two-lane road, concreted over by the WPA. I could see somebody had gotten past the shortages and rationing to throw up some temporary housing a little north of the tracks, ratty little one-story jobs made of cinder blocks. They would probably tear it all down once the war ended.

I adjusted my hat and tie and walked toward the crowd a hundred yards back down the tracks. It didn't look good. Too many suits, and not the Hanny's special I had on, but nice ones, and men in them who were all looking at me. Fifty feet away, on the other side of the track, stood a new Lincoln and, outside it, four tough-looking guys carrying Thompsons. Just a routine job. Before I got far, Joe Fisher walked up, moving fast on his wide, thick legs.

"Bull, what's all the company about?" He nodded toward the men in suits.

"Beats me, but looks like Espee brass."

"Your problem," Fisher smirked. His face wasn't built for it. It was thick and immovable, the color and texture of adobe.

"Who are the ones with the Tommy guns?" I asked.

"I was going to ask you that."

Fisher was a Phoenix homicide dick, and he wasn't a bad guy when you compared him to his pals, one of whom awkwardly crossed the tracks and poked me in the chest.

"Jimmy Darrow." He spoke my name accusingly. "This ain't a railroad problem. Take a powder."

Frenchy Navarre's coat was open so you could see the two revolvers he carried in shoulder holsters. He wanted you to see them. He had a failed boxer's face and a killer's heart. I'd seen a lot of guys like him in the war, the Great War. My war. I pushed his hand away just slowly enough, tossed aside my cigarette, and walked past him.

More railroad honchos than I'd ever seen in little Phoenix, Arizona, surrounded me. The introductions were perfunctory: the general manager, a vice president, the head of the mechanical department, and the chief special agent. Names I had only seen on company stationery and timetables.

The chief special agent did most of the talking. "Darrow, you need to work with these local officers to get this cleared up, and I mean soon."

"Sure," I said. Best behavior. "Any dope you can give me on this?"

Heads shook adamantly.

"Son, we need you to double-check everything on this line, make sure it's shipshape." This was the basso of the general manager.

"Yes, sir." I stood awkwardly, waiting to be dismissed.

The chief drew me aside. He had the type of kindly face that I had grown to hate on sight.

"It's wintertime, see, and all the bosses are here for the nice weather," he said conspiratorially. "So they have nothing to do but go out and do our jobs for us, get it?"

"Sure."

In a louder voice, he said, "We need to make sure this line is secure. I want a report by tonight. Let's make it 8 p.m. Sharp. I'm at the Hotel Adams." I said my yessirs all over again. The chief took my arm. "Remember, serve in silence."

I waited for them to climb into a shiny black Caddy, then I lit a Lucky.

Another train trundled slowly by, the big grimy 2-8-0 locomotive making the ground shake. *Southern Pacific Lines*, proclaimed the tender. It must have had twenty cars, old Harriman coaches, faded black from smoke. Through the open windows, I saw the passengers. Black and brown faces in olive green. Colored troops. They looked with curiosity at our little party. The locomotive smoke sent me into coughs that made my lungs feel like they were on fire. For a moment, I bent over with my hands on my pants legs while my head stopped spinning. I felt better when I took a drag on my cigarette. After the train passed, I crossed over to where Fisher and Navarre had parked their Ford.

"Here it is," Fisher said, standing by the open trunk.

He pointed to an old citrus crate. *Big Town Oranges*, the label said. Inside I found a bulging, bloodstained towel. They let me unwrap it.

"You find it this way?"

"No, genius," Frenchy said. "We gotta save it. Evidence. You see that train, Fisher? More niggers than in Nigger Town and they're giving 'em guns." His small, dark eyes focused on me. "What the hell are you doing here, goddamned bull? Go roust some lowlifes down at the yards." He stalked off.

"It was found in the middle of the tracks, right back there." Fisher pointed to where the brass had been standing. "Cut off neat as can be. Mexican found it."

It had been a pretty foot once, pale, petite, with tiny well-shaped toes and the kind of ankle that gives men the shakes when it's attached to a live woman. It was held in a new strap-around black shoe, with a medium heel made of leather. And all had been sliced off at the shin. A railroad car will do that. This was no hobo.

"Where's the rest of her?"

Fisher spat into the dust. "Beats the hell out of me. We've been a mile up and down the tracks in either direction, looked in the ditches, nothing. There was blood on the tracks but no woman. Trail of blood didn't even go as far as the road." He pulled out a handkerchief and ran it over his forehead before replacing his fedora. "She musta been a looker."

The Westward Ho Hotel was the tallest building in Phoenix. It had sixteen stories and refrigeration. When I walked in a little after noon, the lobby was crowded with men in pricey suits and expensive cigar smoke. There wasn't a single uniform. You'd think the world was at peace and nice girls weren't getting their feet cut off by trains. Actually, I wasn't sure she was a nice girl, which was one reason I had come to the hotel. I crossed the lobby and told the elevator operator, an ancient colored man, to take me to the eighth floor. I walked down the hall past three doors on carpet so soft it massaged my feet through the soles of my shoes. I put my hat in my hand and knocked on the fourth door once.

Strawberry Sue might have struck you as the prettiest girl you'd ever seen, if you saw her from behind and the dress fit right—and maybe twenty years ago it would have been true from the front too. But the sun had ravaged her skin, leaving her face rough and cut with lines and creases. Her face looked like the desert. I thought her figure was nice, but it went out of style in the '20s. She was small, so thin I could almost touch my middle fingers if I wrapped my hands around her waist, and her hair was bright orange, worn unfashionably in a ponytail like the child of the ranch she was. Her real name was Ruby, but she hated it. The radio was talking about the big Allied landings in North Africa. I asked her to turn it off. She poured me a Scotch while I took off my shoes. As I sipped the drink, she pulled down her hair and took off my tie real slow.

Afterwards, we lay on the soft bed and I stroked her hair while she had her head in the notch where my neck met my shoulder. "My spot," she called it. She didn't seem to mind the scar there that looked exactly like the shape of the Grand Canyon. I had to smoke Chesterfields because that was what Sue smoked and I was out of my brand.

"You could fall asleep and get some rest, Stuck-On," she said. "I'd take care of you. You wouldn't have to be scared of nothing."

"I'm doing good, Sue." I let out a long blue plume of smoke and talked a little business.

"She doesn't sound like the kind of girl I associate with." Sue was like that, using big words, reading books, trying to better herself. I admired it.

"She looked like she could have been a high-end call girl, from what I saw of her. Nice shoe. Pale, nice skin."

"Why would she end up under a train?"

"Maybe she steamed up a certain friend of yours."

She made a small, indeterminate sound.

"He's done it before, when a girl crossed him," I said.

She stroked the hair on my chest with her small hands. "Don't talk about that now, Stuck-On . . . You know why I call you that?"

I knew why but just ran my hand against the softness of her red hair and tapped some ash in the direction of the ashtray.

"Cause I'm stuck on you, silly," she said. "Why don't you get a real job and we can run away?"

Instead of answering her, I climbed out of bed and walked to the window. It faced north and I studied the palm-lined streets below, where neat bungalows had crew-cut lawns. They gave way to citrus groves and fields, dairies and livestock, and finally the desert. Camelback Mountain was miles away but it looked like I could lean just a little out the window and touch it. Phoenix was an oasis. It was a shame, some of the people an oasis attracts.

"What about it, Sue?"

She lay there naked, her small arms wrapped around her smooth young-girl breasts. "I haven't heard anything, Stuck-On. Honest. I'd tell you. There's lots of new people in town. Maybe it was the Japs?"

I looked back out at the crisp blue sky. "Most of the Japs are gone, you know that. They sent 'em to the camps. Their land's just dying out there."

"Maybe it doesn't have anything to do with call girls, or him."

I used her fancy shower and felt better than I had in a month. Downstairs, I stopped at the smoke shop and nearly made it out the door. But he was fast for a fat man and suddenly his big saggy face was inches from mine.

"Well, Frank Darrow's son. How's Strawberry Sue this fine day?"

I moved back a step so I didn't have to smell his cologne. "I'm sure she's good."

He laughed, a disconcerting gurgling sound, and offered me a cigar. I shook my head. Duke Simms was in his fourth term as a

Phoenix city commissioner, but he wore suits and smoked cigars that didn't come with a municipal paycheck. I wished I'd never met him.

"Who are all these people?" I indicated the crowded lobby.

"Businessmen, entrepreneurs. You know what that word means?"

"Friends of yours?"

"Yes, indeed. This is a business-friendly city, Jimmy."

"Why the hell aren't they in the service?"

"Now, don't be that way. They're supplying the air bases, building our defense plants." His chest swelled and he ran his stubby fingers down his lapels. "This town is changing, son. You're not even going to recognize it."

I shook my head and tried to walk past him, but he blocked my way.

"Come outside, son," he drawled, "I was just thinking of you." He wrapped an arm around me and steered me out onto the sidewalk, far enough away from the door to give us some privacy. Simms wore a bright red tie and had a matching handkerchief in his coat pocket. An American flag sprouted from his lapel. "What's going on down at the Espee these days?"

"What do you want, Simms?"

"Such a blunt young man, and after having had a good time just now."

My fingers ached from making a fist.

"I need a little reciprocity," he went on. "Just a little shipment coming to the freight station tonight."

"Things are different," I said. "It's wartime."

The gurgling came again from the back of his throat. "Is that why I had to pay to bring in thirty new clean girls from Texas and Oklahoma? Wartime, yes, indeed. Now, son, we have an understanding."

"Tell me about a girl who had her foot cut off by a train west of town."

He ignored me and put his hand on my bad shoulder, digging his fingers in. I set my face so the pain wouldn't show. "Our understanding is you get to be entertained by Miss Sue complimentary, and you do some things for me. It's worked out well. And it's not as if Strawberry Sue is a spring chicken. Get it? If you went back on our deal, who knows . . . ?"

He released my shoulder and the sensation of knitting needles probing somebody else's flesh replaced the pain. I managed, "You're a son of a bitch."

"I am," he agreed. "But you have to live with certain disagreeable realities." He smiled through yellow teeth. "Here's what I need."

I rode a crowded streetcar back downtown, then waited for a long string of boxcars to be pulled along Jackson Street before I could walk the block to the depot. They told of faraway places: Baltimore and Ohio, New York Central, Pennsylvania, Frisco, Missouri Pacific, Burlington, Denver, and Rio Grande Western. Anywhere but here. The station sat at the end of the street, gracefully reigning over the surrounding hotels and warehouses. Mail and Railway Express Agency trucks crowded before the long building adjacent to the waiting room.

The Western Union sign hanging from one arch of the building was like a beacon for me. I wasn't sure what the hell the brass wanted me to do about the girl attached to the foot, but I could send wires to station agents east- and westbound from Phoenix. Had anyone reported a passenger who didn't arrive? Had any conductors noticed anything funny on their trains? Later, I'd take a car and check the rail yards, the Tovrea stockyards, Pacific Fruit Express icing docks, the bridge over the Salt River—make sure the line was secure, whatever the hell that meant. It didn't seem to have much connection with the severed foot. Logan was conveniently gone.

When I was finished, I walked back downstairs to the waiting room which was nearly deserted. Out on the tracks, a switch engine was moving baggage and mail cars, but the next passenger train wasn't due to depart until 4:30. The high ceiling of the room held a fog of cigarette smoke and dust, caught in the rays of the sunlight. Over by the newsstand, a couple of young GIs were horsing around, their uniforms new, their faces untouched by death. For just a second I saw myself in a magic mirror, May 1918, and my shoulder throbbed and everything in the world seemed broken. A bird colonel brushed past, glaring at me as if he expected to be saluted. The big wooden benches looked lonely. On one of them, a bum pretended to snooze under a sweat-stained Panama hat. One of the ticket agents watched me from under his eyeshade, then cocked his head as if he were trying to toss it as a shot put. From that direction, two women were coming my way.

"You're the railroad police?"

I said I was. The question came from a short, stooped old woman in a blue dress that was too light for the season, even in Phoenix. With her was a younger woman, blond, blue-eyed, fair-skinned, and pretty in a damaged way, like a china bowl that had been shattered but carefully glued back together, the cracks showing only on close examination.

"That man said you could help us. It's our Mary." The old woman stared at me as if I should understand, and somewhere something crawling in my gut winked at me.

"It's my sister Mary," the blonde said. "She was coming home from Los Angeles. She's been in school, you see, and she was coming home for a visit. She was supposed to be on the train last night. She sent us a telegram telling us to expect her."

The old woman grabbed my sleeve. "We've been here all night waiting!"

"She never showed?"

Two heads shook in unison, and I wondered if it could be that easy.

"Do you live here in town?"

"We live out a ways," the mother said, sticking her chin at me. "In Palmcroft."

I nodded: nice big houses by the new city park. She wanted to let me know money was involved. She didn't bother with anything so unsavory as introducing herself to me. I sat them down on a bench.

Fifteen minutes later, Joe Fisher and Frenchy Navarre walked in and heard the story for the second time. Mary Becker took a train out of Los Angeles, due to arrive in Phoenix just past 9. The girl was nineteen. The younger woman, Anna, did most of the talking, with the mother nodding. Becker. I knew the name. They owned big cotton farms west of town.

"She's a very sweet, innocent girl," Anna said. "I just can't bear to think that anything could have happened, that someone might have taken advantage of her."

"Wouldn't have been the first time," the old lady said.

"Mother!" Anna looked at the two cops, then me. "You have to help us." She reached in her handbag and passed us a photograph. It showed a pretty girl with curly dark hair and large, knowing eyes. She was standing on a pier, smiling at the photographer. "That's Mary."

Navarre took it and studied it, handed it to Fisher, who tucked it in his pocket. "Go up to the station house and make a missing person's report," Navarre said. "We'll see what we can do. But you gotta understand, it's wartime. Lot of people coming through, lot of people on the trains."

"Maybe she was just delayed," Fisher said softly.

The cops rose in unison and I followed. Navarre turned on his heel once we were through the front doors. "I can't believe you'd waste our time with this shit."

"I dunno, Frenchy. You have a missing girl and so do they. Maybe that's too complicated for you."

He pushed up his chest, showing the crossed shoulder holsters. "Don't think you're special because you're with the railroad, you cocksucker. Any time you want to find out, let me know." He strode angrily to the car.

"Show them the shoe, Joe. That'll settle it, one way or another."

Fisher looked at me sadly and said, "He thinks he's got a lead. What're you gonna do?" He handed me the snapshot.

I went back in and sat down with Anna and her mother. The benches were starting to fill up for the afternoon Santa Fe train.

"Anybody in Los Angeles you can call? Any friends of Mary's?"

"She lived with three other girls in a very nice apartment," Anna said. "We talked to them long distance this morning. They drove her to the depot and saw her get on the train."

I asked why she was coming home. The old lady's face had hardened into a sullen mask while Anna and the cops had talked. Now she looked at me fiercely. "That's none of your concern. My daughter is missing from one of your trains. That should be your concern."

Anna touched my arm. "Mother is very tired. Mary was coming home on family business. It's nothing."

I found myself studying the blonde's ankles. She probably thought I was just being fresh. They were nice ankles, naked thanks to the nylon shortage. I pulled out my smokes and offered them. Anna took one and I studied her face while I lit her cigarette. It looked like a face that might tell me things if the mother wasn't there. Then I asked her what her sister might have been wearing on her trip home.

After I left them, I made a few checks with the dispatcher. He was already in a bad mood. Extra engineers and firemen had been called in and he didn't know why. The section foreman had been out all day on the line. "Nobody gives me the word," he mumbled. After a few minutes of commiseration, he told me that the train Mary Becker boarded in Los Angeles had arrived on time the night before. It had been divided into three crowded sections, the last one coming in shortly after 10. It stayed fifteen minutes then departed for Tempe, Mesa, Tucson, El Paso, and points east. Next I went to the baggage room through the double doors just beyond the ticket counter. Anna had described Mary's luggage: a matching suitcase and overnight bag, burnt-yellow and streamlined, with three brown stripes. The baggage men let me be: they were loading carts for the Santa Fe. It only took a few minutes of prowling to find the set. It looked almost new and the tag said, M. *Becker*, with an address in Los Angeles. I told the head baggage man to set them aside and headed back to the waiting room.

The women were gone.

It would have to wait. I needed to check the line and report to the chief at 8 o'clock "sharp." I pushed through the front doors and heard a woman yell. She sounded a lot like Anna Becker. Looking around an archway, I spotted her with a man, standing beside a roadster with the top down. The car glistened red in the afternoon sun. So did Anna's golden hair. She was in an agitated conversation with the man, chopping the air with her hands. Twice I made out the name Mary, said with urgency. They couldn't see me. The thick pillars and archways of the station portico concealed me. Anna moved enough that I could take him in: dark hair in a crooner's hairstyle, a kid's face but the muscular body of a twenty-five-year-old. He was wearing a leather jacket and driving gloves. I didn't see many able-bodied men his age around, and I wondered how he'd bugged out of the draft. He didn't look like 4-F material, but you couldn't tell. He sneered at something Anna said and she screamed, "How could you! What kind of man are you?" That's when he hit her, so hard that the sound echoed in the portico.

That was enough. I knew what kind of man he was. But when I stepped out, the car was already speeding up Fourth Avenue, Anna's blond hair fluffing out in the wind. I tapped the roof of a taxi and got in. In only seconds the cabbie had caught up. They paused at the light at Jefferson, then turned right. I didn't know what I was doing. At that moment, I would have showed the kid in the leather jacket what it was like to be hit by somebody his own size. By the time we reached Second Street, however, I had hold of myself again. They turned south and parked. I sent the cab half a block past, paid him, and got out.

We were a long way from Palmcroft. The sidewalk was filthy and broken. The buildings were seedy single-story affairs with fading paint and dark entrances, broken up by seedier three- and four-story hotels. It was the heart of the Deuce, where the bars, brothels, hock shops, and flop houses intersected with the remains of Chinatown and the busy produce warehouses. It had enough to interest soldiers on liberty, Indians, old cowboys without pensions, off-duty farmers, miners, and railroad men. The street was crowded, so Anna and the kid didn't notice me. He walked around to the passenger side, opened the door, and yanked her arm sharply. She came out of the car flashing a pale leg up to her thigh. Then they disappeared into a doorway. I didn't need to walk close to see where they'd gone. It was a bar I knew well, the Phone Booth, and it was sure as hell a long way from Palmcroft. A cop walked by twirling his billy, a reminder that I could mind my own business, the railroad business I got paid for. I lit a cigarette and leaned against a brick wall, covering up the Pepsodent ad, hating some of the things I knew. One was that the Phone Booth was quietly owned by Duke Simms, and that he used a private room in the back for special meetings. I hated knowing about those too. Even with 65,000 people, Phoenix was still a very small town.

I walked out of the Hotel Adams at 8:15. A dry chill was drifting in from the desert and the sidewalks were jammed with soldiers and airmen in town on liberty. I was wearing a fresh shirt and tie, and the chief special agent seemed pleased with my report. To me, there didn't seem much to it. I had checked the line through town, run some bums out from under the Tempe bridge, and looked over the blocks of boxcars down at the SP yard, searching for broken seals on the doors or other signs of pilferage. I had left word for Joe Fisher where he would find Mary Becker's luggage. I carried my own kind of bag and it was full of questions, maybe even a little kit of suspicions inside. Who was the punk who had slapped Anna, and why had she been so upset? She had yelled at him and said the name of her sister. And she had ended up at a place nice girls shouldn't even know existed in this town. Now all I could do was buy an evening paper and read it as I walked vaguely in the direction of the depot.

I was about to cross Jefferson Street when a car nearly ran me down. I jumped back and recognized the familiar black Ford. I followed it into the driveway by police headquarters. It was full dark, but the streetlights showed Frenchy Navarre getting out of the backseat, then pulling out another man. The handcuffs on the man's wrists glistened under the light. He was a kid really, a colored kid in fatigues, and his head and body slumped against the car. Navarre leaned in close and was talking to him. When the kid's head came up, I could see a bloody membrane where his lower jaw should have been. Then Fisher came around from the driver's side and they led him into the station. I let them get inside, and followed.

Navarre had the kid at the booking desk when he looked around and saw me. "Get lost, bull." He momentarily turned back to his prisoner to punch him in the kidney. The boy crumpled in agony. Navarre's hand looked odd, but then I saw it, a seven-inch blackjack protruding, and it had fresh blood on it.

"Here's your murderer," Navarre said. "Nigger playing soldier, really trying to rape a white woman."

"No, sir, I swear I didn't . . . don't know nothing 'bout this," the boy pleaded with me, slurring his words through his ruined mouth. He spat a bloody tooth to the floor.

"Well, how you explain this, nigger?" Navarre held out an ankle bracelet. It had dried blood on it. "Tried to pawn it after you raped that girl and put her on the train tracks."

"No, no . . ."

"Wasn't too smart coming into Phoenix, was it, boy? We make our niggers behave, keep 'em south of the tracks. So the government gives you a uniform, gives you a gun, makes you think you're special. You're just a black nigger, you murderous son of a bitch."

"Gotta call my commanding officer," the kid said.

"Shut up!" Navarre roared, his eyes bright and primal like an animal's.

I tried to catch Fisher's eye. This seemed all wrong. Anna Becker had mentioned nothing about an ankle bracelet.

"Did you find the body?" I asked.

Navarre brandished the blackjack toward me. "We don't need anything more than what we got to send this nigger to the gas chamber. Now get the hell out, bull."

With that he advanced on me in three fast strides, raising the sap with one hand and reaching inside his coat with the other. I took a step backward and I was faster. He had a .38 Police Positive in his left hand, but it was frozen uselessly in mid-air. My Colt .45 was five inches from his broad, veiny, ugly nose. His eyes were obsidian, dead.

"Kill him!" Navarre commanded, but his voice shook.

Nobody moved. Nobody spoke.

"I'll kill *you*, Darrow!"

But his arm remained where it had been, the pistol pointed out into the room.

I aimed, staring at him down the heavy barrel of the automatic. "You like to hurt people . . . you like it . . ." Those were all the words that would come out.

Then I felt Joe Fisher next to me and the spell broke. "Let it go, Jimmy." A stocky desk sergeant pushed Navarre away and I holstered the Colt.

"James, you're walking like an old man. That's not right."

I turned to see Mose, resplendent in his immaculate sleeping-car porter uniform. We stood at trackside, and it was oddly quiet. The usual call of train whistles was silent. My eyes roved over the station tracks and saw spikes and blocks of wood driven into the switches that connected the array of tracks to the main line. Alarm shot through me: *Secure the line.*

"Why are the tracks spiked? No train can switch off the main line."

"You're gonna see, boy," Mose said, his teeth huge and white.

"What are you doing here anyway, Mose? You should have departed an hour ago. Nothing seems to be moving."

He gave his deep, melodious laugh. "Some things moving. The pilot train came through twenty minutes ago, right on schedule."

"What the hell are you talking about?"

Mose clapped me fondly on my good shoulder. "Son, you would be the only person on the Espee who don't know."

I was going to protest more but a thick, sharp whistle echoed through the dry air. I leaned over and could see a headlight in the distance. I pulled out my nearly empty pack of Luckies, offered one to Mose, and lit them both.

"I've got to go to the freight station, do Simms's dirty work."

Mose stared toward the black masses of the South Mountains. "You got your reasons, son."

Now the train was close enough that I could hear the engineer start to sound the bell.

"There's no goddamned justice in this town." I said it in a conversational voice, to no one in particular, drowned out by the locomotive's approach.

"You just finding that out?" Mose shook his head and laughed. "Oh, Jimmy, you a piece of work."

Then the train was on us, passing quickly. It was double-headed, with two powerful steam locomotives. Then a pair of baggage cars rolled by, one with an odd set of antennae on top, followed by a pair of sleepers. The last car rumbled heavily. It had new dark

green paint that glowed under the platform lights and fresh lettering on the side said, *PULLMAN*, but unlike every other car it
had no number. The shades were down. Yet the rear window had
light, and there . . . right there inside. The familiar patrician head,
the jaunty jut to the chin, even the cigarette holder in his mouth,
just like in the newsreels. He looked at us. Mose stiffly saluted.

Then the train was gone. Nothing was left but the red marker
on the last car, which quickly went around the slight curve and
continued east.

Mose put his arm around me. "On his way home from a tour
of bases on the coast, and the Espee handled it all the way," he
said proudly. "See, boy, happy days are here again."

I walked toward the freight station and the song was in my
head. But my head played it too slow, like a dirge.

THE EIGHTH DEADLY SIN
BY CHARLES KELLY

Hassayampa Valley

Father Carty O'Toole could see the hard-knocked Dodge pickup beating down on him from a half-mile away, dust huffing from its tires and settling on the mesquite, a tiny torpedo tracing the western edge of the White Tank Mountains. Walberto must have the goods today. Sweat clutched at O'Toole's crotch beneath his black robes, his heart bounced. The buzzing of the cicadas in the crazy heat tweaked his nerves. He had a Colt .357 Python stuffed full of potential detonations hidden in the confessional. Fine. But the varnish smell of the sin-box was cut through by the stringency of Hoppe's No. 6 gunpowder solvent, and that could give away O'Toole's play. He steadied himself, fought for faith. Surely, God would not let that happen, assuming God wasn't taking a day off. That happened from time to time in the Hassayampa Valley.

O'Toole stood well back in the shadow of the vestibule of Mission Santa Dolores, taking what comfort he could from the relative coolness offered by the packed-earth walls. Built in the 1920s, a replica of older and more-honored antiquities, the church had been long abandoned, replaced by a modern church twenty miles away with the soaring lines of a department store. The mission was too old and shabby and isolated to serve the spiritual needs of the population oozing westward from Phoenix, but O'Toole had not let it languish. Carrying out a bit of personal penance, he had set himself the task of dusting and polishing the pews, swabbing down the tile, cleaning the plaster angels and cherubs that festooned the reredos behind the altar. In this heat, it had been exacting work for a fat man pushing sixty. But the police were so bothersome in this part of the world. Better to stay out of their way.

He'd had to break the lock on the door to get in, but of course that was no problem for him. He'd been at the cleaning for a week, while he waited. It gave him a cover story if someone came by, but nobody did. And aside from the psychic payback it offered him, it was something to do. There was no television or even a radio in the abandoned priests' quarters out back, his comestible needs and water supplied by a Coleman camp refrigerator, his literary cravings fulfilled by some dusty paperbacks replete with the adventures of hard-nosed men and abandoned women. A small electric generator fed the battery that kept his cell phone alive.

The truck was closer now, growing larger, a Dodge Ram driven with more enthusiasm than sense—that was Walberto's way. Slipping through thirsty desert scrub and sandy dirt, it looked shallow and indistinct. Twenty-five yards away, the snarling of its engine snapped off. It clanked and stopped near a paloverde on the perimeter of the dirt-track turnaround. Was there a passenger? Hard to tell because of the dazzling brightness. Apparently not, for only Walberto emerged, closing the door with a *thunk*.

His hands were empty, no package. Disappointed, O'Toole examined the rest of him. A black ball cap, a Dallas Cowboys warm-up jacket over a white T-shirt, jeans, cowboy boots tooled in Texas. O'Toole didn't like the warm-up jacket, not one bit. In this heat, it must feel like a microwave on full power. He examined Walberto's bony outline, but the jacket flapped loosely, showing nothing. Walberto darted forward, swift without effort, merging with the darkness of the vestibule.

"You're hiding, Father," Walberto said, smiling into the shadow as his eyes adjusted, his mouth slashed across by gapped teeth.

"It's the heat," O'Toole said.

"The heat, of course." He fell silent, making O'Toole ask.

"Did you bring it?" He glanced over Walberto's shoulder at the pickup. Was there someone else?

"Sure," said Walberto, stepping in front of O'Toole to cut off his view. "It's in my pocket."

O'Toole scanned the outline of the jacket. Those pockets seemed quite small. Without taking his eyes off Walberto, he jerked his head toward the darkness beyond them.

"Come in," he said. "Let's go deeper into the church."

"Sure," Walberto said. He moved closer, so his whisper would carry. "I had to kill the man."

O'Toole's heart went cold, and he cursed his own greed. This is what his self-imposed mission to the illegal migrants had come to. As if he hadn't known it all along. Two months ago, he'd been at loose ends in Buffalo. No parish for him, nothing he could sneak into at any rate, even with the Catholic Church in America desperate for priests. Then he got a call from an old friend in Arizona. Opportunities existed. Migrants being held in safe houses in Phoenix—indeed, all over the Valley of the Sun—needed to hear the word of the Lord. The smugglers liked the idea—a dose of religion helped the migrants accept the rotten conditions—and the money for a bit of spiritual soothing was good, very good. The smugglers' money, Walberto's money.

O'Toole swallowed, but couldn't lubricate his throat. His voice was a dry wheeze. "Let's go deeper into the church."

The black-robed man turned, and his feet clattered on the tile. He listened for Walberto's feet. At first O'Toole heard nothing, and the sweat on his forehead gathered and flowed. His knees almost buckled, but he kept moving. Then he heard the tick-tock of the cowboy boots, and regained his movement. It's all about appearances, he thought. Act strong, be strong. And get to the Python.

O'Toole was making for the shadowy alcove just short of the altar. That was where the confessional reared up, encompassing two upright boxes—one for the sinner, one for the dispenser of penance. But Walberto's voice, very quiet, stopped him.

"Let's talk here," the coyote said. "I don't like to get too far from the daylight."

O'Toole turned, and Walberto waved to one of the splintered pews. Trying to think of a reason not to, O'Toole shuffled to a seat and settled down. He half-turned as Walberto slipped into the pew behind him, but the coyote put a firm hand on his shoulder and waggled his head. "Face front, Father. Kneel. Act like you're praying. I'll do the same. I'll do my best, but you'll probably be better than me. You've had more practice."

O'Toole complied, clacking the kneeler down and settling heavily into place, though it was a pointless charade. The likelihood of anyone coming to this abandoned place, anyone who needed to be fooled, was quite remote. He was acutely aware of Walberto kneeling just behind him, like a Mafia assassin in the rear seat of a car. O'Toole knew that situation. The man in front had to pretend everything was all right, or the bullet would come quicker. But in facing front, the target had to fight the panic of not knowing. The muscles in O'Toole's neck bunched. I'm getting a headache, he thought. Why? Will that help me survive? The stupidity of his bodily reactions confounded him.

Walberto's breath poisoned the air. "Tell me the story again."

O'Toole was incredulous. "You mean the story about the relic?"

"Umm-hmm. The relic. The reason I killed the man."

Wonderful. Story time, as they both sat in the shadow of the gallows. Or was it the shadow of the lethal-injection gurney? Who cared? The result was the same: O'Toole on a slab. He found his voice, heard himself wheedling: "You were to pay him a little, promise him more when we did the deal."

"He didn't believe me, he thought I was going to stab him. He was right."

O'Toole's breakfast—a stale ham sandwich—rose dangerously. "That wasn't necessary."

"Sure it was. Tell me the story."

And O'Toole did, just as he had told it to strengthen the faith of migrants stashed away in Buckeye, Phoenix, Glendale, even Scottsdale, eating take-out sandwiches, drowsing with the curtains drawn, waiting for the next stage of their journeys. They thought it emerged from deep theological study O'Toole had pursued in shadowed monasteries. In fact, he'd done most of his research online.

The True Cross, the Cross of Golgotha, on which Christ was nailed, disappeared for centuries after the Crucifixion. In AD 326, it was discovered by the mother of Constantine I, the Empress Helena, on a journey to Israel. In a place adjoining the tomb where Christ was buried, she found three ancient crosses in a cavern. A sick woman, placed on one of them, rallied.

"It restores health, then," Walberto breathed with satisfaction.

"So it is said," O'Toole agreed, and continued.

The True Cross was kept in the Church of the Holy Sepulchre in Jerusalem until the year 614, when it was taken in a Persian raid. It became a prize in the wars between the Romans and Muslims, changing hands often. Still held by Muslims at the time of the Third Crusade, it disappeared. But bits of the cross that had come off were collected and returned to Europe. Some fragments were enclosed in altars, some placed in tiny golden reliquaries. But some had surfaced even earlier and were considered special for their size and mystic powers.

"Any relic larger than a toothpick is quite potent," said O'Toole.

"And one as long as five or six inches . . ." Walberto whispered, like a child who knows a story by heart.

O'Toole completed the thought, ". . . would be a stunning find."

Walberto remained entranced. He said, "Radegunda, Queen of the Franks, obtained from the Emperor Justin II, in 569, a remarkable relic of the True Cross."

O'Toole was amazed. It was almost the exact wording of the

Catholic Encyclopedia, a volume from which O'Toole could quote extensively, and had quoted to Walberto. The coyote, whose typical reading consisted of the ingredients lists from the backs of Campbell Soup cans, had remembered.

"Yes," said O'Toole. "This was one of the relics catalogued in 1870 by the Parisian scholar Rohault de Fleury in his masterly *Mémoire sur les instruments de la Passion.*"

Walberto tapped impatiently on the pew in front of him, his massive signet ring making a sound like a door-rapper. "And how did it get here, all the way from France, after all that time?"

"The provenance shows that," rejoined O'Toole. "Stolen in France, carried to the new world, treasured for centuries in a monastery high in the Sierra Obscura in northern Mexico, then spirited away fifty years ago to the mission in Magadalena, then . . ."

". . . brought to Phoenix two weeks ago by Jorge Canto, a muralist in that mission . . ."

". . . to pay his passage across the border."

"Jorge Canto, who now lies dead of seven wounds in his chest and back on a bed in Room 23 of the Painted Robin Motel in Buckeye," Walberto concluded with some relish. "A crucifix on his forehead." O'Toole could hear him tapping his head, as if trying to spring loose a thought. "What's that prov thing?"

"Provenance," said O'Toole. "The papers you stole from Canto last week and gave to me. That's why I told you to get the relic. They prove it's authentic."

"Oh, sure."

O'Toole was put off. "You don't believe it?"

"Faith is very hard, Father. You know that."

"Yes."

"A man is easily tempted. You've heard of the seven deadly sins?"

O'Toole felt a surge of annoyance. Was this Dallas Cowboys fan really trying to instruct him on matters of faith?

"Yes," said O'Toole. "The seven deadly sins—lust, gluttony, greed, sloth, anger, envy, and pride."

"Sure," said Walberto. "*Luxuria, gula, avaritia, acedia, ira, invidia,* and *superbia*. In Colombia, the priest taught us in Latin."

Jesus, this was too much.

"I know Latin," O'Toole said heavily.

"Of course. But do you know there is an eighth deadly sin?"

O'Toole sighed.

Walberto's laugh crackled. "The eighth deadly sin is overconfidence. I don't know how to say it in Latin."

Touché. It occurred to O'Toole that "Walberto" was a name of Germanic origin, meaning "one who remains in power." The coyote had the upper hand now, and O'Toole had to get it back. "I can market the relic," O'Toole said. "I have a buyer. I told you that. In San Francisco. One hundred thousand dollars."

He half-turned to see if Walberto was now holding a weapon, but the coyote's hands were empty, and he waved O'Toole back to the front. "One hundred thousand dollars," said Walberto. "No, I think it's worth more now. Here, see what you think. Don't turn around again, just put your right hand out to the side, palm up."

O'Toole did so, and felt a hard scrap thrust into his grip. His pulse hammering, he brought it up before his eyes. A sliver of pine wood, seven inches long at least, calcified by age. He could see places where other slivers had been torn away, and he looked back through the centuries, thinking of the remnant being passed from hand to hand, hidden under cloaks, enclosed in velvet and leather cases, being spilled rudely on a carpet by burglars, slipped into pockets foul with tobacco, held reverently up to the light of forgotten dawns, always on the move, its destiny to wind up here, in his hand.

Walberto's voice was urgent. "Put your finger in the blood."

There was a crusty black splotch—not large—near one tip of the large splinter. O'Toole tried it with a thumb, and the surface broke and wept red. Hastily, he wiped his thumb on his robe, his heart beating faster.

"The blood of Jorge Canto," intoned Walberto, "shed by us for the forgiveness of sins. And, I think, for two hundred thousand dollars minimum."

O'Toole turned the remnant over to hide the red spot, and noted older, darker stains on the wood. He thought of Christ's hands, torn by the nails, and the spear that had slashed into his side, bringing forth blood and water. Could the blood of Golgotha really have survived all these centuries, locked in the fibers of the wood? His faith urged him toward that conclusion, but Walberto had a different interpretation.

"You're beginning to see it now, aren't you, Father? Plenty of dudes like Jorge have died for that relic. That's what makes it valuable. The price went way up the second I slipped that knife through his ribs."

The coyote paused, and O'Toole could not bring himself to reply. He felt a crawling sensation between his shoulder blades, and envisioned Walberto's knife blade, plunging again and again through skin, scraping bone, exploding blood vessels, releasing scarlet geysers of life-juice. Silence fell as they knelt there in the sweaty heat, with the shadows of the church smothering them. Then, somewhere outside the church, O'Toole heard a light scraping sound.

"Shit!" whispered Walberto. "There's somebody out there. Let's take this into the sin-box. We don't want to be seen together."

A happenstance visitor? O'Toole didn't believe it. He hadn't heard a vehicle engine since Walberto had pulled up, and even the sound of moving feet—some hiker extending his distance over desolate territory—would have reached them in the dead quiet within the church walls. Most likely it was a wild dog or an actual coyote, some beast that could have made the approach without attracting notice.

"All right," O'Toole whispered back. He rose quickly, his big legs twitching, and started for the priest's side of the confessional.

Walberto took his arm. "Let me go in that side," the smuggler whispered, grinning. "I always wanted to try out that priest's seat. Besides, maybe you have a sin to confess."

O'Toole felt tightness in his throat. His mind blanked. Dumbly, he nodded, thinking desperately about favorable possibilities. The pistol might not be easy to see. Out of caution, he had tilted a missal up against it when he'd placed it on the small shelf next to the priest's seat.

He made his way to the penitent's door on the confessional and creaked it open. It stuck a bit. Things in the church had never worked exactly right for O'Toole. He wondered about that. On the other side, he could hear Walberto bumping around, then settling down. O'Toole knelt on the hard bench, his face inches from the mesh that covered the square hole between them.

The coyote's breath rippled the cloth. "Aren't you going to say it, Father?"

"Say what?"

"What you're supposed to say—*Bless me, Father, for I have sinned.*"

Despite his nervousness, O'Toole felt anger rising in his throat. "You're not a priest."

The coyote was unfazed. "And are you a priest, Father? For sure? You sure do some slick things for a man of the cloth."

"A man has to live," O'Toole replied.

"Yes, that can be a problem." Walberto seemed to be shifting around in the enclosed space. One of his elbows thumped the thin wall between them. "But once a priest, always a priest, even if you're an asshole, right?"

O'Toole thought about his sins. Miserably, he replied, "Yes."

"This is supposed to be a confession," Walberto said, his voice now cheerful. "Have you been guilty of the eighth deadly sin, overconfidence? I think so. You thought you'd get this relic from me easy. But you won't. The price goes up when somebody dies. And it would go up crazy for a priest."

O'Toole heard metal clanking on wood from the other side

of the confessional. His mind raced. His fatness in the confined space locked him in, he'd never be able to shift and lunge through the door in time. He was like a doomed cow in a butcher's chute, waiting for the electric knife to buzz and slash its carotid arteries away.

"Look," said Walberto teasingly, "there's a gun in here."

O'Toole could see the round muzzle of the .357 poking at the mesh, could see Walberto mockingly pushing his own face into the cloth right next to it.

"There's a gun in here too," O'Toole said, sweeping the tiny Beretta M21A from under his robes and firing twice. Blood bubbled on the screen as the .22-caliber long-rifle bullets punched into the coyote's forehead. The hard chunks of meat that had been Walberto clanked and vibrated against the confessional. Then there was silence.

O'Toole reholstered the pistol and put a hand to his chest. It took him some time to calm his pounding heart, some time to get his breath down into the range in which it no longer whistled and strained. He was sweating like a man in a steam bath. He tilted his head against the cool wood next to the penitent's window, let his headache subside, and, eventually, composed himself.

At last his thoughts turned to the relic and to spiritual duties. There was one more thing he had to do for Walberto.

He crossed himself, compressed his hands, and leaned forward.

"Oh Lord," O'Toole prayed, "be merciful to him, a sinner."

DIRTY SCOTTSDALE

BY DIANA GABALDON

Desert Botanical Garden

I t was high noon, and 110°. The cops were in shirtsleeves, the homeowner was wearing plaid bermuda shorts and a *wtf?* expression. The body floating facedown in the swimming pool was wearing a navy-blue wool suit, which was odder than the veil of blood hanging like shark bait in the water.

The girl by the pool was more appropriately dressed—if you could use that word to describe the triangles of turquoise fabric that covered her nominally private parts.

"The poor dope," I said, shaking my head. "He always wanted a pool. Well, in the end he got himself a pool—only the price turned out to be a little high."

The girl looked at me. She had a hot-pink towel clutched dramatically to her mouth, eyes wide above it. Turquoise eye shadow to match her suit, and a lot of waterproof mascara.

"Tom Kolodzi," I said, with a jerk of the head toward the uniformed cops. "I'm with the police." You notice I didn't say I *was* the police. "You know the guy in the pool?"

Her eyes got wider, and she shook her head. I took out my notebook and flipped it open, turning to shield it from the cops.

"Your name?"

She blinked, and lowered the towel. Her mouth was blurred with red, and she looked like a little kid who'd been eating a popsicle, breast implants notwithstanding.

"Chloe Eastwood."

"Any relation to Clint?" I smiled, friendly.

"Who?"

I should have flipped a coin and said, *Call it, friendo*. Instead, I asked, "Do you live here?"

She nodded like a bobble-head doll, her eyes going back to the body. "I just . . . I just came out to tan, and . . . there he was."

"You called it in?"

She shook her head, blond ponytail swishing over baby-oiled shoulders.

"I screamed and Cooney came running out, and the yard guys and everybody." She waved vaguely toward the house where three nervous-looking Mexicans were clustered. A Mexican woman too, with a blond boy of five or six clutching her leg. "I guess Cooney called."

Her eyes went to the homeowner: Mr. Bermuda Shorts, shoulders hunched in aggression. One of the uniforms caught sight of me and opened his mouth to order me out. The two uniforms exchanged a quick look, though, then stared right through me before turning deliberately toward the pool.

I relaxed a little. I'd been doing a ride-along—you always want to get acquainted with the cops in a new place—when the 410 call came through. They'd told me to stay in the car, of course, but didn't lock me in. It could get up to 140 in a parked car, and they didn't want to explain a dead reporter in the backseat. They didn't want to explain a live reporter in their crime scene, either; if I kept my mouth shut, they'd pretend they had no idea how I got there, and leave it to homicide to throw me out.

There was a sudden hum, and a *whoosh* made everybody jump. A timer had come on, and water was rushing down a pile of rocks at the end. It sounded like Niagara Falls, and Gonzales turned and started yelling at the homeowner, who looked confused and belligerent, like a bear in the underwear aisle at Macy's.

"Cooney doesn't know how to work the pool stuff," my new friend said, contemptuous. "My mom always has to do it."

I took out my cell phone and snapped as fast as I could while everyone's attention was distracted. The blood in the water was beginning to eddy away from the floating body.

I nodded to Chloe.

"Be right back. Don't go anywhere."

I stepped behind a pair of palm trees, and hit 1 on my speed dial.

"Paulie?" I said, low-voiced as I could over the artificial falls. "Where are you?" She was supposed to be at Scottsdale and Shea, shooting a traffic accident; if she was still there . . .

"Kolodzi?" Her voice was outraged. "Are you calling me from the men's room? That's just *gross!*"

"No. Get this—10236 North Forty-eighth Street. Body in the pool." I saw the fresh-sawed stubs on the palm tree by my face and had a brain-wave. "There's a ladder lying on the ground out front—" The Mexicans had been trimming the palm trees; I'd seen the dead palm fronds on the curb. "It'd be a killer shot from the roof." And maybe the cops wouldn't see her before she got it.

The click in my ear coincided with silence; somebody'd turned off the falls. I pocketed the phone and rejoined the party.

One cop was missing; so was the Mexican woman. The palm tree trimmers were edging slowly toward the side of the house, eyes focused on the cop talking to Cooney. The little blond boy had joined Chloe on the lounger—not willingly.

"I wanna *see!*"

"Knock it *off*, Tyrone! Mom'll be here any minute! Get back here, I said! The cops are gonna put you in jail if you get *near* that pool!"

"Aw, will not, fuckface!"

"Don't talk to your sister like that," I said. I don't have kids myself, but I have nieces and nephews. I learned the Voice of Doom from my siblings.

Tyrone gave me a startled glance.

"Siddown," I said, in the same tone of voice.

He did, muttering "Crap" under his breath.

"See?" his sister hissed at him.

Sirens were coming. I could hear the roar of a fire engine over the scream of an ambulance. 911 was taking no chances.

A minute later, the pool gate clanged open and four EMTs charged in, intent on rescue. One grabbed a pool skimmer and began trying to snag the body with it.

"Hey!" The cop grabbed his arm. "The guy's *dead*, goddammit! This is a murder scene!"

"He's not dead till a doctor says so," a female EMT informed him.

"Back off!" He'd wrestled the skimmer away from the EMT and stood with it braced like a quarterstaff, daring any of them to mess with his body. "He's fuckin' dead!"

"He will be if you don't let us get him out of there!"

"What. The. Fuck. Is. Going. On. Here?" said a voice behind me. Whoever it was had a pretty good Voice of Doom too; it cut through the argument like a hot wire through ice cream.

I turned to see a tall blond woman in a sun hat, Hawaiian shirt flapping open over a white bikini. Chloe and Tyrone's mother; the breast implants must be hereditary.

"Cooney!" she barked. "What are you doing? What's—" She caught sight of the guy in the pool and stopped dead, her mouth hanging open far enough for me to see that one of her molars was gold.

Cooney came trundling over, sweating and apologetic.

"It's okay, Pammy—"

"Don't call me Pammy! Who are you?" she demanded, swiveling a laser eye on me. "Are you in charge here? Who's that in my swimming pool?"

"Tom Kolodzi, ma'am," I said, offering her a hand. "Do you know the man in the pool?"

"Of course not!" she snapped, taking my hand by reflex. Hers was cold and damp and covered by a latex glove. She let go fast, peeling the glove off with a snap. "Sorry. I was drowning squirrels in the garage."

"Squirrels?"

"Ground squirrels," she said through her teeth. "They eat the goddamn plantings. Are they going to get that—him—out of the pool?" Her eyes kept sliding toward the water, where the body had resumed its dead man's float. Another siren—police, this time.

Slamming car doors and a radio crackle, and the brass was with us. The homicide lieutenant didn't glance at me, and made short work of the EMTs, who retreated, muttering, under the edge of the patio roof, from which misters had begun to spray. The Mexican tree trimmers had evaporated during the cops' confrontation with the EMTs. The scene-of-crime people arrived on homicide's heels, and a police photographer was taking shots of everything in sight, including me and the squirrel-killer. I wanted to look up at the roof to see if Paulie had made it, but didn't want to draw attention to her if she had.

The dead guy beached, flotsam in a navy-blue wool suit. Everybody leaned forward to look at his face—not least, Pammy.

I was looking at her, and saw the blood leave her face and her mist-on tan go yellow. Saw her glance, laser-sharp, at Chloe. Chloe's mouth fell open, and her mother grabbed her shoulder, fingers digging in, before she could squeak.

"Take your brother in the house, darling," Pammy said, in a pleasant mommy voice. "He doesn't need to see this, and neither do you." Chloe nodded like a robot, and took Tyrone's hand. He didn't resist; he'd seen the dead guy's face too, and was the color of skim milk.

Nobody looks good soaking wet and dead, but this guy probably wasn't a GQ model on his best day. Maybe fifty, with a good-sized gut, long strands of graying hair on a balding head. Weak chin, and a nose that was trying to make up for it.

There was a little black hole in his shirt front. The shirt was white, pasted to his body; I could see the curly black hairs on his chest through the cloth. I looked away in time to see Cooney, who was talking to one of the plainclothes people, glance in my direction and shake his head with a puzzled frown. Time to go.

The dead guy's chest filled the screen of Paulie's Mac. The black eye of the bullet hole sat in a vortex of water-swirled chest hair. She zoomed in so all you saw was the hole, then pressed something and the picture went from black-and-white to full color.

"Guh!" said MaryAnne, recoiling.

"Isn't that cool?" Paulie asked me, ignoring the editor. "See the shades of blue all around the hole?"

"Yeah," I said. "Really cool." It was, but my stomach agreed with MaryAnne, who had clamped a hand to her mouth.

"We can't run that!" she said, removing the hand and then putting it right back.

"I know, I know," Paulie said impatiently. "Don't worry, I got plenty more. Thanks for the tip, Kolodzi," she said, giving me an eye. "I almost died of heatstroke on that roof, but it was worth it."

She looked like she'd been boiled alive, even after an hour in the chill of the newsroom, but she'd used her time well.

There were some prize-winning shots of the body in the pool, as well as close-ups of Chloe, Cooney, Pam—several focused on her chest—and a heartbreaker of Tyrone, looking small and stricken and not saying "Crap." Still better, Paulie'd heard everything said on the pool deck.

"Nobody knew the dead guy—or that's what they said. But look at this." She tapped a key and a soggy white rectangle popped onto the screen. A zoom in and I could see it was a wad of stuck-together business cards.

Howarth ap Gruffydd, PhD, one read. *Director, Llangeggellyn Botanical Institute.*

"Damn," said MaryAnne. "What the heck is a Welsh botanist doing dead in Cooney Pratt's swimming pool?"

"Maybe the gardener did it," Paulie speculated. "He's gone."

"What, one of the guys with the ladder?" I asked.

She shook her head, cheeks sucked in to get the last dregs of Mr. Pibb through her straw.

"Nope, those guys were door-to-door palm tree trimmers. You know—cash only, and probably illegal." A good bet, given the way they'd faded at the sight of the police. "There's a regular yard guy, though; a guy named John Jaramillo. He should have been there today. But he wasn't." She popped the lid off her cup and tilted it up, sloshing ice.

"The cops asked for his phone and address, of course," I suggested. She gave me a smug look and held out her arm. She'd scribbled the numbers with what looked like eyeliner.

Harvey, the new intern, came hustling in, a sheaf of printouts in hand. I'd sent him to do a quick search on the Pratts.

"I sent a lot of stuff to your e-mail, but I thought you'd like these . . . Jesus, is that guy dead?" He goggled at the screen, where Paulie's best shot of Dr. ap Gruffydd had replaced the business card.

"No, it's a YouTube video of Hillary Clinton after the Democratic primary," MaryAnne said. "Can't you tell?"

I made Harvey give me the quickie version on the Pratts, which he did, pausing occasionally to gape at the screen, where Paulie and MaryAnne were busy choosing shots.

Cooney Pratt was a real-estate developer; he'd made his money bulldozing desert and putting up tract homes, having either the good judgment or the luck to get out before the housing market collapsed. Pam was his third wife, occupation: housewife.

"No shit," I said, eyeing a close-up of Pam's chest before dropping my gaze back to the paper. The Pratts were rich *and* social; there were several shots of Pam, veneers gleaming, arms linked with two or three other low-cut ladies, laughing their heads off in support of some worthy cause. Harvey had helpfully compiled a list: the Pratts were benefactors of everything from the Phoenix Symphony to the Desert Botanical Gar—

"The Desert Botanical Garden?" I looked up and MaryAnne's

eyes locked with mine. I shrugged; why not? Where else would you expect to find a botanist?

They had three of the pictures I'd sent from my cell phone up now, discussing which one to use.

"That one," MaryAnne said, pointing. She had one eye closed, the other squinting. "What if we zoom it?"

"Crap up close is just close-up crap," Paulie said, shaking her head. She zoomed it, though. Her hand hovered for an instant, then dropped again to zoom out.

"Maybe the other way? Yeah. Yeah, that's better."

The shrinkage didn't improve the definition, but the picture now was arresting. The body hung like a jellyfish, doing its dead-man's float in the midst of a distinct red nimbus.

"Jesus," I said. MaryAnne was making approving noises, and Paulie took my remark as praise for her artistic acumen too, but that wasn't why I'd said it. I sighed.

"Subpoena time."

Paulie put a possessive hand on the computer in reflex.

"Run it first," I said, and she relaxed a little. "But I have to call; the cops can estimate time of death from that." I touched the screen, at the edge of the blood cloud. "Look. I don't know if he drowned or died from the gunshot, but if it was the shot, it didn't kill him right away. He bled a lot after he went in the pool."

"So?" said MaryAnne.

"So you put any liquid in any other liquid and don't stir it, the first liquid will still move—slowly—at a constant rate. Diffusion?"

From wariness to blankness. I sighed.

"You can figure out what that rate is, roughly. The pool water wasn't disturbed until the waterfall came on; the cloud of blood was intact—and you can see the edges of it in the photo. So you can tell about how long it would have taken for blood to spread that far through the water after it stopped pumping out of Dr. ap Gruffydd."

"They teach you that in the Boy Scouts, Kolodzi?" MaryAnne asked.

"High school physics. We need to give it to the cops," I repeated. "You want to do it, M-A? Or me?"

She shook her head.

"You. They're gonna want to talk to whoever took the picture. See if you can trade it for an unofficial time of death. Then see if the Desert Botanical Garden is missing a visiting botanist. Fast."

I didn't see a patrol car in the DBG parking lot, but a small knot of employees was clustered between the Membership table and a glass-fronted Admissions booth, talking excitedly—the cops were here.

"Director's office?" I asked the woman at Membership, polite but authoritative. "I'm here about Dr. ap Gruffydd."

She was flushed from the heat, but pinked up even more with excitement.

"Oh! Oh. Yes, of course. I think they're all at the main office, that's up behind Dorrance Hall—go past the cactus and succulent houses and turn right, there are signs. Oh, no—wait!" She snatched a sheet of little purple stickers, each one adorned with a butterfly, and affixed one carefully to my lapel. "There you are."

I thanked her, and flashing my purple butterfly at the gate, went in. It wasn't just the employees who were buzzing; the trees were full of cicadas, and the whole place hummed like it was electrified.

A big thunderhead passed over, and I breathed shade, grateful. The monsoon rains were coming, but not here yet. I passed the cactus and succulent houses, side-by-side series of huge metal arches covered with steel mesh, and wondered whether they were a lightning hazard; I could see the flicker of heat lightning over the Superstitions to the east.

I shucked the jacket I'd worn to impersonate authority. My shirt was sweat-soaked, but dried almost instantly; clouds or no clouds, the humidity was maybe six percent. Yeah, it's a dry heat.

Meaning that instead of being poached when you walk outside, you're flash-fried.

I turned up the Quail Path and blinked at something—a cactus? It had stickers—that looked like an orgy of underfed octopi, skinny bewhiskered tentacles writhing over twenty square feet of ground and up into the branches of the nearest tree. And that wasn't even the weirdest thing I passed.

The administrative offices were in a discreet building above a little café with an enclosed patio. I was about to crash the party when I caught a glimpse of the Scottsdale homicide lieutenant from the Pratts' pool deck and went down to the café instead.

I bought a bottle of water and asked the girl behind the counter if she knew where Dr. ap Gruffydd's office was.

"Oh, are you with the police?" she breathed, excited. "Isn't it just *awful*?"

"Yes," I said. "Did you know the doctor?"

"Oh, not really." She looked torn between regret and relief. "He'd only been here three months or so, and he wasn't around most of the time because he kept going down to Tucson to see people about orchids—the Mexican government wouldn't let him go in anymore, something about his visa, so he'd have these orchid hunters come meet him at the border."

That was interesting; Harvey hadn't had much time, but you don't get a lot of random hits on a name like Howarth ap Gruffydd. He was an expert on the orchidaceae of Latin America; had written two books on orchids, contributed to botanical journals, and otherwise seemed not to have gotten his name in the media. The girl was still talking.

"I helped with the catering for the reception for him up at the Wildflower Pavilion, though, and he talked to me a little bit then."

"Yes? What did he say, do you remember?"

She giggled, but then put a hand over her mouth, shocked at herself.

"Oh, I'm sorry—I didn't mean to laugh! It's just—he was talking Welsh to all the ladies; it was so cool. And he said something to me in Welsh too, and he smiled and winked so I think it was a compliment, but I don't really *know* what he said, you know?"

A few minutes further conversation got me the information that Dr. ap G had had a temporary office behind the herb garden, to which she helpfully gave me directions.

The herb garden wasn't hard to find. Aside from signs and the pungent smells of everything from oregano and pineapple sage to ten different varieties of mint, it was marked by a fifteen-foot turquoise metal sculpture that looked like a twisted tree trunk, until you got close enough to see that it had feet, rudimentary wings, and several openings out of which live rosemary plants were growing. *St. Earth Walking*, read a bronze plaque behind it.

"Yeah, if you say so," I said to it, and walked up to the office building as though I owned the place.

It was empty, all the office doors locked. A board near the entrance listed the occupants; Dr. ap G's office was near the far end of the hall. It was locked too; the cops hadn't arrived here yet, but it wouldn't be long. There were a few cartoons about orchids taped to the door—and seven or eight snapshots of the reception the refreshment girl had mentioned; there was an open-sided pavilion, the hills of Papago Park visible in the background.

Most of the people looked the same—round white faces with manic grins. But one open-mouthed blond laugher had a gold tooth showing—and a hand possessively on the sleeve of the Welsh botanist, who must have been telling her something side-splitting in Welsh.

Voices outside. I wanted to grab the snapshot, but I knew better than to take evidence, especially if I might get caught with it. I made it out the far door just as the one I'd come through opened.

Outside, the thick blanket of heat settled over me. I took a wrong turn and ended up panting like a dog on a path above the gardens, where five or six . . . things . . . stood like a prehistoric village. They were made of twigs and branches, twisted together and shaped into giant balls, with openings that might be doors or windows. It was getting late—the clouds over the Superstitions were black, and the mountains themselves glowed a weird, intense lavender. I stepped inside one of the balls and pulled out my cell, debating who to call.

Paulie first, to check in. My voice mail. Next, John Jaramillo. I'd called his number on my way to the gardens, and got *his* voice mail. I punched in the code to block caller-ID and tried again.

"Hello?" said a voice that didn't sound like a Mexican gardener.

"May I speak to Mr. John Jaramillo?" I said in my best telemarketer voice, pronouncing it Jar-a-milo, rather than Har-a-meeyo.

"He's not here. Who's this?" Definitely a cop.

"This is Sean with Mesa Verde Time-Shares," I said chattily. "I'll call back later." I pressed the button and stood still, evaporating. A hot wind was coming up, big thermals pushing the clouds up into thunderheads a half-mile high, the air underneath them rushing in to fill the space. From here, I could see a good chunk of the area where Scottsdale runs into Phoenix, urban sprawl beyond the gardens' border.

Pam Pratt? No. My chances of getting to her before the cops did were nil.

One avenue left to try, before I adjourned to Rosita's for a cold beer or six and a plate of chicken enchiladas. I flipped the phone open again and hit 12 on my speed dial.

The phone on the other end picked up after one ring. The only reason girls of that age don't pick up right away is that they're already talking to somebody else.

"Callie?"

"Uncle Tom! What's happening?"

"I need a friend, Callie," I said to my eldest niece. "Think you can find me someone on Facebook who knows a Chloe Eastwood?"

* * *

The morning brought several items of information: a callback from the police lab with an unofficial time of death—between 2 and 3 a.m. A discreet call to one of the original uniforms, who reluctantly told me that the adult Pratts had been at a party, which they hadn't left until 6 a.m.; socialites had more fun than I realized. Chloe hadn't been home either—her best friend, two houses down, was also having a party. The only people home between 2 and 3 a.m. had been Tyrone and his nanny, both asleep.

Paulie had called around to her photographer acquaintances and ended up in possession of e-mailed photos of Dr. ap G's blowout. These not only confirmed Pam Pratt's prior knowledge of the doctor, but yielded another nugget—an image of Cooney Pratt, drink in hand, shooting daggers at the Welshman, who was in the act of slipping some sort of wildflower, stem first, into Pam's cleavage.

And finally, a call from Callie, with the results of her Facebook research: JRose, who was on the "friend" lists for both Callie and Chloe Pratt.

"She says she'll meet you at the Coffee Plantation by the Shea 14," Callie said. "You know where that is?"

"Sure. Thanks, Callie. Have you ever met this girl in person?"

"Of course not," she said, sounding surprised. "But she likes historical fiction and her pictures are cute."

JRose was cute in person too. A shapely redhead with big blue eyes and a breezy manner, more than willing to help out her friend Callie's Uncle Tom. She hadn't been at the party on the night of the murder, but would try to find out how long Chloe had been there.

"Discreetly," I said.

"I can do discreet," she replied, and lowered her lashes in illustration.

"You know Chloe well?"

"Not that well, but I know her f2f. She doesn't usually go to parties like that," she said, twirling a straw in her caramel macchiato. "She parties, but it's mostly at the clubs. I've seen her now and then, with her mom. Her mom's a coug," she added, scornful and amused.

"Coug—what, short for cougar?"

"*Rowr,*" she said, clawing one hand and showing her canines. Then laughed, her face going back to sweetness. "Older ladies, like married with kids. They go to clubs and hit on younger men. Cougs are ladies who are way too old to be wearin' what they're wearin', and doin' what they're doin'."

"What are they wearing?" I asked. My informant cupped both hands in front of her chest.

"*Big* fake boobs. And like miniskirts with no Underoos."

"Yeah? You can tell?"

She rolled her big blue eyes at me. "Oh, *everybody* can tell! They get all drunk and fall around, and everybody's like, 'Oh, put it *away!*'"

This was beginning to sound entertaining.

"Chloe and her mom. They hang out, you said . . . like, *what* places?"

"Oh, the Devil's North, that's the big hangout for cougs. Or at Eli's, down by Claimjumpers on Shea."

"Devil's North?" I'd heard of Eli's, but—

"The Devil's Martini," she explained, and paused for a slurp of her macchiato.

"You said, 'too old to be doing what they're doing.' What *are* they doing?"

"I told you," she said promptly. "Hitting on younger men. There was this photo on DirtyScottsdale.com, this coug right up with this little kid celebrating his twenty-first, and the caption says, *Oh, you're twenty-one? Well, I'm twenty-seven—I don't think that's too much difference, do you?*" She laughed.

"Only she was maybe *thirty*-seven! That's just gross."

"But there are older guys who hit on younger women in clubs, aren't there?"

"Oh, sure."

"Isn't that a double standard?"

"Oh, totally," she agreed cheerfully, and gave me a look of appraisal that was a lot older than she was. I lifted a finger for the bill, hoping *37* wasn't flashing on my forehead.

I'd heard of DirtyScottsdale.com, but hadn't had occasion to look at the site before. It's a do-it-yourself local tabloid covering the club scene; people take pictures of each other drunk, behaving badly, in unflattering or compromising positions, and send them to the site, usually anonymously, often with scurrilous captions.

Some of them were truly funny; some were embarrassing, like the shot of a young woman, very drunk, urinating in a parking lot. All of them were vulgar and most were kind of sad.

I found Chloe in the archives, leaning up against the wall next to a door that said *Ladies*. Her eyes were unfocused and there was a sloppy smile on her face. The tie of her halter dress had come undone—or been untied on purpose—and she was clutching the fabric to one of her breasts. The other one was left to fend for itself, and with thoughts of Callie, JRose, and girlish innocence, I paged down fast.

"Whoa." I paged back up, even faster.

Dr. ap Gruffydd looked a lot better alive, though with the scraggly ponytail, he still wouldn't do better than tenth runner-up in the Llangeggellyn beauty pageant. He was laughing, holding up a woman who was draped over him like a honeysuckle vine on a trellis. One of his hands cupped her butt—literally; she'd slid down him, and her short shiny red skirt had ridden up on one side, and damned if JRose hadn't been right about the Underoos.

I called Paulie and asked her to clip the two photos and make me decent prints. They might come in handy.

* * *

I came back from lunch to find a message from Pamela Eastwood Pratt. Would I meet her at 3 o'clock for a quick drink at Bloom? Mrs. Pratt had tracked me down and gotten my number pretty quick. Which also meant that she knew what I did for a living. Why would a socialite murder suspect want to talk to a journalist?

I turned the possibilities over in my mind as I drove—anything from a front-page confession to a clumsy attempt to redirect suspicion elsewhere by planting a story. Or given what I'd been finding out about Chloe, maybe an attempt to warn me away from her. I touched the pocket where I'd stashed the photos; whatever Mrs. Pratt had in mind to tell me, those might steer her closer to the truth.

Bloom is an upscale restaurant with floral stained-glass panels, circular blue-leather booths, and excellent food. It's mobbed for lunch and dinner, but if you go between 2 and 5, you can hear yourself think. And the wine list is good.

"Mrs. Pratt," I said, sliding into the booth opposite the lady in question.

"Call me Pamela," she responded, making a face. "Pratt— what a godawful name."

"Sure. Pam—"

"*Pamela.*" She smiled. "Pam is nice, and Pammy . . ." She waved a hand, dismissive. "Well, that says oatmeal cookies and and flannel jammies with dancing kittens. Pammy is . . . you know. *Beige.*"

"Whereas Pamela . . ." I said, obliging.

She leaned back in her chair a little, giving me the full benefit of her cleavage. She already had a glass of red wine, held carelessly by the stem.

"Oh, *Pamela* . . . now, Pamela says Tanqueray martini, hold the vermouth, red silk, hot jazz and hotter men, don't bother to take your boots off at the door, and you can leave the lights on, mister, cuz I left shy behind in kindergarten." She laughed, and I caught a glint of gold molar.

"Pamela." I lifted my water to her, and we smiled at each other. Then she set her wine down; to business.

"I Googled you," she said abruptly.

"That makes two of us," I said, and she blinked, but then steadied. She'd already Googled herself; she thought there was nothing unfit for public consumption. DirtyScottsdale.com didn't always have names attached to their photos; the shot of her as an anonymous cougar wouldn't show up.

"If I say this is off the record . . . ?" One plucked eyebrow rose.

"Then it is."

Some people think speaking to a reporter "off the record" is like speaking to an attorney or a priest. I wouldn't quote her. That didn't mean I wouldn't make use of whatever she told me.

"I want you to find my gardener."

"What do you think I am, an employment agency?"

The cougar glinted briefly in her eyes, but she kept it on the leash.

"John Jaramillo. He's been supplying my daughter with drugs from Mexico. Now he's gone and I have a dead botanist in my swimming pool. Think there's a connection there, Sherlock?"

"Yeah. Maybe not the same one you're thinking of, though." I took the photo out of my pocket and laid it on the table.

"Crap," she said, sounding exactly like Tyrone. She frowned at the photo. "I *really* need to get to the gym."

"Connection?" I prompted. "Like between you and the good doctor?"

She made a *pfft!* sound and flicked the photo back at me.

"He was better in bed than you'd think from his looks," she said. "I hadn't seen him since the night this was taken, though, until he turned up in my pool."

"Right. And you don't think the cops would like to know about this?" I tapped a finger on the photo, and the server, who was setting down my glass of Riesling, glanced at it.

"Wow," he said. "Nice butt."

"Thanks, sweetie," she drawled, leaning back in her chair and giving him a laser eyeball. He glanced from the picture to her, and did a double-take.

"Is that *you*? Er . . . ma'am?"

"Meet me in the parking lot after work and find out." The cougar stretched voluptuously, flexing her shiny pink claws. The server, who might have been nineteen, turned purple and fled.

She laughed, but was dead serious when she looked back at me.

"The cops know. I was rattled when he turned up in the pool, but once I had a minute to think, I realized that as soon as they identified him, they'd head for the DBG and find out I knew him. So I called them and fessed up. I didn't know about that—" She cast a displeased glance at the photo. "And if I get my hands on the little shithead who took it—but never mind . . ." She waved a hand. "It's Chloe."

"Chloe took the picture?" It hadn't looked as though Chloe were in any shape to hold a camera.

"No." Pamela gave me a sharp look. "Chloe is why I want you to find John Jaramillo."

Noticing that Chloe's glazed eyeballs coincided with Chloe's clubbing, Pamela had figured logically that she was getting drugs at one or another of the clubs, and thus had put on her cougar costume and gone prowling with her daughter.

"What did Chloe think of that?" I asked.

She shrugged. "If I didn't go, she didn't go. Besides, I took dates along—" She glanced at the photo of herself and ap Gruffydd. "I wasn't following her around all night. Or at least I didn't let it look that way."

I'd already figured that Pamela was much shrewder and more observant than I'd originally thought. She was shrewder than Chloe too, and it didn't take long for her to tumble to the fact that Chloe wasn't getting drugs at the clubs—she was taking drugs *to* the clubs.

"I caught her dealing in the restroom one night." Pam was rolling her empty wine glass slowly between her palms, looking down into the dregs. "Dragged her out into the parking lot and . . . made her tell me where she was getting it."

"From the gardener."

"Yep." She looked up, fixing me with a hard gaze. "You have a reputation for digging things up, Kolodzi. And you're a little less sleazy than the average private detective."

"Gee, thanks."

"And you want to know who killed Griff."

"Griff?"

She sighed impatiently.

"It's spelled Gruffydd, but it's pronounced Griffith. He didn't like Howarth." For the first time, her voice betrayed a little emotion over the Welshman's death. I was a long way from trusting her, but I was beginning to like her a little.

She shrugged. She was wearing a sleeveless pink top, and the hairs on her forearms were standing up in the chilled air.

"So. You find John Jaramillo, the cops convict him of murdering Griff, he goes down, Chloe's source dries up, and you get a story—a story that doesn't include Chloe."

I considered that—but the other picture, of Chloe by the ladies' room, bleary and undressed, with her sweet young breast adrift and vulnerable, was still resting in my pocket.

"Okay," I said. Reminded of photos, though, I pulled out the third one I'd brought—the shot of Cooney Pratt glaring at ap Gruffydd. "You seem pretty convinced that Jaramillo's responsible. And I could see it happening by accident, maybe—the Welsh guy comes by to see you, and stumbles into the middle of a drug deal, maybe. But your husband would seem to have an actual motive."

Pamela stared down at the wildflower in the photo, then flicked the shot back at me and stood up.

"Forget Cooney," she said, and putting a hand on my shoulder, leaned down and whispered confidentially in my ear, "He really *is* a prat, you know."

Not much happened for two days. The police released driblets of information, nothing helpful. A crane fell into a hole on a light-rail construction site. The D-Backs lost two games in a row. And Cooney Pratt's alibi developed holes big enough to swallow a backhoe.

Pamela's alibi was solid; she'd been at a killer bridge tournament at the Hyatt Regency Gainey Ranch, in sight of eighty other people. But Cooney had been with the noncombatants, who'd spent the night in the lobby bar, the spa, the giant heated pool . . . or one of the bedrooms. People had seen him, all right—but there were gaps. And it was a five-minute drive from the hotel to his house.

Meanwhile, John Jaramillo had dropped off the face of the earth. His wife refused to be interviewed, though gossip in his neighborhood said she wasn't that broken up over his absence.

I was debating whether to try some of Jaramillo's other gardening clients, or invite Cooney Pratt out for a drink and show him pictures, when the phone rang.

"I've found him!" Pamela's voice was high, and nervous, for her.

"Who, Jar—"

"The gardener, yes." She swallowed, audibly. "Do you want a story? Come right away—meet me at my house. Come *now.*"

"It was the damn squirrels," she explained, leading me down her front drive. "I kept trapping more and more of the little buggers, and finally realized they were coming from the house next door, crawling through the breeze blocks in my wall."

"Yeah?"

"So I looked at the house next door." I looked too. The next-door house was vacant, with a realtor's sign.

"And?"

"The morning it happened? The murder? I had a hangover, and I was drowning those fucking squirrels in the garage, and I was *so* irritated by the racket from the air conditioner next door. Then, of course, there was lots more racket from the pool deck, and I forgot all about it."

I looked up at the roof. The AC unit now was off. The yard of the empty house was spiked with fried weeds sprouting through pink gravel. There wasn't a soul in sight, bar a garbage truck cruising slowly, picking up the big round turquoise dumpsters, tossing the trash, then slamming them back on the pavement. Half the dumpsters had fallen over from the impact and lay on their sides, wheels spinning.

"Class warfare," Pamela said, seeing me look. "The garbage guy hates rich people. Wait till he's gone."

We did, and she filled me in rapidly on her deductions. The house wasn't being shown; nobody would show a house with the yard in that condition. But if the house was empty—why run the air conditioner?

"Jaramillo," she said, narrowing her eyes at the empty house. "It's got to be him. That's where he keeps the drugs."

It was possible. Obviously nobody was there now; not with the AC turned off. On the other hand, the cops took a dim view of breaking and entering. I mentioned this, and Pam pulled out a key, flourishing it under my nose.

"We traded keys with the people who used to live here—you know, in case of emergencies."

The key was for the kitchen door. The house was unfurnished and silent, but I stopped dead, the back of my neck prickling. I'd thought she was imagining things, but she wasn't. The air was thick and stifling and probably at least 115°, but it didn't have that dead feel that abandoned houses have.

What it did have was one very bad smell. I thought it was time to call the cops right then, but Pam had gone ahead of me, through a door, and she gave a strangled scream.

I went after her and found myself in a narrow room furnished with a washer, a dryer, and a corpse.

There were flies and he'd been dead long enough that the flesh was sagging off his bones and had a greenish tinge. Pam was standing behind the body, holding a gun.

"Told you I found him," she said.

"Yeah. Let's put the gun away, shall we, and call the cops."

She swallowed, and pointed the gun directly at me.

"Oh, come on!"

"I'm sorry," she said, though she didn't sound sorry. "I can't let Chloe be arrested for killing him. Everybody knows you've been looking for him. So you found him, and he shot you, and you shot him. By the time anybody finds you, nobody will be able to tell how long either of you's been dead, and . . ." Her voice was shaking, and so was her hand.

A shadow behind the door moved. My eyes flicked to it, and Pamela made a little throaty noise. "Oh, don't even *try* that . . ." she began, and then went "*Uk!*" as a slender Hispanic guy in dark jeans and a black T-shirt stepped out and hit her on the head with the butt of his gun.

Pamela's weapon spun out of her hand as she went down and hit the washing machine with a booming noise, but I didn't try to dive for it.

"Who the hell are you?" the Hispanic guy said, looking me over.

"A newspaper reporter. Should I ask who you are?"

"No, that wouldn't be a good idea." He spoke good English, but it wasn't his first language. He glanced at the body and shook his head, then peered back at me, thoughtful.

"Okay," he said, making up his mind. "You going to help me get him out of here, all right?"

"Er . . ." I raised an eyebrow at Pamela, who was groaning on the floor.

"Yeah, right. Put the lady in the closet." He waved the gun toward what looked like a broom closet—though you don't usually see broom closets with deadbolts on the outside.

Pamela was bleeding from her scalp, and vomited when I dragged her up onto her feet. It was a messy business, but I got her in the closet and the door bolted. I was streaming with sweat by the time I finished, and wondered whether there was any air in the closet. Then I looked up and saw small holes drilled through the wood—ventilation.

"For troublemakers," the guy said with a shrug. "Just in case, you know?"

I looked at the body, and wiped the back of my hand across my mouth. His stomach had swelled up like a balloon, and it was too damn easy to imagine what it'd be like if he popped.

My friend was thinking along the same lines.

"Garbage bags," he said, gesturing with the gun toward the door to the garage. "Move slow."

The garage was crowded with filled garbage bags, some of them broken and spilling. Fast-food wrappers, fragments of stale tortillas, empty refried-bean cans. Several small furry things scuttled out of the pile, and the guy kicked at one but missed.

"Rats," he said with a shrug.

"Ground squirrels."

My pal shrugged and motioned to an open box of giant leaf bags. I took two, and, holding my breath and keeping a grip on my belly muscles, slipped one over Jaramillo's head and the other over his feet. The guy with the gun tossed me a set of keys.

"Back the truck into the driveway."

The truck might have been Jaramillo's; it was a pickup with a ratty trailer made of white wire mesh, rakes and shovels in holders at the back, piled with garden trash. I wrestled Jaramillo's body into the trailer, then got behind the wheel, at my friend's urging.

"Drive."

Within ten minutes we were headed south on the 101. The

pickup had good AC and my hands and arms were freezing in the blast of cold air, but I was still drenched in sweat.

"How did you get them in there?" I asked at last, breaking the silence. A SWAT negotiator I'd interviewed once told me that what you do in a hostage situation is get the perp talking. Keep them talking, because if they're talking, they aren't shooting.

My captor blinked.

"The illegals," I said. "You're a coyote, right?"

"Yeah," he said softly.

"Heck of an idea. Hiding them in Scottsdale, I mean. How'd you get them in and out of the house?"

He lifted one shoulder, off-handed.

"Yard trucks, hoopties. You drive a truck like this down any street in Scottsdale, three, four Mexicans in the back—who looks at yard guys? Everybody's got yard guys. A beater car pulls up at the end of the street, two women get out—*domesticas*, nannies." He smiled, but there wasn't much humor in it. "They belong here."

"How many people were in that house when the cops came?"

"Sixty-three."

"Jesus." Sixty-three people huddling in that house, afraid to move for fear of making a sound. Probably afraid of more than the cops too.

"Was he—" I jerked a thumb toward the trailer behind us, "in there, then?"

He sighed and shifted his weight a little. "Yeah."

"Dead?"

"Yeah."

Conversation lapsed until we hit the 202 and turned west.

"You kill him?" I asked, trying to keep it casual.

"No." His eyes widened a little in surprise, and he shook his head. "I don't kill people. Unless I have to," he added.

I figured a coyote probably had to, sometimes. I hoped he wasn't figuring this was one of those occasions.

"Who shot him?"

"My partner. Go I-10, south." He waved the gun at a highway sign. A big raindrop hit the windshield with an audible *splat!* and we both jumped. I pressed, to keep him talking.

"Did he stumble into it—Jaramillo? If anybody was going to notice extra yard guys in the neighborhood, I'd guess it would be a gardener."

My friend made a little sound, maybe surprise, maybe contempt. "No, he was part of it. How you think we found those— that house?" He'd started to say "houses." There were more of them.

"Dangerous, wasn't it? For him, I mean. Having it so close?"

"Yeah, it turned out pretty dangerous for him." He glanced through the rear window at the trailer. It was starting to rain in earnest now, and I switched the wipers on.

"He had an angle?" I guessed. "He was using your . . . er, your business, to bring in drugs?"

The guy stiffened a little. "If he did, I didn't know about it," he said, sounding defensive.

"What, you got morals about drugs?"

"What you think I am, *chingadero?*"

"Fine, you don't smuggle drugs. Just people."

"You think it's the same?" He sounded incredulous, and I had to concede that he had a point.

"Nope. Just trying to figure out how Jaramillo got dead." We were well out of the city by now. The rain was pelting down, and I had to slow the vehicle.

"Him," he said in disgust. "You're right, he got his own deal going, he don't tell us. But not drugs. Flowers."

What with everything, I'd temporarily forgotten about Dr. ap Gruffydd's murder, but that word brought it back with a bang.

"What kind of flowers?"

He shrugged. "I don't know. Like this." He pushed the button on the glove box. It fell open, and I glimpsed a bundle of brown burlap, with something yellow sticking out of it. I figured it was an orchid, but couldn't take my eyes off the road to make sure.

"Where'd it come from?"

"One of the guys we bring over. Most of them, they're from Sonora, Sinaloa, Michoacán . . . This guy, he's from Quintana Roo. In the jungle." He nodded toward the road ahead. "I don't know where Johnny finds him, but he puts him in touch with . . . with my partner."

The orchid smuggler had joined the group of illegals and been brought to the house in Scottsdale, next door to the Pratts. Jaramillo's plan, insofar as my companion knew, had been to work late, then sneak into the supposedly empty house and get the orchid, which he'd take to the botanist.

But the good doctor had been too anxious to wait, fearing that his precious orchid would perish before he'd got his hands on it. So he'd picked up Jaramillo from his house and gone with him to the Pratts' at night, sneaking into the backyard under cover of the nearby party. Ap Gruffydd had waited by the pool while Jaramillo hopped over the wall and went to get the orchid.

"But the guy who had it, he wanted his money, and Johnny, he don't got it yet, because the guy—the other guy, who wants the flower—he couldn't get it from his bank, because it was night." He shrugged again.

So Jaramillo had hopped back over the fence to tell ap Gruffydd; and the botanist, inflamed by the nearness of an orchid, had declared that he'd go talk to the fellow himself, at least see the flower.

Jaramillo had tried to stop him, but couldn't, and next thing anyone knew, the Welsh botanist was face to face with sixty-three illegal Mexicans—and a couple of alarmed—and armed—coyotes. The unnamed partner had pulled his gun, and Jaramillo, seeing his deal going south, had lunged to intercept him.

"So that's how Johnny got dead," my companion said with a sigh. Ap Gruffydd had run, of course, and made it back over the wall, but had made the mistake of turning—whether with thoughts of going back to rescue his orchid or just to see whether anyone was coming—and been shot in the chest by the coyote, aiming from the top of the wall.

"Over a flower," my friend repeated, shaking his head. "Get off here, okay?"

We took the exit ramp toward Eloy, but within a few minutes of leaving the highway, he directed me down a dirt road. The lightning had been following us, snaking across the sky in big white bolts. Now the storm started to catch up, and the thunder came louder and more often. It didn't matter much; we'd run out of conversation.

The truck lurched and splashed along, the trailer bouncing from side to side. I could see Eloy off in the distance, tiny flickers of light that disappeared every few seconds in the blinding flash of the lightning.

Where the fuck were we going? I wondered. Actually, I wondered how far I was going, because I didn't think my friend was planning to head back to Mexico with me in tow. I was still sweating, and the truck was full of the tin-can reek of fear.

"Why—" My mouth was dry, and I had to work my tongue to make words. "Why did you go back? Why not leave him—" I jerked my head backward, "leave him there?"

The coyote looked surprised.

"I couldn't leave him there to rot. He's married to my—" he cut off sharp, frowning. "He's family," he said, and repeated, "I couldn't leave him there."

Two miles farther and we came to a gate, where another dirt road led off toward the mountains. Far south, I could see the outline of Picacho Peak, stark in the lightning flashes.

"Turn it around here," he said, moving the gun in a small circle. "Aim it back the way we came, then get out."

This would be it, then. The truck lurched into the ruts of the road we'd just traveled, pointed back toward Phoenix. I was looking for something to say, anything, but not one word came to me. There wasn't anything but the smell of ozone and fear, and the small vivid details that I knew I'd remember forever because they were the last things I'd see: the cracked gray dash, a plaid dish towel somebody'd left on the seat, the coyote's wrist watch, a Swatch with a green metal band.

"You got a phone? Leave it on the seat."

I fumbled it out, dropped it on the seat, and following the motion of his gun, opened the door into the rain. *Run*, I thought, putting a foot on the side board. *Drop, roll, stand up, and run*. I couldn't make it, I knew that. But I'd try.

"Hey," he said behind me, softly. I glanced over my shoulder, and he tossed something at me. I caught it by reflex. The orchid, in its burlap wrapping.

"Name it for your girlfriend, okay?" he said, and gave me a very small smile. His feet came up and hit me in the ribs. I fell out and landed on my knees in the mud. An arm wearing a Swatch reached out, grabbed the handle, and pulled the door shut. The roar of the engine shocked me out of numbness and I stumbled to my feet just in time to avoid being run over.

The truck bumped slowly away.

I stood there with lightning striking all around me, and watched him drive off. One more of all those wonderful people out there in the darkness.

GROWING BACK

BY ROBERT ANGLEN

Apache Junction

E ddie Keane came screaming out of the motherfucker of all bad dreams. He could still feel the blood coating his belly, arms, and face. A dry and crusty scab, it filled his mouth with copper, sealed his eyelids, glued him to the bed sheets. Eddie lay trembling on the narrow bunk. He couldn't get over how real the shit seemed, like this meth-and-dust concoction he'd once needled off a biker's spike. Toxic crystal kept him bouncing five days straight and some freakish creatures had gotten into his skull before he crashed.

Eddie figured this was worse. His brain was stuck on sleep, caught in the bloody cocoon of his subconscious. He waited for the dream to die. Except it didn't. Slowly, he became aware of the stillness around him, the strange and utter silence. Not possible. Noise was built into this place; it lived in the walls. The rattle of pain, fear, and tormented prayer hummed 24-7 through the tiers of steel cages, a living current fed by 450 inmates locked into a brutally dull routine.

Now nothing. Dreamland. Then a crazy thought. Maybe this wasn't a dream. Eddie panicked, struggling to get up, wake up, seized by the conviction that if he rolled over and opened his eyes he would no longer be in his jail cell. He'd be home again, lying in bed next to the body of his wife. Same as the night he beat her to death with a bottle of Old Granddad.

Eddie remembered the white-hot hatred pumping through his veins. Her lying there, head propped on one hand, as if what she'd said wasn't the whackiest thing to ever come out of her mouth.

"You pregnant, Cheryl?" Eddie's high instantly lost. "That it?"

"No, honey. I'm just saying, wouldn't it be nice? Us making something good."

Good? Two hours ago she'd been fucking an aluminum pole at a Van Buren syphilis shack, working her cooze overtime to snatch up dollar bills from businessmen too shit-faced to tell talent from tweak.

Now she was talking about wanting a kid.

"That's speed talk, Cheryl. Nonsense," he said. "You're too stupid to breed."

Her expression crumpled into a humiliated wad. She sat up, smearing a tear track. "Goddamn. Why you gotta be so mean?" She struck him loosely. Spat. Hit him again. "Admit it. You're just afraid. Of what will come out. Well, you oughta be. Cause ain't nothing good's ever coming out of you."

Eddie finally understood what the jigs were always going on about. She'd gone Oprah on him. Well, he knew how to change the channel on that action.

Cheryl's eyes went double-ought, her mouth still working but no sound coming out, the red imprint of his hand fading across her cheek. Thing about cunts, no matter how many times you smack them, they always look surprised the next time.

Eddie lay back and groped around for the whiskey bottle on the floor. Cheryl would suffer him out for a few minutes, then she'd do that stupid laugh thing, make like she'd been pulling his chain. He would apologize. They would fuck. Love all around.

He never saw her coming. She hit him hard enough to send the bottle skidding across his gums. He lashed out and caught a wad of her hair. Pulled her face into his fist. Blood splattered. Bones crunched. Broken teeth rattled against the wall. Eddie straddled her, not thinking, just swinging. He let the Fury work through his muscles with each satisfying thunk until his rage was spent. That's when he looked down and saw that he was still holding the bottle. Unlike Cheryl's face, it was intact. Goddamn. Old Granddad sure knew his stuff. Eddie tipped back the bottle and took a long hard pull before passing out.

So maybe he hadn't meant to do her all the way. Wasn't like he could take it back. And damned if he was going to start crooning like a fish on his first night in stir, begging for a second chance. Accident or not, Eddie knew if he were given another chance, he'd beat the shit out of her a second time.

Judge knew it too. That raven-eyed executioner sat high up on his throne, hair so slick and shiny he might have been wearing a cowl over his long black robe. Even his smile was more warlock than magistrate, a greedy thing that seemed to anticipate the inevitable sentence.

Eddie held the judge's baleful gaze, unflinching, grinning at his inquisitor through the old scar that split his lips. Eddie craned his neck so the swastika brand showed over the collar of his white shirt and kept his fists bunched on the defense table, blue-inked knuckles facing forward: *FURY*.

The judge gave Eddie a look of pure indulgence.

"Tell me, Mr. Keane. What made you this way?"

"What way is that, Your Honor?"

"Maybe it's better you don't know. You're twenty-eight years old. What if I give you twenty years to come up with the answer?"

"Wow," Eddie aped. "That's like a whole 'nother life."

Something sharp and dangerous flickered behind the judge's opaque eyes. For a fleeting second Eddie actually felt the stab of it, an invisible hook piercing deep.

"Exactly," the judge said. "Another life."

Prison sounds pushed out of the darkness, a jumble of clangs, shouts, and overlapping voices that dissolved the mocking tone of the judge's voice. Life? Fuck you, Hoodoo Man. Prison don't scare me.

"What you saying, bitch?" The terse shout exploded in Eddie's ears. Without warning a pair of hands slammed him backwards. "I cut you, *puta*. Then we see who's scared."

Eddie crashed into a wall of bodies. More hands caught him, kept him from falling. He jerked around to see a blur of hard, half-remembered faces yelling encouragement. A flat steel object was shoved into his palm. "Take the greaser out, Eddie! Shank his ass!" He was propelled toward his opponent, a squat Latin killer stripped to the waist, *La Eme* brands and prison tats stretched over exaggerated muscles. And Eddie realized he was standing in the middle of a memory.

The men surrounding him weren't the ones doing time with him now; this place wasn't the Special Management Unit where he spent twenty-three hours a day in lockdown. None of this was now. It was four years ago, Florence, Central Unit. Small-time drug dispute between gangs on the outside, Eddie tapped by the AB to settle it inside.

Mind reeling, he watched the Mexican bob and weave in front of him, stick razor flashing. He remembered the spic's name. El Gato. But unlike the first time they squared off, Eddie's reflex was disbelief. "No way this is happening."

"Oh, it's happening, *ese*. Tell me you don't feel this." The Mexican lunged and Eddie screamed, the blade slicing across his face. Liquid fire filled his mouth. The meat of his shredded lips bounced against his teeth and puffs of air seeped through a hole in his cheek.

"Now, I cut that teardrop off your face, *pendejo*."

This isn't real! It's the past! Eddie's brain screamed. But the pain was real. Same for Eddie's reaction, the surge of strength, the narrowing of vision, and the dark detachment as the Fury took over.

He let the spic have his second of victory, then struck from a crouch, twisting his own blade into the Mexican's middle. El Gato looked down, mystified, battle forgotten as astonished fingers tried to rejoin the severed green lines of tattoos over a bulging white ribbon of muscle. Eddie charged. *Stick, stick, stick!* He followed the Mexican to the cement. Shouts erupted. A siren went off. Someone yelled, "Guards!" Eddie shook off the warning and rose over the spic's body. He coughed up a ball of blood and tissue, spat the clotted mess onto the dead guy's upturned face. "Gato, shit!" he screamed. "Pussy!"

Eddie's mind unzipped.

The kill scream was still tearing out of his throat when his senses went black and a ripping sound filled his head. *Shit just opened up*, Eddie thought. Reality evaporated. Gone went the fight scene, the mad crush of inmates, the warble of alarms. One instant Eddie was breathing blood over the spic's body, the next he was back in a cell, staring into a mirror.

And crazy stared back at him.

Eddie leaned into the strip of sheet metal above the cell's sink, not trusting the reflection. He recognized the face but it belonged to someone else, some other Eddie.

The knife wound was gone.

No bloody track. No itch of stitches. No trace of the jagged white scar. He could still feel the icy kiss of El Gato's razor. Remembered the patchwork repair job by prison docs and the forever-after taste of antiseptic.

But the reflection face was unmarred, as if the fight never happened.

"Keane! Visitor!" Eddie jumped away from the mirror. The CO stood three paces from the bars, khaki-bland, indifferent. "Stand your gate. You know the drill. Move before you're told, you forfeit your privilege."

"Who?"

"Says he's your father."

Eddie barked a laugh. "Right. My father's—"

He'd been about to say *dead*—before memory stopped him:

The old man stooped over a plastic visitor's chair, humiliated and embarrassed, talking about death. Cancer. Eating him from the asshole out. Sitting there, too selfish to beg sympathy, too full of pride to realize that's what he was doing. Looking into that bulldog face, Eddie had experienced an overwhelming urge to embrace his father, to let go all of the history and hate between them. Because for the first time his father was here, reaching out to his only son.

Then the flash of judgment in those rummy eyes, the same smug look on the old man's face that had chased Eddie out of childhood. And bitter realization. His father hadn't come to make peace. He was making a point. Like a miser arranging bundles of cash in the bottom of his coffin. Preparation. Telling Eddie death didn't change anything. *I own you.*

Eddie felt the hurt, fresh. Which made zero sense. The old man was five years dead and gone. Cancer had done a bang-up job. Turned his body into a busted stack pipe that kept leaking until the guy in the unit below complained about raw sewage dripping from his ceiling.

So, anyone care to explain how the old man could be waiting to talk with him?

Slowly, Eddie swiveled back to the mirror. The face—stripped of its hardest time and wounds—was his. Only years younger. And Eddie knew he hadn't been remembering events. He'd been reliving them.

Growing backwards.

"C'mon, Keane," the guard pressed. "Enough preening. Let's go."

Eddie wanted to scream in protest. He could already hear the old man's voice, the leathery gloat roughing its way past Redman chaw.

"See you got yourself branded. Didn't take long."

"Thought you of all people would understand."

"I understand fine, boyo. Skinheads made you their punch."

"I'm nobody's—"

"You're everybody's punch, Eddie. Always been, always be."

Eddie shook his head against his father's words. Told himself that if he refused to leave his cell, his father would stay a memory, stay dead. The face in the mirror told him different. Against his own volition, Eddie let the guard take him—to what?

His past.

The dark cord of memory dragged Eddie toward its umbilicus. Time warped as his life played out in reverse. Days and weeks compressed into emotions, tight fistfuls of grief and rage that pummeled Eddie with savage intensity. Single events stretched out in slow-second madness, suspending him in acts of cruelty and degradation. He fought to reassert his indifference, tap into the Fury's narcotic rage. But Old Granddad had left the building. And Eddie fell victim to his own torment.

Zip.

There was the kid's face, fear flushed with betrayal and begging Eddie not to let it happen. Eddie backed out of the showers as the crew of Level 5 meat packers moved in. He had sold the kid's drug debt to the faggots for pennies on the dollar. Call it a refinancing plan. Watching the attack, the men throwing themselves at the quivering and mewling flesh, Eddie got a hard-on. He imagined his dick as a knife. Not fucking. Cutting.

Zip.

DT demons whispered in Eddie's ears. He was in the hole. A sensory-deprivation chamber where the Arizona Department of Corrections turned out snitches and bitches. Eddie fought the voices. He talked over them, yelled, sang, recited goddamn Motörhead lyrics until he ran out of words and gushed gibberish. They had dropped him cold turkey into an SMU II isolation cell. All Eddie needed to do was renounce the brotherhood. Roll over. Three days later the detox demons came, ripping his insides, twisting his spine, loosening his bowels. He blew chunks, gagged air, shouted at the walls. Then he beat on them, hitting the concrete as if working a heavy bag. Each blow accompanied by the mash of gristle and Eddie's roar. "You!" *CRUNCH.* "Don't!" *CRUNCH.* "Own me!"

Zip.

Flesh burned, sizzled, and popped. His skin came off in searing layers, filling the cell with a burnt-onion stench. It took two of them to hold Eddie down as the heated metal blade worked a dollar-sized patch on his neck. "Cross's got six sides," the knife-man said. "We're three down." From the corner of his eye, Eddie saw the knife pass through a guttering flame. He sucked in a lungful of the crispy air. He was kindred now. Full-fledged AB. Silently he repeated the pledge that he'd just said aloud. *My life is this and this is for life.*

The car baked in the dirty sunrise, a primer oven. Eddie sat behind the wheel, windows down, stewing in sweat. He could taste the grit trapped in the heat haze rising above the rows of battered single-wides. The vial of crystal death lay on the passenger seat, all sparkle and sunshine. Eddie cranked up the radio on some rage metal and tried to stave off the shakes. He didn't want to be here. Scrunching his eyes shut, he fiercely tried to make believe this backwards bullshit was part of a monstrous bad trip. But Jackyl's hammer-jammer guitar clash—"Mental Masturbation!"—removed any doubt about where he was or who would soon come stumbling out of the mud-colored trailer.

Here was the Wagon Wheel Mobile Home Park, another artifact of Apache Junction's dismal Western heritage. The city had tried everything to cash in on cowboys short of issuing Stetsons and spurs to the hookers on its greasy main drag. Probably would have if the hookers had been willing to stick around.

You could still find actual Indians on the Apache Trail, usually pulling all-nighters in stop-and-robs or passed out in bars named Rooster Cogburn's. The redman Eddie sought operated an auto salvage yard to front a methamphetamine distributorship. He was too glazed on his own product to care that Eddie greeted him as "Tonto" or ask why Eddie dropped twenty extra for a corroded car battery.

Eddie spent the next hour scraping the terminals onto a sheet of butcher paper and cutting the acid into the crystal, creating the ultimate shot of high test. He spent the rest of the night sick over what he planned.

Still wasn't sure he could go through with it.

But he knew that he would. Because, let's face it, this was the past. He saw the trailer's door swing open. At the same time, a hand drew back a piece of foil blocking the front window and a familiar wedge of blond hair appeared. Her eyes found his. She nodded. A second later, Wade Gramble stuck his face through the side window of Eddie's car, his greeting stretching all the way back to grade school: "Edddieeeeee Spaghetti!"

Eddie once again saw his best friend for the last time. Knock-off Ray-Bans over that fuck-a-duck grin, undiminished by a junkie-thin frame and the chemicals oozing from his pores and soaking his Doctor Who T-shirt.

"Got us a caper, bro," Wade said, dropping beside Eddie and extending his fist for a bump. "Easy peasy, lemon squeezy. Scoping VIN numbers off junkers, waiting in line at the DMV. Dude I know, his sister's into some Armenians who're tossing out serious Franklins for bogus registrations."

Eddie had gone schizophrenic. He had become two people. Inside Eddie wanted to grab Wade by the shoulders, bust the remaining Chiclets out of his grille, and scream at him to run. But Outside Eddie was doing the talking. Cool and laid back, an actor ghosting through lines perfected in a single performance six years ago.

"Maybe I got something better," Eddie said.

"Better how? That's like free money, bro."

Eddie opened his hand on the vial. "This do?"

"Dude! Beats waiting in line every time."

She straddled his lap, backlit by purple neon, grinding as the Red Hot Chili Peppers caterwauled about Californication. Her face was so close he could taste butterscotch from the candies she chain-popped between sets. They were in a private VIP booth, their love lounge.

"It doesn't have to be this way," Cheryl said, voice husky. "You can make me yours, for all of the time."

"You don't belong to me," Eddie said. "You're Wade's. He loves you."

"Wade ain't like you, Eddie. He's weak." Cheryl arched her back. "I hear things. I'm afraid he's going to get you busted. Or worse. He's not the friend you think he is."

It would take Eddie years to wise up to Cheryl's lies and manipulations. He couldn't see his hands in the dark. But he knew how his fists would one day smash her face.

"You always get what you want?" he said.

"What I deserve, you mean." She stroked him.

Eddie closed his eyes.

"Open your goddamn eyes, boyo!" the old man barked. "You owe her that much."

Eddie obeyed, blinking into focus a cheap pine casket atop a floral-strewn dais. Inside, rose-colored satin framed his mother's deflated features, rouged and painted into a plastic sheen. He and the old man were alone in the mortuary. "She looks pretty much the same as the last time you beat her," Eddie said. "Only happier."

"Is that why you came here? To lay blame?"

Eddie really couldn't say. He wanted to mourn her, but the only genuine sentiment he'd been able to summon for his mother was conflict. A fitting eulogy. "Guess I wanted to make sure she was finally safe from you."

"Jesus, but you're a weak sister." Eddie could hear the alcohol burn in his father's pitiless voice. "No way you came from me. I knew the moment she spat you outta her cunny lips I wasn't your father. But I gave you my name anyway. Know what they call that? A legacy."

"Swell legacy, Dad. Look what you did for her."

"What about what you did, Eddie? The shame you put her through. The way you took advantage of her. You forget about that? Need me to remind you?"

"Shut up!" Eddie swung at the old man, who deflected the punch and clamped Eddie's jaw in one meaty hand. Squeezing, he pushed Eddie against the casket, crashing over vases, toppling arrangements, and scattering blossoms across his mother's body.

"Let me clue you in, boyo. I gave your mother what she wanted. You call it battery. She called it love. We made our peace a long time ago. How about you?" The old man pushed Eddie's head toward his mother's, crushing his face onto her lipstick-encrusted mouth. "Here's your chance, Eddie. Tell her you're sorry. Kiss her goodbye."

Pink underwear kept Eddie from escaping America's toughest jail. Well, maybe escape was overblowing it. Security was so loose he could've walked out the front gate.

But then he wouldn't have access to pink underwear. He couldn't believe the money he was making off the things. Hell, he was wearing three pairs at a time just to keep up with demand. And supply? Eddie was kicking back to the laundry crew so they'd keep quiet on the count.

Putting inmates in pink underwear was the brainchild of the Maricopa County Sheriff, who thought degrading men by forcing them to eat green bologna sandwiches, watch the Disney Channel, and work on chain gangs made him America's Toughest Sheriff.

Of course, the sadistic fuck also built a jail out of tents on the floor of the goddamn Gila Desert. And on that one, Eddie had to give the sheriff props. Satan's front porch had nothing on a thousand men crammed ten to a tent in 120-degree summers.

Eddie processed into Tent City a couple of months after his nineteenth birthday, which he'd celebrated by racking up a misdemeanor assault charge and causing a near riot at a Mesa bar. Charges would have been worse except when police arrived Eddie was being stomped into the ground by a group of seriously pissed off *vatos*. Seems Eddie had inflicted a grievous insult to their culture when he cold-cocked one of their homies then shoved his hat under the *pachuco's* ass and asked if that was where the candy came out.

Eddie thought he should send the greasers a complimentary pair of pinks. He'd gotten the idea for his underwear caper from a stroke rag, some freak of nature writing about how she got off when her boyfriend gave her the Dirty Sanchez. If chicks were willing to brag about licking their own shit, what would they be willing to shell out for an inmate's dirty drawers?

Anybody could sell clean boxers. In fact, Eddie was pretty sure the sheriff had a side business doing just that. What he offered was lived-in stuff. Pissed in, shit on, cum-filled and bloody, the messier the better. He had Wade set it up with a classified and a post box. First week, they got a dozen orders. Doubled it the next week. Finally had to bribe a couple of deputies to get the boxers out.

Eddie felt like a captain of friggin' industry. Escape. Are you kidding?

"Knuckles, bro? Fury. That some kind of promise?"

"A reminder. Finally stood down the old man."

"Righteous. He back off?"

"Nah. Kicked the shit outta me."

They were barreling west on U.S. 60 in a Lexus that Wade had boosted from a movie theater parking lot, where they had just seen *Starship Troopers* for the upteenth time. Wade geeked over science fiction. Eddie didn't mind. It gave them somewhere they could go together and disconnect. For them, sci-fi wasn't a theme. It was a place.

"Remember when we use to fly paper airplanes off the Alma School overpass?" Eddie said. "Like we were X-wings making a run on Death Star. See if we could make it to the pavement before getting crunched."

"Yeah. Till you taped an M-80 to one. Nearly caused that trucker to jackknife."

"Man, I'll never forget that dude's face."

"Funny stuff, Eddie. Long time ago."

"Not for me."

Eddie's body devolved. The pain was exquisite. He saw his muscles thin out and flatten. His limbs shrank. Broken bones snapped fresh, bulging under his skin, then fused together as if they had never been broken at all. Tattoo blue vanished. He could literally see his manhood fade as he slipped into adolescence, his life clicking away like slides in an old-style Viewmaster, the selector switch set to suffer.

He tore through the boy's pod, his clothes, books, finally fingering the three-by-five picture under the mattress. Eddie hated the boy. He was a pampered puss, a crybaby. One of those kids who didn't think he belonged in juvie, no matter his crime.

The picture proved it. Family Vacation 101. Silly smiles backdropped by Arizona red rock, the boy front and center, arms draped around a bored little sister and brainiac brother. Mom and Dad flashed peace signs over their heads.

The boy treated the picture like a piece of magic, rubbing it through his pocket, peeking glances and talking to it when he thought no one was watching. It only made Eddie hate him more. It confirmed that whatever the boy had done, it would eventually be forgotten. Not so for Eddie. The picture people knew it. Their smiles ridiculed him.

Eddie dropped the picture on the floor between his feet. He unbuttoned his pants and began jacking off.

The old man came out of Eddie's bedroom wagging a pipe and baggie. He was dressed in his police uniform and he put the weight of the badge behind his voice.

"You're a walking felony, Eddie. Guess it'll be Christmas in Durango for you," he said. "I'll process you through intake myself."

Eddie held the old man's eyes. Kept quiet even as his father shoved him bodily into the back of the patrol car. What could he say? The pipe wasn't his. Neither was the dope.

"Go ahead, Eddie. Cry entrapment. Tell them how I planted the evidence. Nobody's going to hear anything you say." The old man cranked his head back and laughed through the metal cage. "Done you same as we do the niggers. Nobody hears them either."

Desert twilight crept like a sepia claw toward the end of the hall-way where Eddie cowered outside of his parents' bedroom. He strained to hear the voices on the other side of the door, primed for violence.

He knows. Eddie screwed his mind down on the thought, rejecting it. Impossible.

Then the door opened and the old man loomed over him in the shadows. Eddie tried to look past him to where his mother waited in the room. Surely she would defend him. He was just twelve. How could it be his fault? "Mom?"

She averted her gaze, giving him up to the old man.

"Shhh, boy." His father's face cracked into an indecipherable jigsaw of emotions. Eddie could see anger, fear, and hate clamoring to escape. "She can't talk to you."

Slowly, the old man raised his fist, showing Eddie the torn and frayed lamp cord coiled around it like a whip. "This is going to hurt you a whole lot more than it will me."

The old man let it out then, a shrieking fit of laughter that grew louder with each successive crack of the cord, until even Eddie's screeches were lost to it.

"I'll protect you. I swear."

"Just hold me."

"Like that?"

"Put your hands down. Lower."

"Here?"

"Lower. Oh, that's nice."

"Can I kiss you?"

"Please. How does that feel?"

"It tickles, kinda."

"Now?"

"You're soft."

"Don't stop."

"Why are you crying?"

"Because you make me feel beautiful."

"You are beautiful."

"And you won't ever hate me, Eddie?"

"Never."

"And you promise you won't ever leave me?"

"No. I love you, Mom."

Eddie crouched beside a yucca, unable to pull his eyes from the girl's window. He'd imagined squalor and Third World filth, a ghetto repackaged into an East Mesa ranch house. But the girl's room shined pastel princess beneath decorative fixtures, all canopy, ruffles, and lace.

It looked, well, normal. They lived better than Eddie. Not like niggers at all.

The girl, whose name was Rhonda and shared Eddie's sixth-grade class, glided through the pink and white fairy tale, her face a caramel question mark beneath a frizz of black hair. Eddie resented the fluttery feeling she gave him. He wished she were white. He'd followed her home to prove to himself that she wasn't worthy of his affection, to see the urban decay her kind would bring to his neighborhood, the way his father always said.

Voices charged him in the darkness. "Peeping motherfucker! Get him!" Eddie was lifted off his feet and thrown into the yucca's spiny fronds. He could see faces in front of him. Black faces. "Whatcha doing perving on my little sister?"

Eddie's heart hammered with the old man's warnings. The niggers were flesh eaters. Savages. They had tricked him with their pretty house, pretty girl. But he could smell their violence, the blood and mud from where they spawned. He struggled to break away and a voice growled, "Keep doing that and we'll fuck you up more, white boy."

Eddie started crying. "Daddy, I'm sorry."

The blond skank jitterbugged in the spotlight.

"Vampire," Ed Keane, Sr. said, chasing her with the beam. "Turn to ash if she don't suck pipe before sunup."

Eddie cringed at the palsied ghoul-whore. But he was excited too. "Shouldn't you arrest her or something?"

"What for? She's no threat. Except to your dick."

Saturday morning ride-along. Eddie in the shotgun seat of his father's shop, touring Mesa's underworld. The only time he enjoyed being with his father. Before the day, and the drinking, got hot. They were in the avenues off Mesa Drive. A menagerie of stucco and cinder block fortified with iron bars and junked cars. Speed bumps that once protected kids at play now protected drug dealers from police raids.

"Real people used to live here. Families. Back when I was a kid, before old Mesa High burned down and the mud people took over." The old man hit the steering wheel. "Politicians have turned their back on the city. Call it good growth. It's abandonment. Of course, they'll deny it. Hold out their little Main Street shops as proof. Expect us to defend it."

Eddie loved watching the old man work the streets, holding dominion over the freaks and the loons. Bust them or blast them, help or hurt. Decided on an arbitrary scale that his father called justice. The old man patted his leg. "Can I tell you something?"

"Okay."

"You remember when I shot that guy last year?"

"The rapist. Yeah."

"What if I told you I shot him in cold blood?"

"I thought he came after you. With his knife."

"He had a knife, all right. But he wasn't holding it when I shot him."

"So you killed him for no reason. Why?"

"Because I could. It gave me satisfaction."

Eleven-year-old Eddie did not see the fire in his father's eyes, only the power of its glow. He swelled with pride at the knowledge he'd been entrusted to guard.

"Are you still one of the good guys?"

"I'm still wearing the badge, aren't I?"

"You think maybe when I grow up I can be a police?"

Eddie sat ramrod straight, arms folded in his lap. His mother sat across from him at the table. They stared at each other over their untouched plates of food. Had been that way since his father sat down at the table, pulled out his handgun, and set it beside his utensils. "I'd appreciate a little quiet time tonight," he said.

A domestic-violence lullaby put Eddie to sleep. Woke fast when the book bag tied to his doorknob rustled. Early Daddy Defense System. In the light from the hall he saw his mother slip into the room. She knelt before his bed, face pitted from abuse. She kissed his forehead, sobbed, kissed his mouth. Her breath was copper-hot with blood and alcohol. Awkwardly, Eddie tried to embrace her.

That first time couldn't really be called sex. But as she pressed herself against him, Eddie saw relief spill into his mother's features. Terror replaced by a strange and haunting nothingness. Eddie decided he would do anything to see that look of peace on his mother's face. In the morning he wasn't sure if he had dreamed the episode.

"Eddie, get out of bed," she called. "Oatmeal's getting soggy."

The puppy's neck had been twisted so severely that its dead eyes were staring back at its haunches. Its body lay on the patio next to a scattering of dead leaves. A stain on the carpet and the smear on his father's polished shoe told the story.

"I asked you to start picking up after your dog!" the old man yelled. "Now pick up your dog. Trash bag and shovel are waiting for you."

His dog's name was Bandit. Eddie had carried him home on his bike from the store, made a house out of cardboard and towels, snuck him in at night, and let him chase his toes under the covers. He tried not to look at the creature, whose only crime had been reliance on Eddie. Tears filled his eyes.

"Don't you dare cry, boyo," his father said. "Dog's a lesson. Everything gets taken away."

The house breathed pain. The wrongness of it stopped Eddie cold at the back door. Bandit must've sensed its threat too. The dog sniffed and nipped at Eddie's shoes, growling defensively as he tried to get past.

Eddie bent down and stroked Bandit's fur, overcome by sadness at what was to become of his little friend. He thought of how the spade vibrated as he tamped down the dirt around the trash bag. He picked the dog up and pressed his face into its fur.

It took a moment for the significance of the gesture to register.

Eddie knew the horror show that awaited him inside. He was eight years old again, home from a half day of school with plans to dump his bag, snag a juice, and get gone.

He remembered the frigid blast of air-conditioning that froze the sweat on his back and legs, the gurgle of the fridge, and how the light from the boxed windows formed a floating cage across the kitchen. He saw the empty whiskey bottle on the table and his father's gun belt slung over one of the chairs. He passed quietly through the light bars, aware that a low keening had interrupted the preternatural stillness.

It was coming from the end of the hall, his parents' room, where Eddie found his father choking his mother blue. The old man was sitting astride her on the bed, still dressed in full uniform. Beneath him, his mother's naked body writhed. She snorted for air, blowing snot and blood in an arc that reached almost to the ceiling. Her arms and legs pinwheeled and her bony ass bucked off the mattress.

Eddie remembered standing there, transfixed, doing nothing.

But in his memory he had not stopped to pick up the dog. Something had changed. For the first time since beginning his macabre descent into the wayback, Eddie had no compulsion to follow his past. He stepped out of it. Instead of walking through the kitchen, he went to the table and lifted his father's gun from its holster.

The automatic was heavy. He held it two-handed, the way his father had demonstrated: *Got to hold firm on those jigs.* Eddie carried it like that down the hall, Bandit at his heels the whole way.

Eddie didn't stop at the bedroom door this time. He raised the gun. "Get off her."

The old man spun around, surprised and angry at Eddie's transgression. "Do yourself a favor, boyo," he said. "Whatever you're doing, undo it. Pronto."

"I'm trying."

"You must be stupid sick—" The old man stopped when he saw the gun. "What in the fuck-all name of Christ are you thinking?"

"Ending you."

Eddie backed away as his father rolled off the bed. His mother didn't move. "So that's your plan? You're going to shoot your own father?"

"Y-Yes," Eddie said.

"R-R-Really? You fucking whelp. I own you." Booze fused with rage in the old man's eyes. "Are you listening to me? You're mine. I made you. Now drop that gun. Do you hear me?"

Eddie didn't hear. He was twenty years away, in a courtroom, staring down the black-cowled judge. He again felt the scorn of that penetrating gaze and the righteousness of the single question the judge had posed. *What made you?*

"I know," Eddie answered, and snapped back to the old man. He fired three times, center mass. His father's face vanished in an explosion of smoke and gore. Eddie wondered if his sentence was over.

He'd served his time. Done life.

PART II

Where the Sidewalk Ends

AMAPOLA

BY LUIS ALBERTO URREA

Paradise Valley

Here's the thing—I never took drugs in my life. Yes, all right, I was the champion of my share of keggers. Me and the Pope. We were like, Bring on the Corona and the Jäger! Who wasn't? But I never even smoked the chronic, much less used the hard stuff. Until I met Pope's little sister. And when I met her, she was the drug, and I took her and I took her, and when I took her, I didn't care about anything. All the blood and all the bullets in the world could not penetrate that high.

The irony of Amapola and me was that I never would have gotten close to her if her family hadn't believed I was gay. It was easy for them to think a gringo kid with emo hair and eyeliner was *un joto*. By the time they found out the truth, it was too late to do much about it. All they could do was put me to the test to see if I was a stand-up boy. It was either that or kill me.

You think I'm kidding.

At first, I didn't even know she existed. I was friends with Popo. We met in my senior year at Camelback High. Alice Cooper's old school back in prehistory—our big claim to fame, though the freshmen had no idea who Alice Cooper was. VH1 was for grandmothers. Maybe Alice was a president's wife or something.

You'd think the freak factor would remain high, right? But it was another hot space full of Arizona Republicans and future CEOs and the struggling underworld of auto mechanics and hopeless football jocks not yet aware they were going to be fat and bald and living in a duplex on the far side drinking too much and paying alimony to the cheerleaders they thought could never weigh 298 pounds and smoke like a coal plant.

Not Popo. The Pope. For one thing, he had more money than God. Well, his dad and his Aunt Cuca had all the money, but it drizzled upon him like the first rains of Christmas. He was always buying the beer, paying for gas and movie tickets and midnight runs to Taco Bell. "Good American food," he called it.

He'd transferred in during my senior year. He called it his exile. I spied him for the first time in English. We were struggling to stay awake during the endless literary conversations about *A Separate Peace*. He didn't say much about it. Just sat over there making sly eyes at the girls and laughing at the teacher's jokes. I'd never seen a Beaner kid with such long hair. He looked like some kind of Apache warrior, to tell you the truth. He had double-loops in his left ear. He got drogy sometimes and wore eyeliner under one eye. Those little Born Again chicks went crazy for him when he was in his devil-boy mode.

And the day we connected, he was wearing a Cradle of Filth T-shirt. He was staring at me. We locked eyes for a second and he nodded once and we both started to laugh. I was wearing a Fields of the Nephilim shirt. We were the Pentagram Brothers that day, for sure. Everybody else must have been thinking we were goth school shooters. I guess it was a good thing Phoenix was too friggin' hot for black trenchcoats.

Later, I was sitting outside the vice principal's office. Ray Hulsebus, the nickelback on the football team, had called me "faggot" and we'd duked it out in the lunch court. Popo was sitting on the wooden bench in the hall.

"Good fight," he said, nodding once.

I sat beside him.

"Wha'd you get busted for?" I asked.

He gestured at his shirt. It was originally black, but it had been laundered so often it was gray. In a circle were the purple letters, *VU*. Above them, in stark white, one word: *HEROIN*.

"Cool," I said. "Velvet Underground."

"My favorite song."

We slapped hands.

"The admin's not into classic rock," he noted. "Think I'm . . . advocating substance abuse."

We laughed.

"You like *Berlin?*" he asked.

"Berlin? Like, the old VH1 band?"

"Hell no! Lou Reed's best album, dude!"

They summoned him.

"I'll play it for ya," he said, and walked into the office.

And so it began.

Tía Cuca's house was the bomb. She was hooked up with some kind of Lebanese merchant. Out in Paradise Valley. The whole place was cool floor tiles and suede couches. Their pool looked out on the city lights, and you could watch roadrunners on the deck cruising for rattlers at dusk. Honestly, I didn't know why Pope wasn't in some rich private school like Brophy or Phoenix Country Day, but apparently his scholastic history was "spotty," as they say. I still don't know how he ended up at poor ol' Camelback, but I do know it must have taken a lot of maneuvering by his family. By the time we'd graduated, we were inseparable. He went to ASU. I didn't have that kind of money. I went to community college.

Pope's room was the coolest thing I'd ever seen. Tía Cuca had given him a detached single-car garage at the far end of the house. They'd put in a bathroom and made a bed loft on top of it. Pope had a king-size mattress up there, and a wall of CDs and a Bose iPod port, and everything was Wi-Fi'd to his laptop. There was a huge Bowie poster on the wall beside the door—in full Aladdin Sane glory, complete with the little shiny splash of come on his collarbone. It was so retro. My boy had satellite on a flat screen, and piles of DVDs around the slumpy little couch on the ground floor. I didn't know why he was so crazy for the criminal stuff—*Scarface* and *The Godfather*. I was sick of Tony Montana and Michael Corleone! Elvis clock—you know the one, with the King's legs dancing back and forth in place of a pendulum.

"Welcome," Pope said on that first visit, "to Disgraceland."

He was comical like that when you got to know him.

He turned me on to all that good classic stuff: Iggy, T. Rex, Roxy Music. He wasn't really fond of new music, except for the darkwave guys. Anyway, there we'd be, blasting that glam as loud as possible, and it would get late and I'd just fall asleep on his big bed with him. No wonder they thought I was gay! Ha. We were drinking Buds and reading *Hustler* mags we'd stolen from his Uncle Abdullah or whatever his name was. Aunt Cuca once said, "Don't you ever go home?" not mean like. Friendly banter, I'd say. But I told her, "Nah—since the divorce, my mom's too busy to worry about it." And in among all those excellent boys' days and nights, I was puttering around his desk, looking at the *Alien* figures and the Godzillas, scoping out the new copy of *El Topo* he'd gotten by mail, checking his big crystals and his antique dagger, when I saw the picture of Amapola behind his stack of textbooks. Yes, she was a kid. But what a kid.

"Who's this?" I said.

He took the framed picture out of my hand and put it back.

"Don't worry about who that is," he said.

Thanksgiving. Pope had planned a great big fiesta for all his homies and henchmen. Oh, yes. He took the goth-gansta thing seriously, and he had actual "hit men" (he called them that) who did errands for him, carried out security at his concerts. He played guitar for the New Nouveau Nuevos—you might remember them. One of his "soldiers" was a big Irish kid who'd been booted off the football team, Andy the Tank. Andy appeared at our apartment with an invitation to the fiesta—we were to celebrate the Nuevos' upcoming year, and chart the course of the future. I was writing lyrics for Pope, cribbed from Roxy Music and Bowie's *The Man*

Who Sold the World album. The invite was printed out on rolled parchment and tied with a red ribbon. Pope had style.

I went over to Tía Cuca's early, and there she was—Amapola. She'd come up from Nogales for the fiesta, since Pope was by now refusing to go home for any reason. He wanted nothing to do with his dad, who had declared that only gay boys wore long hair or makeup or played in a band that wore feather boas and silver pants. Sang in English.

I was turning eighteen, and she was fifteen, almost sixteen. She was more pale than Popo. She had a frosting of freckles on her nose and cheeks, and her eyes were light brown, almost gold. Her hair was thick and straight and shone like some liquid. She was kind of quiet too, blushing when I talked to her, shying away from all us males.

The meal was righteous. They'd fixed a turkey in the Mexican style. It was stuffed not with bread or oysters, but with nuts, dried pineapple, dried papaya and mango slices, and raisins. Cuca and Amapola wore traditional Mexican dresses and, along with Cuca's cook, served us the courses as we sat like members of the Corleone family around the long dining room table. Pope had seated Andy the Tank beside Fuckin' Franc, the Nuevos' drummer. Some guy I didn't know but who apparently owned a Nine Inch Nails–type synth studio in his garage sat beside Franc. I was granted the seat at the end of the table, across its length from Pope. Down the left side were the rest of the Nuevos—losers all.

I was trying to keep my roving eye hidden from the Pope. I didn't even have to guess what he'd do if he caught me checking her out. But she was so fine. It wasn't even my perpetual state of horniness. Yes it was. But it was more. She was like a song. Her small smiles, her graciousness. The way she swung her hair over her shoulder. The way she lowered her eyes and spoke softly . . . then gave you a wry look that cut sideways and made savage fun of everyone there. You just wanted to be a part of everything she was doing.

"Thank you," I said every time she refilled my water glass or dropped fresh tortillas by my plate. Not much, it's true, but compared to the Tank or Fuckin' Franc, I was as suave as Cary Grant.

"You are so welcome," she'd say.

It started to feel like a dance. It's in the way you say it, not what you say. We were saying more to each other than Cuca or Pope could hear.

And then, I was hit by a jolt that made me jump a little in my chair.

She stood behind me, resting her hands on the top of the chair. We were down to the cinnamon coffee and the red grape juice toasts. And Amapola put out one finger, where they couldn't see it, and ran her fingernail up and down between my shoulder blades.

Suddenly, supper was over, and we were all saying goodnight, and she had disappeared somewhere in the big house and never came back out.

Soon, Christmas came, and Pope again refused to go home. I don't know how Cuca took it, having the sullen King Nouveau lurking in her converted garage. He had a kitsch aluminum tree in there. Blue ornaments. "*Très* Warhol," he sighed.

My mom had given me some cool stuff—a vintage Who T-shirt, things like that. Pope's dad had sent presents—running shoes, French sunglasses, a .22 target pistol. We snickered. I was way cooler than Poppa Popo. I had been over to Zia Records and bought him some obscure '70s CDs: Captain Beyond, Curved Air, Amon Duul II, the Groundhogs. Things that looked cool, not that I'd ever heard them. Pope got me a vintage turntable and the first four Frank Zappa LPs; I couldn't listen to that shit. But still. How cool is that?

Pope wasn't a fool. He wasn't blind either. He'd arranged a better gift for me than all that. He'd arranged for Amapola to come visit for a week. I found out later she had begged him.

"Keep it in your pants," he warned me. "I'm watching you."

Oh my God. I was flying. We went everywhere for those six days. The three of us, unfortunately. Pope took us to that fancy art deco hotel downtown—the Clarendon. That one with the crazy neon lights on the walls outside and the dark gourmet eatery on the ground-floor front corner. We went to movie matinees, never night movies. It took two movies to wrangle a spot sitting next to her, getting Pope to relinquish the middle seat to keep us apart. But he knew it was a powerful movement between us, like continental drift. She kept leaning over to watch me instead of the movies. She'd laugh at everything I said. She lagged when we walked so I would walk near her. I was trying to keep my cool, not set off the Hermano Grande alarms. And suddenly he let me sit beside her, and I could smell her. She was all clean hair and sweet skin. Our arms brushed on the armrest, and we let them linger, sweat against each other. Our skin forming a thin layer of wet between us, a little of her and a little of me mixing into something made of both of us. I was aching. I could have pole-vaulted right out of the theater.

She turned sixteen that week. At a 3 o'clock showing of *The Dark Knight*, she slipped her hand over the edge of the armrest and tangled her fingers in mine.

This time, when she left, Pope allowed us one minute alone in his garage room. I kissed her. It was awkward. Delicious. Her hand went to my face and held it. She got in Cuca's car and cried as they drove away.

"You fucker," Popo said.

I couldn't believe she didn't Facebook. Amapola didn't even e-mail. She lived across the border, in Nogales, Mexico. So the phone was out of the question, even though her dad could have afforded it. When I asked Pope about his father's business, he told me they ran a duty-free import/export company based on each side of the border, in the two Nogaleses. Whatever. I just wanted to talk to Amapola. So I got stamps and envelopes. I was thinking, what is this, like, 1980 or something? But I wrote to her, and she wrote to me. I never even thought about the fact that instant messages or e-mail couldn't hold perfume, or have lip prints on the paper. You could Skype naked images to each other all night long, but Amapola had me hooked through the lips with each new scent in the envelope. She put her hair in the envelopes. It was more powerful than anything I'd experienced before. Maybe it was voodoo.

At Easter, Cuca and her Lebanese hubby flew to St. Thomas for a holiday. Somehow, Pope managed to get Amapola there at the house for a few days. He was gigging a lot, and he was seeing three or four strippers. I'll admit, he was hitting the sauce too much—he'd come home wasted and ricochet around the bathroom, banging into the fixtures like a pinball. I thought he'd break his neck on the toilet or the bathtub. The old man had been putting pressure on him—I had no idea how or what he wanted of Pope. He wanted the rock 'n' roll foolishness to end, that's for sure.

"You have no idea!" Pope would say, tequila stink on his breath. "If you only knew what they were really like. You can't begin to guess." But, you know, all boys who wear eyeliner and pay for full-sleeve tats say the same thing. Don't nobody understand the troubles they've seen. I just thought Pope was caught up in being our Nikki Sixx. We were heading for fame, world tours. I thought.

And there she was, all smiles. Dressed in black. Looking witchy and magical. Pope had a date with a girl named Demitasse. Can you believe that? Because she had small breasts or something. She danced at a high-end club that catered to men who knew words like "demitasse." She had little silver vials full of "stardust," that's all I really knew. It all left Pope staggering and blind, and that was what I needed to find time alone with my beloved.

We watched a couple of DVDs, and we held hands and then kissed. I freed her nipple from the lace—it was pink and swollen, like a little candy. I thought it would be brown. What did I know about Mexican girls? She pushed me away when I got on top of her, and she moved my hand back gently when it slipped up her thigh.

Pope came home walking sideways. I had no idea what time it was. I don't know how he got home. My pants were wet all down my left leg from hours of writhing with her. When Pope slurred, "My dad's in town," I didn't even pay attention. He went to Cuca's piano in the living room and tried to play some arrangement he'd cobbled together of *Tommy*. Then there was a silence that grew long. We looked in there and he was asleep in the floor, under the piano.

"Shh," Amapola said. And, "Wait here for me." She kissed my mouth, bit my lip.

When she came back down, she wore a nightgown that drifted around her legs and belly like fog. I knelt at her feet and ran my palms up her legs. She turned aside just as my hands crossed the midpoint of her thighs, and my palms slid up over her hip bones. She had taken off her panties. I put my mouth to her navel. I could smell her through the thin material.

"Do you love me?" she whispered, fingers tangled in my hair.

"Anything. You and me." I wasn't even thinking. "Us."

She yanked my hair.

"Do," she said. "You. Love me?"

Yank. It hurt.

"Yes!" I said. "Okay! Jesus! Love you!"

We went upstairs.

"Get up! Get up! Get the fuck up!" Popo was saying, ripping off the sheets. "Now! Now! Now!"

Amapola covered herself and rolled away with a small cry. Light was blasting through the windows. I thought he was going to beat my ass for sleeping with her. But he was in a panic.

"Get dressed. Dude—get dressed now!"

"What? What?"

"My dad."

He put his fists to his head.

"Oh shit. My dad!"

She started to cry.

I was in my white boxers in the middle of the room.

"Guys," I said. "Guys! Is there some trouble here?"

Amapola dragged the sheet off the bed and ran, wrapped, into the bathroom.

"You got no idea," Pope said. "Get dressed."

We were in the car in ten minutes. We sped out of the foothills and across town. Phoenix always looks empty to me when it's hot, like one of those sci-fi movies where all the people are dead and gone and some vampires or zombies are hiding in the vacant condos, waiting for night. The streets are too wide, and they reflect the heat like a Teflon cooking pan. Pigeons might explode into flame just flying across the street to escape the melting city bus.

Pope was saying, "Just don't say nothing. Just show respect. It'll be okay. Right, sis?"

She was in the backseat.

"Don't talk back," she said. "Just listen. You can take it."

"Yeah," Pope said. "You can take it. You better take it. That's the only way he'll respect you."

My head was spinning.

Apparently, the old man had come to town to see Pope and meet me, but Pope, that asshole, had been so wasted he forgot. But it was worse than that. The old man had waited at a fancy restaurant. For both of us. You didn't keep Big Pop waiting.

You see, he had found my letters. He had rushed north to try to avert the inevitable. And now he was seething, they said, because Pope's maricón best friend wasn't queer at all, and was working his mojo on the sweet pea. My scalp still hurt from her savage hair-pulling. I looked back at her. Man, she was as fresh as a sea breeze. I started to smile.

"Ain't no joke," Pope announced.

We fretted in silence.

"Look," he said. "It won't seem like it at first, but Pops will do anything for my sister. Anything. She controls him, man. So keep cool."

When we got there, Pope said, "The bistro." I had never seen it before, not really traveling in circles that ate French food or ate at "bistros." Pops was standing outside. He was a slender man, balding. Clean-shaven. Only about five-seven. He wore aviator glasses, that kind that turn dark in the sun. They were deep gray over his eyes. He was standing with a Mexican in a uniform. The other guy was over six feet tall and had a good gut on him. What Pope called a "food baby" from that funny movie everybody liked.

The old man and the soldier stared at me. I wanted to laugh. That's it? I mean, really? A little skinny bald guy? I was invincible with love.

Poppa turned and entered the bistro without a word. Pope and Amapola followed, holding hands. The stout soldier dude just eyeballed me and walked in. I was left alone on the sidewalk. I followed.

They were already sitting. It was ice cold. The way I liked it. I tried not to see Amapola's nipples. But I noticed her pops looking at them. And then the soldier. Pops told her, "Tápate, cabrona." She had brought a little sweater with her, and now I knew why. She primly draped herself.

"Dad . . ." said Pope.

"Shut it," his father said.

The eyeglasses had only become half-dark. You could almost see his eyes.

A waiter delivered a clear drink.

"Martini, sir," he said.

It was only about 11 in the morning.

Big Poppa said, "I came to town last night to see you." He sipped his drink. "I come here, to this restaurant. Is my favorite.

Is comida Frances, understand? Quality." Another sip. He looked at the soldier—the soldier nodded. "I invite you." He pointed at Pope. Then at her. Then at me. "You, you, and you. Right here. Berry expensive." He drained the martini and snapped his fingers at the waiter. "An' I sit here an' wait." The waiter hurried over and took the glass and scurried away.

"Me an' my brother, Arnulfo."

He put his hand on the soldier's arm.

"We wait for you."

Popo said, "Dad . . ."

"Callate el osico, chingado," his father breathed. He turned his head to me and smiled. He looked like a moray eel in a tank. Another martini landed before him.

"You," he said. "Why you dress like a girl?" He sipped. "I wait for you, but you don't care. No! Don't say nothing. Listen. I wait, and you no show up here to my fancy dinner. Is okay. I don't care." He waved his hand. "I have my li'l drink, and I don't care." He toasted me. He seemed like he was coiled, steel springs inside his gut. My skin was crawling and I didn't even know why.

"I wait for you," he said. "Captain Arnulfo, he wait. You don't care, right? Is okay! I'm happy. I got my martinis, I don't give a shit."

He smiled.

He pulled a long cigar out of his inner pocket. He bit the end off and spit it on the table. He put the cigar in his mouth. Arnulfo took out a gold lighter and struck a blue flame.

The waiter rushed over and murmured, "I'm sorry, sir, but this is a nonsmoking bistro. You'll have to take it outside."

The old man didn't even look at him—just stared at me through those gray lenses.

"Is hot outside," he said. "Right, gringo? Too hot?" I nodded—I didn't know what to do. "You see?" the old man said.

"I must insist," the waiter said.

"Bring the chef," the old man said.

"Excuse me?"

"Get the chef out here for me. Now."

The waiter brought out the chef, who bent down to the old man. Whispers. No drama. But the two men hurried away and the waiter came back with an ashtray. Arnulfo lit Poppa's cigar.

He blew smoke at me and said, "Why you do this violence to me?"

"I . . ." I said.

"Shut up."

He snapped his fingers again, and food and more martinis arrived. I stared at my plate. Snails in garlic butter. I couldn't eat, couldn't even sip the water. Smoke drifted to me. I could feel the gray lenses focused on me. Pope, that chickenshit, just ate and never looked up. Amapola sipped iced coffee and stared out the window.

After forty minutes of this nightmare, Poppa pushed his plate away.

"Oye," he said, "tú."

I looked up.

"Why you wan' fock my baby daughter?"

Sure, I trembled for a while after that. I got it, I really did. But did good sense overtake me? What do you think? I was full-on into the Romeo and Juliet thing, and she was even worse. Parents—you want to ensure your daughters marry young? Forbid them from seeing their boyfriends. Just try it.

"Uncle Arnie," as big dark Captain Arnulfo was called in Cuca's house, started hanging around. A lot. I wasn't, like, stupid. I could tell what was what—he was sussing me out (that's a word Pope taught me). He brought Bass Pale Ale all the time. He sidled up to me and said dumb things like, "You like the sexy?" Pope and I laughed all night after Uncle Arnie made his appearances. "You make the sexy-sexy in cars?" What a dork, we thought.

My beloved showered me with letters. I had no way of knowing if my own letters got to her or not, but she soon found an Internet café in Nogales and sent me cyber-love. Popo was drying up a little, not quite what you'd call sober, but occasionally back on the earth, and he started calling me "McLovin." I think it was his way of trying to tone it down. "Bring it down a notch, homeboy," he'd say when I waxed overly poetic about his sister.

It was a Saturday when it happened. I was IM-ing Amapola. That's all I did on Saturday afternoons. No TV, no cruising in the car, no movies or pool time. I fixed a huge vat of sun tea and hit my laptop and talked to her. Mom was at work—she was always at work or out doing lame shit like bowling. It was just me, the computer, my distant girlie, and the cat rubbing against my leg. I'll confess to you—don't laugh—I cried at night thinking about her.

Does this explain things a little? Pope said I was whipped. I'd be like, that's no way to talk about your sister. She's better than all of you people! He'd just look at me out of those squinty Apache eyes. "Maybe," he'd drawl. "Maybe . . ." And I was just thinking about all that on Saturday, going crazier and crazier with the desire to see her sweet face every morning, her hair on my skin every night, mad in love with her, and I was IM-ing her that she should just book. Run away. She was almost seventeen already. She could catch a bus and be in Phoenix in a few hours and we'd jump on I-10 and drive to Cali. I didn't know what I imagined— just us, in love, on a beach. And suddenly the laptop crashed. Just gone—black screen before Amapola could answer me. That was weird, I thought. I cursed and kicked stuff, then I grabbed a shower and rolled.

When I cruised over to Aunt Cuca's, she was gone. So was Pope. Uncle Arnie was sitting in the living room in his uniform, sipping coffee.

"They all go on vacation," he said. "Just you and me."

Vacation? Pope hadn't said anything about vacations. Not that he was what my English profs would call a reliable narrator.

Arnie gestured for me to sit. I stood there.

"Coffee?" he offered.

"No, thanks."

"Sit!"

I sat.

I can't relate the conversation very clearly, since I never knew what the F Arnie was mumbling, to tell you the truth. His accent was all bandido. I often just nodded and smiled, hoping not to offend the dude, lest he freak out and bust caps in me. That's a joke. Kind of. But then I'd wonder what I'd just agreed to.

"You love Amapola," he said. It wasn't a question. He smiled sadly, put his hand on my knee.

"Yes, sir," I said.

He nodded. Sighed. "Love," he said. "Is good, love."

"Yes, sir."

"You not going away, right?"

I shook my head. "No way."

"So. What this means? You marry the girl?"

Whoa. Marry? I . . . guess . . . I was going to marry her. Someday.

Sure, you think about it. But to say it out loud. That was hard. Yet I felt like some kind of breakthrough was happening here. The older generation had sent an emissary.

"I believe," I said, mustering some balls, "yes. I will marry Amapola. Someday. You know."

He shrugged, sadly. I thought that was a little odd, frankly. He held up a finger and busted out a cell phone, hit the speed button, and muttered in Spanish. Snapped it shut. Sipped his coffee.

"We have big family reunion tomorrow. You come. Okay? I'll fix up all with Amapola's papá. You see. Yes?"

I smiled at him, not believing this turn of events.

"Big Mexican rancho. Horses. Good food. Mariachis." He laughed. "And love! Two kids in love!"

We slapped hands. We smiled and chuckled. I had some coffee.

"I pick you up here at 7 in the morning," he said. "Don't be late."

The morning desert was purple and orange. The air was almost cool. Arnie had a Styrofoam cooler loaded with Dr. Peppers and Cokes. He drove a bitchin' S-Class Benz. It smelled like leather and aftershave. He kept the satellite tuned to BBC Radio 1. "You like the crazy maricón music, right?" he asked.

"... Ah ... right."

It was more like flying than driving, and when he sped past Arivaca, I wasn't all that concerned. I figured we were going to Nogales, Arizona. But we slid through that little dry town like a shark and crossed into Mex without slowing down. He just raised a finger off the steering wheel and motored along, saying, "You going to like this."

And then we were through Nogales, Mexico, too. Black and tan desert. Saguaros and freaky burned-looking cactuses. I don't know what that stuff was. It was spiky.

We took a long dirt side road. I was craning around, looking at the bad black mountains around us.

"Suspension makes this road feel like butter," Arnie noted.

We came out in a big valley. There was an airfield of some sort there. Mexican army stuff—trucks, Humvees. Three or four hangars or warehouses. Some shiny Cadillacs and SUVs scattered around.

"You going to like this," Arnie said. "It's a surprise."

There was Big Poppa Popo, the old man himself. He was standing with his hands on his hips. With a tall American. Those dark gray lenses turned toward us. We parked. We got out.

"What's going on?" I asked.

"Shut up," said Arnie.

"Where's the rancho?" I asked.

The American burst out laughing.

"Jesus, kid!" he shouted. He turned to the old man. "He really is a dumbshit."

He walked away and got in a white SUV. He slammed the door and drove into the desert, back the way we had come. We stood there watching him go. I'm not going to lie—I was getting scared.

"You marry Amapola?" the old man said.

"One day. Look, I don't know what you guys are doing here, but—"

"Look at that," he interrupted, turning from me and gesturing toward a helicopter sitting on the field. "Huey. Old stuff, from your Vietnam. Now the Mexican air force use it to fight las drogas." He turned to me. "You use las drogas?"

"No! Never."

They laughed.

"Sure, sure," the old man said.

"Ask Amapola!" I cried. "She'll tell you!"

"She already tell me everything," he said.

Arnie put his arm around my shoulders. "Come," he said, and started walking toward the helicopter. I resisted for a moment, but the various Mexican soldiers standing around were suddenly really focused and not slouching and were walking along all around us.

"What is this?" I said.

"You know what I do?" the old man asked.

"Business?" I said. My mind was blanking out, I was so scared.

"Business." He nodded. "Good answer."

We came under the blades of the big helicopter. I'd never been near one in my life. It scared the crap out of me. The Mexican pilots looked out their side windows at me. The old man patted the machine.

"President Bush!" he said. "DEA!"

I looked at Arnie. He smiled, nodded at me. "Fight the drogas," he said.

The engines whined and chuffed and the rotor started to turn.

"Is very secret what we do," said the old man. "But you

take a ride and see. Is my special treat. You go with Arnulfo."

"Come with me," Arnie said.

"You go up and see, then we talk about love."

The old man hurried away, and it was just me and Arnie and the soldiers with their black M16s.

"After you," Arnie said.

He pulled on a helmet. Then we took off. It was rough as hell. I felt like I was being pummeled in the ass and lower back when the engines really kicked in. And when we rose, my guts dropped out through my feet. I closed my eyes and gripped the webbing Arnie had fastened around my waist. "Holy God!" I shouted. It was worse when we banked—the side doors were wide open, and I screamed like a girl, sure I was falling out. The Mexicans laughed and shook their heads, but I didn't care.

Arnie was standing in the door. He unhooked a big gun from the stanchion where it had been strapped with its barrel pointed up. He dangled it in the door on cords. He leaned toward me and shouted, "Sixty caliber! Hung on double bungees!" He slammed a magazine into the thing and pulled levers and snapped snappers. He leaned down to me again and shouted, "Feel the vibration? You lay on the floor, it makes you come!"

I thought I heard him wrong.

We were beating out of the desert and into low hills. I could see our shadow below us, fluttering like a giant bug on the ground and over the bushes. The seat kicked up and we were rising.

Arnulfo took a pistol from his belt and showed me.

"Amapola," he said.

I looked around for her, stupidly. But then I saw what was below us, in a watered valley. Orange flowers. Amapola. Poppies.

"This is what we do," Arnulfo said.

He raised his pistol and shot three rounds out the door and laughed. I put my hands over my ears.

"You're DEA?" I cried.

He popped off another round.

"Is competition," he said. "We do business."

Oh my God.

He fell against me and was shouting in my ear and there was nowhere I could go. "You want Amapola? You want to marry my sobrina? Just like that? Really? Pendejo." He grabbed my shirt. "Can you fly, gringo? Can you fly?" I was shaking. I was trying to shrink away from him, but I could not. I was trapped in my seat. His breath stank, and his lips were at my ear like hers might have been, and he was screaming, "Can you fly, chingado? Because you got a choice! You fly, or you do what we do."

I kept shouting, "What? What?" It was like one of those dreams where nothing makes sense. "What?"

"You do what we do, I let you live, cabrón."

"What?"

"I let you live. Or you fly. Decide."

"I don't want to die!" I yelled. I was close to wetting my pants. The Huey was nose-down and sweeping in a circle. I could see people below us, running. A few small huts. Horses or mules. A pickup started to speed out of the big poppy field. Arnulfo talked into his mike and the helicopter heaved after it. Oh no, oh no. He took up the .60 caliber and braced himself. I put my fingers in my ears. And he ripped a long stream of bullets out the door. It was the loudest thing I'd ever heard. Louder than the loudest thing you can imagine. So loud your insides jump, but it all becomes an endless rip of noise, like thunder cracking inside your bladder and your teeth hurt from gritting against it.

The truck just tattered, if metal can tatter. The roof of the cab blew apart and the smoking ruin of the vehicle spun away below us and vanished in dust and smoke and steam.

I was crying.

"Be a man!" Arnulfo yelled.

We were hovering. The crew members were all turned toward me, staring.

Arnie unsnapped my seat webbing.

"Choose," he said.

"I want to live."

"Choose."

You know how it goes in *Die Hard* movies. How the hero kicks the bad guy out the door and sprays the Mexican crew with the .60 and survives a crash landing. But that's not what happened. That didn't even cross my mind. Not even close. No, I got up on terribly shaky legs, so shaky I might have pitched out the open door all by myself to discover that I could not, in fact, fly. I said, "What do I do?" And the door gunner grabbed me and shoved me up to the hot gun. The ground was wobbling far below us, and I could see the Indian workers down there. Six men and a woman. And they were running. I was praying and begging God to get me out of this somehow and I was thinking of my beautiful lover and I told myself I didn't know how I got there and the door gunner came up behind me now, he slammed himself against my ass, and he said, "Hold it, lean into it. It's gonna kick, okay? Finger on the trigger. I got you." And I braced the .60 and I tried to close my eyes and prayed I'd miss them and I was saying, *Amapola, Amapola*, over and over in my mind, and the gunner was hard against me, he was erect and pressing it into my buttocks and he shouted, "For love!" and I squeezed the trigger.

PUBLIC TRANSPORTATION

BY LEE CHILD

Chandler

He said he wouldn't talk to me. I asked him why. He said because he was a cop and I was a journalist. I said he sounded like a guy with something to hide. He said no, he had nothing to hide.

"So talk to me," I said, and I knew he would.

He scuffed around for a minute more, hands on the top of the bar, drumming his fingers, moving a little on his stool. I knew him fairly well. He was edging out of the summer of his career and entering the autumn. His best years were behind him. He was in the valley, facing a long ten years before his pension. He liked winning, but losing didn't worry him too much. He was a realistic man. But he liked to be sure. What he hated was not really knowing whether he had won or lost.

"From the top," I said.

He shrugged and took a sip of his beer and sighed and blew fumes toward the mirror facing us. Then he started with the 911 call. The house, out beyond Chandler, south and east of the city. A long low ranch, prosperous, walled in, the unlit pool, the darkness. The parents, arriving home from a party. The silence. The busted window, the empty bed. The trail of blood through the hallway. The daughter's body, all ripped up. Fourteen years old, damaged in a way he still wasn't prepared to discuss.

I said, "There were details that you withheld."

He asked, "How do you know?"

"You guys always do that. To evaluate the confessions."

He nodded.

I asked, "How many confessions did you get?"

"A hundred and eight."

"All phony?"

"Of course."

"What information did you withhold?"

"I'm not going to tell you."

"Why not? You not sure you got the right guy?"

He didn't answer.

"Keep going," I said.

So he did. The scene was clearly fresh. The parents had gotten back maybe moments after the perpetrator had exited. Police response had been fast. The blood on the hallway carpet was still liquid. Dark red, not black, against the kid's pale skin. The kid's pale skin was a problem from the start. They all knew it. They were in a position to act fast and heavy, so they were going to, and they knew it would be claimed later that the speed was all about the kid being white, not black or brown. It wasn't. It was a question of luck and timing. They got a fresh scene, and they got a couple of breaks. I nodded, like I accepted his view. Which I did. I was a journalist, and I liked mischief as much as the next guy, but sometimes things were straightforward.

"Go on," I said.

There were photographs of the kid all over the house. She was an only child. She was luminous and beautiful. She was stupefying, the way fourteen-year-old white Arizona girls often are.

"Go on," I said.

The first break had been the weather. There had been torrential rain two days previously, and then the heat had come back with a vengeance. The rain had skimmed the street with sand and mud and the heat had baked it to a film of dust, and the dust showed no tire tracks other than those from the parents' vehicle and the cop cars and the ambulance. Therefore the perpetrator had arrived on foot. And left on foot. There were clear marks in the dust. Sneakers, maybe size ten, fairly generic soles. The

prints were photographed and e-mailed and everyone was confi-
dent that in the fullness of time some database somewhere would
match a brand and a style. But what was more important was that
they had a suspect recently departed from a live scene on foot,
in a landscape where no one walked. So APBs and be-on-the-
lookouts were broadcast for a two-mile radius. It was midnight
and more than a hundred degrees and pedestrians were going to
be rare. It was simply too hot for walking. Certainly too hot for
running. Any kind of sustained physical activity would be close to
a suicide attempt. Greater Phoenix was that kind of place, especially in the summer.

Ten minutes passed and no fugitives were found.

Then they got their second break. The parents were reason-
ably lucid. In between all the bawling and screaming they noticed
their daughter's cell phone was missing. It had been her pride and
joy. An iPhone, with an AT&T contract that gave her unlimited
minutes, which she exploited to the max. Back then iPhones were
new and cool. The cops figured the perp had stolen it. They figured the kind of guy who had no car in Arizona would have been
entranced by a small shiny object like an iPhone. Or else if he
was some kind of big-time deviant, maybe he collected souvenirs.
Maybe the cache of photographs of the kid's friends was exciting.
Or the text messages stored in the memory.

"Go on," I said.

The third break was all about middle-class parents and
fourteen-year-old daughters. The parents had signed up for a service whereby they could track the GPS chip in the iPhone on
their home computer. Not cheap, but they were the kind of people who wanted to know their kid was telling the truth when she
said she was sleeping over at a girlfriend's house or riding with a
buddy to the library. The cops got the password and logged on
right there and then and saw the phone moving slowly north,
toward Tempe. Too fast for walking. Too fast for running. Too
slow to be in a car.

"Bike?" one of them said.

"Too hot," another answered. "Plus no tire tracks in the driveway."

The guy telling the story next to me on his stool had been the one who had understood.

"Bus," he said. "The perp is on the bus."

Greater Phoenix had a lot of buses. They were for workers paid too little to own cars. They shuttled folks around, especially early in the morning and late at night. The giant city would have ground to a halt without them. Meals would have gone unserved, pools uncleaned, beds unmade, trash not collected. Immediately all the cops as one imagined a rough profile. A dark-skinned man, probably small, probably crazy, rocking on a seat as a bus headed north. Fiddling with the iPhone, checking the music library, looking at the pictures. Maybe with the knife still in his pocket, although surely that was too much to ask.

One cop stayed at the house and watched the screen and called the game like a sports announcer. All the APBs and the BOLOs were canceled and every car screamed after the bus. It took ten minutes to find it. Ten seconds to stop it. It was corraled in a ring of cars. Lights were flashing and popping and cops were crouching behind hoods and doors and trunks and guns were pointing, Glocks and shotguns, dozens of them.

The bus had a driver and three passengers aboard.

The driver was a woman. All three passengers were women. All three were elderly. One of them was white. The driver was a skinny Latina of around thirty.

"Go on," I said.

The guy beside me sipped his beer again and sighed. He had arrived at the point where the investigation was botched. They had spent close to twenty minutes questioning the four women, searching them, making them move up and down the street while the cop back at the house watched for GPS action on the screen. But the cursor didn't move. The phone was still on the bus. But the bus was empty. They searched under the seats. Nothing. They searched the seats themselves.

They found the phone.

The last-but-one seat at the back on the right had been slit with a knife. The phone had been forced edgewise into the foam rubber cushion. It was hidden there and bleeping away silently. A wild goose chase. A decoy.

The slit in the seat was rimed with faint traces of blood. The same knife.

The driver and all three passengers recalled a white man getting on the bus south of Chandler. He had seated himself in back and gotten out again at the next stop. He was described as neatly dressed and close to middle age. He was remembered for being from the wrong demographic. Not a typical bus rider.

The cops asked, "Was he wearing sneakers?"

No one knew for sure.

"Did he have blood on him?"

No one recalled.

The chase restarted south of Chandler. The assumption was that because the decoy had been placed to move north, then the perp was actually moving south. A fine theory, but it came to nothing. No one was found. A helicopter joined the effort. The night was still dark but the helicopter had thermal imaging equipment. It was not useful. Everything single thing it saw was hot.

Dawn came and the helicopter refueled and came back for a visual search. And again, and again, for days. At the end of a long weekend it found something.

"Go on," I said.

The thing that the helicopter found was a corpse. White male, wearing sneakers. In his early twenties. He was identified as a college student, last seen the day before. A day later the medical examiner issued his report. The guy had died of heat exhaustion and dehydration.

"Consistent with running from a crime scene?" the cops asked.

"Among other possibilities," the medical examiner answered.

The guy's toxicology screen was baroque. Ecstasy, skunk, alcohol.

"Enough to make him unstable?" the cops asked.

"Enough to make an elephant unstable," the medical examiner answered.

The guy beside me finished his beer. I signaled for another.

I asked, "Case closed?"

The guy beside me nodded. "Because the kid was white. We needed a result."

"You not convinced?"

"He wasn't middle-aged. He wasn't neatly dressed. His sneakers were wrong. No sign of the knife. Plus, a guy hopped-up enough to run himself to death in the heat wouldn't have thought to set up the decoy with the phone."

"So who was he?"

"Just a frat boy who liked partying a little too much."

"Anyone share your opinion?"

"All of us."

"Anyone doing anything about it?"

"The case is closed."

"So what really happened?"

"I think the decoy indicates premeditation. And I think it was a double bluff. I think the perp got out of the bus and carried on north, maybe in a car he had parked."

I nodded. The perp had. Right then the car he had used was parked in the lot behind the bar. Its keys were in my pocket.

"Win some, lose some," I said.

DEVIL DOLL

BY PATRICK MILLIKIN

Tovrea Castle

S poiled little assholes," Blankenship said, looking down at the two bodies. The girl had crumpled onto her side and lay twisted on the concrete floor. The young man remained sitting but his head sagged forward, a thin line of blood trailing from his mouth. Detective Gene Conover stepped out onto the top-floor landing of the castle and stood beside the uniformed cop. It took him a moment to catch his breath.

"What am I looking at here, Tom?" he said.

"I'd say a murder-suicide type of setup. Sid Vicious over here put a plug in his girlfriend and then took himself out."

A crime scene photographer hovered, clicking shots of the dead pair from various angles. He nodded to Conover and retreated. Several other techs and uniforms hung around downstairs.

The detective slipped on a pair of latex gloves and examined the surface of the waist-high retaining hall. He then took out his Maglite and did a complete circle of the small observation deck. Blankenship waited for him to speak.

"ID?" Conover finally asked.

"Nothing on Sid here, but we found the girl's purse. Her wallet was inside. Cash and credit cards hadn't been touched. Name's Kelly Hodge. Mean anything to you?"

Conover shook his head. "Not really. Does she have a sheet?"

"Well, she doesn't have a record exactly, but we know this girl. You've never seen her before, eh?"

Conover leaned over and looked again closely at the two bodies. "I don't think so, Tom. Should I have?"

"She's Ed Hodge's little girl," Blankenship said.

"The liquor guy?"

"The very same. This is gonna be a mess."

The detective squatted down and studied the entrance wound on the girl's chest, noting the size and shape of the powder burns. He was careful to avoid the blood, which soaked her lower torso and pooled out on the concrete floor. Conover also recognized fresh needle marks on her arm.

"I'd say whoever shot her knew what he was doing," he said, glancing over at the gun lying next to the dead guy's feet. One of the techs had already drawn a chalk circle around it.

"Why, because of the pop gun?" Blankenship asked.

"Easy to miss with a .22. The guy shot her directly in the heart. Couldn't have been more than a foot or two away."

"Did himself the same way from the looks of it."

"We'll see about that."

"Looks pretty straightforward, Gene. Scumbag boyfriend shoots the Hodge girl, then punches his own ticket."

"You may be right," Conover said. He stood up and stepped back from the two bodies. "Where are the shell casings?"

"Bagged and tagged already."

"How many?"

"Just the two, and only two missing from the clip."

"Interesting," he said. "Who called it in?"

"Bouncer over at Angels heard the shots." Blankenship consulted his notes. "Dispatch recorded the call at 3:55 a.m. Let's see, guy's name is Everest or Everett. Something like that."

Conover looked out across the desert toward Washington. The all-nude club's neon marquee was clearly visible a couple hundred yards away.

Blankenship bent down on one knee and crooked his neck to the side to read what was written on the girl's shirt. "Wonder what the hell *45 Grave* means," he said. "Some kind of satanic shit?"

"Rock group'd be my guess," Conover said.

"Think they're in some weird cult or something?" Blankenship frowned at the young man's appearance. The kid looked like a collapsed marionette, dyed black hair hanging in front of his eyes, face smudged with sweat and eyeliner.

"I seriously doubt it, Tom."

"Well, it looks like our boy's shirt is pretty accurate, anyway."

Conover noticed the lettering on the young man's shirt, nearly obscured by blood—*Bad Brains*. He humored Blankenship with a smirk.

The detective glanced at his watch. It was just after 6 a.m. He'd wait for the autopsy and ballistics reports to confirm his suspicions. In the meantime, he refrained from saying much to the uniform. Blankenship was basically a decent guy, but he wasn't too smart and he couldn't keep his mouth shut. This was true of a lot of cops Conover had known over the years.

"It's going to be hard to contain for very long. We'll have to break the news to Hodge before the media gets wind of it," Conover said.

"There's gonna be a shit-storm."

"Yes, I imagine there will be."

"Perhaps we can hold off the vultures for a bit. I'll see what I can do," Blankenship said.

"I'd appreciate that, Tom."

The detective ducked under the crime scene tape and walked out the front door. He stood for a moment looking up at the castle. Half the windows were broken or missing and graffiti stained the stucco walls. Must have been something back in the '30s, he thought. But that was fifty years back. These days the property's only occupants were junkies, prostitutes, and squatters.

Conover shook his head and proceeded down the weed-strewn path, Blankenship falling into step behind him. The sun finally appeared over the mountains to the east, and the decrepit, overgrown cactus garden lay exposed in the golden light.

"Anybody contact the Tovrea family yet?" Conover asked.

"We're trying to reach the widow. She lives out in Paradise Valley."

"Right." Conover walked down to where he'd parked his car, an old '73 Dodge Polara. There were now six or seven patrol cars parked in the dirt lot, and the detective noticed the first TV news truck pulling up to the gate out on Van Buren.

"Shit, here we go," he muttered.

Ron Wheeler dug working at Brookshire's Coffee Shop. It was one of the few twenty-four-hour restaurants in central Phoenix and the place was always packed with good-looking chicks, especially after 1 o'clock when the bars closed. The coffee was strong and drinkable, not like that watered-down shit they served at Denny's, and for a greasy spoon the food wasn't bad. He'd only been there for a few months but he was already popular with the customers and the tips were great.

Ron usually worked the graveyard shift, which suited his lifestyle. A few months back he'd moved out of his parents' house into a studio apartment off Twenty-fourth Street and McDowell, just around the corner from the restaurant. In the evening he'd hang out with friends, maybe smoke a little weed, and practice the guitar. Then he'd work all night until 7 a.m., go home, crash until late afternoon, and do it all over again. His best friend Brian Cortaro had a bass guitar and they planned to start a band. Ron was thinking of asking his new girlfriend Kelly if she'd be interested in taking a stab at singing. He'd graduated from East High in '82, two years back, and his twentieth birthday was coming up in a few days.

To celebrate, Kelly had taken him to see X, one of his favorite bands, over at the Silver Dollar Club. Billy Zoom was his guitar god. Ron thought he was the epitome of cool with his slicked-back hair and silver Gretsch, his fingers racing over the fret board while he just stood there with that insane smile. Yeah, Billy Zoom was bad-ass, and Ron's copies of *Los Angeles* and *Under the Big Black Sun* were all scratched to hell from playing them so much. He'd sit there with his crappy Memphis Les Paul copy and twenty-watt Peavey amp and try to figure out the songs. Zoom's guitar parts were deceptive—they seemed straightforward enough, but then the sneaky bastard would slip in a weird jazz chord or some damn finger-picking run that would fuck with Ron's mind.

He'd taken to calling Kelly his "devil doll" after one of his favorite X songs. She definitely had that Exene Cervenka look, like a lot of the girls in the punk scene—tousled Raggedy Ann hair, thrift store dresses, Dr. Martens. Occasionally she'd do the Dinah Cancer thing—leather pants, gauzy black tops, ghoul makeup. Kelly had the body to pull it off, but her stepmother didn't get her fashion sense at all. "You're such a pretty girl," she'd say, "why do you try to hide it so much?"

To Ron she was beautiful, way out of his league. They'd met at a TSOL gig over at the Metro earlier in the year. That night he'd learned that she'd gone to Xavier High, and, although they were almost exactly the same age, Ron suspected that she was more experienced than he was. Several weeks later when they had sex in Ron's twin bed, he'd lied when Kelly asked him if it had been his first time.

After the X show, they drove around downtown and killed the last few beers from the cooler in the backseat. Kelly always had booze around. Ron didn't know much about her father, but he did notice that adults seemed to treat Kelly differently when they found out who her dad was. He'd met the old man only once, when Kelly had invited Ron over for a sit-down meal at the family spread in Paradise Valley. Hodge had seemed irritable and distracted, excusing himself from the dinner table several times to take phone calls. Kelly's stepmother Charlotte was right out of central casting—late-thirties cokehead, former model and dancer, peroxide-blond hair, year-round tan. Bitch even drove a fire engine–red Camaro. Ron thought she looked like Morgan

Fairchild, but not as hot. He'd made up his mind that the old guy was a dick, but Hodge obviously doted on his only daughter.

Ron asked Kelly to pull into a U-Totem on Seventh Street, just north of Roosevelt. Nobody in the car was of legal age but it was easy to buy beer in Phoenix if you knew the right places to go.

"Dude, think your uncle's working?" Brian said from the backseat.

"I don't know, man. Probably." Ron's uncle Cliff was one of those Vietnam vets who'd come back all messed up and just couldn't get it together. Cliff cruised Central on his Electra Glide with a bunch of other bikers, got in fights a lot, had trouble holding a job. When Ron was a little boy, his father would go out looking for Cliff, who often disappeared for weeks at a time. Lately, though, he seemed to be doing a bit better.

They pulled into the parking lot and Ron saw Cliff's long ponytail and beard. He turned around, gave Brian the thumbs-up, and stepped out of the car.

"Be right back. Need more smokes, Kelly?"

She nodded and blew Ron a kiss as he disappeared into the store.

"Damn, you got him whipped," Brian said. "Dude's like a puppy dog."

"Would you stop it with that shit?" she said, laughing. Kelly put a Marlboro between her lips and crushed the empty pack. Brian leaned over the front seat with his Zippo. She cupped her hands around the flame and drew in a lungful of smoke. She let her fingers linger against his wrist for a few seconds longer than necessary.

"It's the truth," Brian said.

"Whatever."

They sat silently in the car. Kelly smoked her cigarette.

"Seriously, man. When are we meeting that guy? I'm not feeling too good," Brian said.

Kelly glanced back and noted the hunger in his eyes, the pale and sweaty sheen of his skin. She sighed and reached into the front of her T-shirt, producing a thin silver chain, from which hung a tiny glass vial. She tapped out a small amount of white powder into Brian's palm. He scooped it up with his pinky's extra-long fingernail, raised it to his right nostril, and inhaled sharply.

"I'm running out too. Don't worry though, I talked with my guy earlier. We're supposed to meet him at Party Gardens at 1:30. He says he's got something special saved for me."

"Cool," Brian said.

"And if you're a good boy, I may even let you have some of it," Kelly added, looking over the seat at him, a glint in her eye.

After a few moments, Ron came walking out of the convenience store. He smiled as he opened the shotgun door and tossed a twelve-pack of Coors on the front seat. "Ask and ye shall receive," he said. He pulled a hard pack of Marlboro reds out of his pocket and handed them over to his girlfriend. Kelly eased the Toyota back out onto Seventh and headed north. She hooked a right on McDowell and they were soon parked behind Brookshire's.

The trio sat in the car drinking beer and smoking cigarettes. The back door of the Lucky Cue pool hall hung open and they watched two teenaged kids pass a joint back and forth. Finally, Ron looked at his watch, swore under his breath, and groped around in the backseat for his crumpled server's apron. He was late again. Ron kissed Kelly on the lips and staggered off toward the restaurant to begin his shift.

Conover pulled into the Erotica Hotel on Fifty-Second and Van Buren. The sign outside offered hourly rates and free XXX movies. The city tried to shut it down many times, but somehow the old flophouse had survived. The place got a lot of business from factory workers at the nearby Motorola plant, who used it for nooners and after-work trysts. The Erotica sat diagonally across from the Tovrea Castle and marked the eastern edge of the Van

Buren strip. Conover, who'd been on the force since the late '60s, knew every square inch of the area. The detective spotted the patrol car as he pulled into the small lot. He parked the Polara and was relieved to see that the officer was Luis Escalante.

"Hey, Gene. Still drivin' that heap, I see."

Escalante stood with arms crossed outside the open hotel room door. Yellow crime scene tape had been stretched across the doorway. Conover noticed that one of the cars out front, a metallic-blue Toyota Cressida, had also been covered with the tape.

"Can't bring myself to get rid of her, Luis," Conover said, stepping out into the late-morning sun's glare. It was nearly October and still well into the nineties.

"On your salary? Shit, you need to get you a flashier ride, homes," Escalante said. "Like our man Bob's."

"Yeah, right. Me and Steve McQueen." One of the other detectives, Bob King, had a green '68 Mustang Fastback, just like the one McQueen drove in *Bullitt*. The vanity plate on the muscle car read: *HEAT*. Conover respected King as a cop, but he disapproved of all the flashy bullshit.

Conover and Escalante had come up through the academy and for years worked the streets of Phoenix together. When Conover got the big bump up to detective, first in robbery and then homicide, their friendship had cooled. Both men knew that Escalante would likely retire in his uniform, and it had caused tension between them for a long time, but things were okay now. It was just the way life had panned out. Conover still trusted him more than most high-ranking officers he knew.

"You're getting a little bit more snow on the roof, hermano," Conover said, walking up to his friend and shaking his hand.

"Shit, least I got some hair left, man," Escalante said, completing their standard opening exchange. Conover ran a hand up to his rapidly receding hairline and grinned.

"I take it this is the Hodge girl's vehicle," he said, pointing at the blue Cressida.

"Registered in Daddy's name, but yep, I'm guessing she's the one who usually drove it. Take a look."

Conover stepped up to the car window and peered inside. The backseat was littered with empty beer cans and cigarette packages. An assortment of cassette tapes lay scattered on the passenger seat and on the floor. A plastic skeleton dangled from the rearview mirror.

"Nice. So they took the party inside, eh?"

"Yeah, and they stepped it up a bit from the looks of it."

The detective left the car and followed Escalante under the hotel's low awning to the open room. He caught himself as he was about to ask if Escalante had touched anything, but he knew that his friend would be insulted at the suggestion. Conover lifted the tape and stepped into the dark room. He stopped just inside to let his eyes adjust, and as the objects in the room materialized, he took stock of the scene.

"Our girl was definitely fucking somebody," Escalante said from outside.

"It would appear so, wouldn't it?" Conover agreed, noting the empty packet of Trojans on the bedside table. The bedspread had been pulled off and lay in a pile on the ancient, grayish-brown carpet. He leaned over the bed and peered at the cigarette butts in the ashtray—five or six lipstick-stained Marlboros and several Kool menthol filters. This last detail gave the detective pause, and he stood in the middle of the room for a moment, thinking.

"Be careful in there, man. You can get crabs just driving by this dump."

Conover didn't respond.

"So, what, you think la chiquita and her boy had one last laugh and then wandered across the street to kill themselves?" Escalante said, breaking the silence. "I just don't see it, bro."

"Neither do I," Conover answered finally. "And it turns out that the kid who died with her out there wasn't her boyfriend." He nodded toward the castle.

"Well, whoever he was, looks like he was nailing her too."

"A distinct possibility," Conover said.

"Then again, how many white boys you know smoke Kools?"

"Not many, these days." Conover looked around the room more closely and his eyes focused on the waste basket. He lifted it with his fingertips and dumped the contents onto the carpet: a bit of tin foil, some wadded up, blood-spotted tissue paper, and a disposable hypodermic needle.

"I'm thinking they had a visitor," Escalante said.

"I'm thinking you're right."

Later that morning, the detective left the crime scene at the Tovrea Castle, checked in with his lieutenant, and then drove out to Paradise Valley to inform Ed Hodge of his daughter's death. He'd arranged to have another detective, Dan Apkaw, meet him there at the Hodge residence. Conover followed the stories over the years like everyone else, the allegations of mob connections, money laundering, drug trafficking. Each time, Hodge's extensive team of lawyers had gotten him off the hook. Hell, there was that *Arizona Republic* reporter back in the mid-'70s who'd been shadowing Hodge for months, digging up all kinds of dirt. The poor guy ended up dead by a car bomb.

Conover followed a narrow street north of Lincoln Drive into the foothills and found the address at the end of a cul-de-sac. He parked behind a new Cadillac Fleetwood Brougham with tinted windows. The homes in this exclusive enclave sat on acre lots, the residents a combination of old Phoenix money, like Hodge, and newer blood—professional athletes, media personalities, and foreign investment bankers. Many of the sprawling mansions sat empty during the hot summer months.

Apkaw pulled up in an unmarked Caprice and parked next to Conover. He stepped out of the car, slipped on his sport coat, and adjusted his tie.

"Thanks for coming along, Dan," Conover said.

"No problem, man."

"Well, I guess we should just get this over with."

The two men proceeded up the drive, passing between white marble columns to an enormous front door. After a few moments, Hodge himself answered. He wore a navy-blue polo shirt over tan linen slacks, and his silver-white hair looked freshly cut and styled. Hodge stared out at the detectives with a frown on his face.

"Edward Hodge? I'm Detective Gene Conover, Phoenix Police Department."

"Yes, what is it?" the man snapped.

"Mr. Hodge, I can't tell you how sorry I am to have to tell you this, but it's about your daughter. She's been the victim of—"

"What is this, some sort of goddamn joke or something? Who the hell is *he?*" Hodge sneered at Apkaw.

"My name is Detective Daniel Apkaw, sir," Dan said quietly.

"I wish it *was* a joke, Mr. Hodge. I'm very sorry to tell you that your daughter has been the victim of a terrible crime. The injuries she sustained were fatal," Conover said.

"That's absurd," Hodge replied. "Where is she?"

"She's been taken to the medical examiner's office downtown."

"This is absurd!" the old man repeated, but this time his voice sounded less certain and his shoulders visibly sagged. "Kelly?" he said. "What did that fucking punk do to my little girl?!"

"Do you mind if we come inside for a moment?" Conover asked gently.

Ron Wheeler sat in the interrogation room across from Detective Apkaw. Tears streaked his face as his shaking fingers lit one cigarette after another. Grief and outrage alternated in his expression, struggling for dominance.

"I can't believe he was fucking her! That fucking asshole! Jesus Christ!"

"You mean you didn't know that Kelly Hodge was sleeping

with Brian Cortaro?" Apkaw asked. "Wasn't she *your* girlfriend, Ron?"

"Yes! Yes! She was my girlfriend. I loved her!"

"Did you kill her?"

"Kill her? What, are you fucking kidding me? No, I didn't fucking kill her!"

"But you were mad at her, weren't you?"

"Why would I be mad at her?!" Wheeler started to cry again. "I loved her. She was so beautiful," he sobbed. "That son of a bitch!"

"Your boss said that you left work early last night . . . at, let's see, approximately 2:45 a.m." Apkaw said. "Is that correct?"

"Yeah, but I was sick! You can ask anyone, I was puking my guts out."

"Boss said you were too drunk to work."

"He did? Shit, yeah, I guess I had a few too many."

"So here's what I think," the detective explained. "You get off work early and Kelly comes to pick you up. Brian was with her in the car. You're really pissed off. This dude's hitting on your woman. You go for a little ride, party a bit more . . . then—"

"No! Goddamnit, I went straight home. Boss called me a taxi. You can fucking check!" Wheeler slumped forward on the table with his head in his hands.

"—then you guys score some junk, shoot up a few speedballs—"

"Speedballs? Are you out of your fucking mind?"

The door opened and Conover motioned for Apkaw to come out into the hall.

"Thanks, Dan. That's enough for now."

"No problem, Gene. Kid's exhausted. You make him for this?"

"No."

"Didn't think so."

"I don't believe Ron Wheeler had any idea what he'd gotten himself into."

* * *

Several weeks later, Conover was in his office sipping a cup of coffee when the telephone rang. It was Blankenship. Some hikers had discovered a badly decomposed body out in the Harquahala Desert. The dead man hadn't even been buried, just dumped out there. He'd been shot execution-style with a .45, and his face was nearly gone, but dental records identified the man as one Anthony Everett, a.k.a. Everett James, a.k.a. James Anthony, and various other aliases.

"Son of a bitch had a rap sheet a mile long."

"Is that right?" Conover asked.

"Damn straight, Gene. He'd been indicted for all kinds of shit—assault, possession with intent to distribute. But here's the thing, almost all of the charges were dismissed."

Conover thanked Blankenship for the call and hung up. The detective sat at his desk, staring out the window a long time.

Later that afternoon, Conover picked up the red Camaro as it headed north on Tatum Boulevard. He lagged several cars behind in the rush hour traffic as the woman turned east onto Shea and continued toward Scottsdale. She pulled into a strip mall just before the light at Scottsdale Road and parked in front of a Nautilus Fitness Club. The detective backed his car into a space at the other side of the parking lot and watched Charlotte Hodge step out of the Camaro. She took a drag off of her cigarette, threw it to the curb, and slammed the door shut. Then she slung her workout bag over her shoulder and disappeared into the club.

Conover waited a moment and then got out of his car. He made his way through the crowded lot to where the blond woman had tossed her cigarette. He bent down and picked up the still-smoldering butt. The green lettering on the filter was clearly visible—*Kool*. Conover smiled and started walking toward the gym.

TOM SNAG

BY LAURA TOHE
Indian School Road

The waitress at Denny's had just turned down his proposal for a drink. His old hook 'em line, "I'll tell you my Indian name," no longer enticed. She wasn't buying his tired act. She tore the check out of her book and slapped it down next to his coffee cup. "You pay up front," she said, and pointed with her chin in the direction of the cash register, then turned away. He watched her walk away and lusted after her ass anyway.

Lately he was losing his touch with picking up women. Hell, maybe it wasn't so lately. He looked at his braids hanging across his chest. His hair was thinning and his braids were getting down to the diameter of a plastic straw, though it was still black thanks to his mother's genes. He was grateful that he didn't have to pour dye on it monthly the way some nose-bleed Indians did.

He was wearing the T-shirt he took from his son's closet. *Path* was written across his chest in big white letters and he had no idea what it meant. His once thin torso had taken a turn south and now stationed itself around his thickened waist. Surprised that he jiggled when he laughed, he took up running in the mornings at the old Indian School grounds. One morning he tripped on the gravel and came down hard. "Damnit!" Tom had rubbed his ankle, hoping it wouldn't swell. Boarding school still kickin' my ass, he thought.

Used to be he could walk into a conference, a bookstore, a nightclub, and the women would turn their heads at the tall, dark, handsome Indian man who could've been on the cover of the romance novels they scooped up in the grocery line, his hair draped over the pulsing pink bosom of the woman in his toned arms. When he was younger he let it hang loose like a wild pony testing the spring wind. Long hair drew the looks and the women. Someone once asked if he was the actor, Wind in His Hair in *Dances with Wolves*. It became a line he used to pick up women. "Did you see *Dances with Wolves*? That was me," he lied to a co-ed who paid for his drinks at the college bar after a poetry reading at MCC. Time was when he could turn the charm on like a light, when women dropped into his lap and all he had to do was scoop them up.

Did he ever love any of them? He wanted to tell one that she was the love of his life, his candle in the wind, his San Francisco peak.

Eliza was a Jew and a former hippie and New Yorker. She was a nurse and rotated among programs and facilities in Phoenix. Tom was working at the Phoenix Indian Center at the time coordinating GED programs for the urbs. Eliza arrived one afternoon to give flu shots to the elderly Indians. Tom helped set up chairs and brought her a cup of coffee during her break, which she accepted though she normally avoided caffeine. She stirred the coffee and impulsively told him she hated that Indians were forced to live on reservations like concentration camps.

"Now their land is being taken from them again and they must live in the cities. Doesn't it just make you angry?" she asked.

"Hell, we're survivors," Tom proclaimed dismissively.

After only four months, Tom decided to give marriage another go around. Their courtship had been a rather staid affair in comparison to the women he'd fucked in the backseats of their BMWs, Audis, and even a red VW bug, their bodies damp and sticking to the leather. Over a spaghetti and meatball dinner Eliza had once asked, "If you had one wish, what would it be?"

He slurped up strands of pasta that resembled roots growing from his mouth.

"May I?" she asked, and picked up his spoon and twirled the pasta onto it and offered it to him.

After a long pause he answered, "If I had one wish, I'd want you to be my wife." Tom knew what to say when women felt most vulnerable.

Since she was already carrying his seed in the darkness of her womb and was soon to finish up her Physician's Assistant training, they decided to make it legal. A child was born, a boy destined to be raised by his mother. Marital bliss faded quickly for Tom and eventually his wandering eye led him back to other women.

One morning a suit arrived at work carrying a yellow envelope. The man caught Tom by surprise, and before he knew it he'd signed the delivery of his divorce papers.

His first wife hadn't been as dramatic. They'd met at the Indian Center before she got a better-paying job at a credit union. On their third date they'd gone to see George Strait sing his love songs in the US Airways Center. They sat way up in the cheap seats and held hands. Afterwards they walked to her apartment and made love for hours on the sofa sleeper she had bought at a garage sale. Carmen was an urb like him but often drove home to the rez on the weekends to be with her family. She'd return Sunday afternoons bringing freshly killed lamb and tortillas in the cooler. Tom made a few trips with her, but his childhood experience of being on the rez gave him excuses to stay in the city. When Carmen told Tom she was pregnant, he joked that he would name the child George, whether it was a girl or boy.

Tom settled into his life as husband and expectant father until he met up with some of his old drinking buddies. They would arrive with loud voices and six-packs of beer in paper bags after Tom and Carmen had gone to bed. Carmen endured for as long as she could Tom's late-night hours and his alcoholic breath as he stumbled into bed beside her. When he wasn't there to take her to the hospital she went alone in a taxi. She went into labor without Tom and when he showed up he was still reeking of last night's party.

She'd merely dropped him off at work one morning and told

him not to come home. He could pick up his things outside their apartment; she'd have them ready. He knew it was coming from the gathering of stony silence between the fights and the daily marital thrashings that their son had to witness. He was sorry that the streets would raise his son just as he had been raised.

He liked how Mandy moved her breasts back and forth across his bare chest, her nipples grazing his. Soft and sexy was how he liked them. Fake ones were only good for eye lust. Mandy owned a Western art gallery in old Scottsdale. He'd met her during one of the Thursday evening art walks when the tourists traipsed among the clichéd Remington-style bronzes and oil paintings of Plains Indian men and women captured in the nineteenth century. One evening he walked into her gallery.

He stopped at a Lakota man holding a drum by a river and whistled low at the painting's five-digit price tag. "Didn't know these old Indians cost this much," he'd said to no one in particular.

"That's a Jordan Stone," came a voice from behind. "I think he's captured the spiritual essence of the old man in the morning light, don't you?"

"Spirituality. 'Morning light.' Isn't that the name of this place?" he asked.

"Morning Light. I just love that image. So I named my gallery that."

Mandy had grown tired of the corporate race in New York City. She was forty-one now with one marriage behind her and no kids because she hadn't made time for any. She considered herself a beginning middle-aged woman whose face and body had a few petals left. During a trip to Phoenix for her brother's wedding in February, the warm winter seduced her, as it had many of the snow birds fleeing steel-gray skies and frozen car batteries. She quit her finance career, sold all her suits, and bought a gallery. Risky, but it meant warm winters and a year-round tan.

Mandy invited Tom to the wine-and-cheese table. She had a storage room in the back where she kept supplies and a futon. After the tourists left, she invited him to the spare room on the pretext of looking at more art. Browsing through the box of canvases, Tom wondered if he might try painting. Mandy dropped onto the futon next to him. It heaved a gust of air and she said impatiently, to Tom's surprise, "Aren't you going to fuck me?"

In one quick turn he lifted the hem of her dress with his left hand and pulled down her thong with his right. He drew it across his face and inhaled her pussy smell in the purple strings, then buried his face between her legs. They spent most of the night working it in the backroom, then drove to her condo. Mandy didn't ask him to leave, so Tom took that as permission to squat permanent residence. Most nights Tom simply reached over and touched Mandy between her legs and they were off following their heat.

"My father was a painter. He came out of the Bambi School of painting at IAIA," he lied. "All Indians are artists," he proclaimed. "Shit, just buy me some paints and a canvas and I can paint better than all those ditwads in your gallery," he boasted.

So she returned with her Lexus loaded with canvas, paints, and an easel. While Mandy worked in her gallery, he painted romantic Plains Indians in buckskins and loin cloths. She hung them in her gallery but there was little interest.

One evening when Mandy was away on one of her buying trips, he walked into the gallery to find her assistant alone. She had just graduated with an Art History degree from ASU and was dreaming of moving on to San Francisco or New York. Over coffee they flirted and ended up in the backroom. Mandy was no fool. She smelled the sheets and promptly fired her assistant and sent Tom solo.

On his way out of Denny's, Tom impulsively picked up the sticky receiver of the pay phone and dropped some coins into the slot. After several rings Mandy answered.

"Hey, Mandy, it's been a long time since we talked."

"Not long enough."

"Come on, Mandy. I thought we were friends."

"What do you want?"

"I just want to talk. Can I come over—Morning Light?"

"Go to hell!"

"You said you were my friend. I heard you say you were my friend."

"Yes, well, friends don't treat each other the way you did to me. Look, I've gotta go. I've got a date with Jay, who makes me laugh."

The line went dead.

The sprain in his ankle was still aching and he tried not to limp as he headed past the Veterans Hospital to the Indian bar on Seventh Avenue. As he stepped into the dank room, the smell of beer and sweaty bodies and things swirling in the darkness assaulted his olfactory sense.

He found a stool at the far end of the Flying Eagle bar. One of the springs had worn halfway through the padding and was poking him in the ass. He ordered a draft. The foam splashed over the rim of the plastic mug when the bartender set it down. Tom threw a crumpled five-dollar bill down on the sticky wooden bar. A cowboy rez band took up one side of the bar and cranked out an old Johnny Horton tune, "Honky Tonk Man." Couples in tight jeans and cowboy boots twirled in little circles. The band sped up the beat with another oldie from CCR. Suddenly, a woman dressed in white pants and jacket appeared among the couples. She moved her body woodenly and alternately picked up her foot, her arms raised stiffly like mannequin arms at her sides. The band kicked up the tempo and she moved even faster. The couples stepped aside and the woman in white had all eyes on her. Goaded on by the attention, she shook her torso and leg in an even more grotesque fashion. When the band stopped, she momentarily paused before leaving the floor, as if waiting for applause. She looked around the room as if to say, *There!* No one clapped except a woman on the other side of the bar.

That's when Tom laid eyes on Crista.

Tom made his way over to the applauding woman, beer in hand. "Some dancer, eh?"

"You from Canada?" she asked, ignoring his question, and took a swallow of her drink in a tall glass.

"Naa. From around here."

"I knew a guy from Canada who ended everything with 'eh?' So I thought . . ."

"Grew up here in Phoenix. My mom's people are from the rez." Tom followed the usual protocol among skins.

"Which one?"

"The big one."

Tom's mother had married her high school sweetheart from the Phoenix Indian School, but after a few years his parents fell apart and he was raised among the city lights and police sirens.

He'd only been to his mother's homeland a few times, and felt out of place among the people who spoke a different language and had to haul water from the community well. His grandmother once remarked that he was too pretty for the harsh life of the rez.

"Navajo or Apache?" she asked.

"Yeah."

"You're tall so you must be Navajo, maybe Apache."

"Yeah."

"Okay, keep your secrets," she said, and took another drink.

"And you, where you from?"

"Up north," she said, and pointed with her lips.

He didn't press further for fear she'd ask him questions for which he had no answers. In the dark he couldn't tell if she was thirty or fifty. She had penetrating eyes, that much he could tell. There was also something in how she laughed, like she was laughing at him.

"What brings you here tonight? I mean besides the 'so you think you can dance' contest and the rah ja jin beat?"

"I'm hunting," she said.

"What are you hunting? A date?" he joked.

"You could call it that."

"You won't find any millionaires in this dump. You'd have to hit one of the nightclubs in Scottsdale."

"I like it fine here."

The beers were beginning to run through his body. The toilets were trashed, so Tom decided to take a leak in the parking lot. He excused himself and stepped outside, among the flashy rez pickup trucks and dented sedans. Cars sped past him on Seventh Avenue. He pissed against the wall of the 99 Cent store and as he zipped up, he thought he saw a blur of movement out of the corner of his eye.

"What the fuck?"

The bar was now reeling with more noise and drunken bodies. He looked for Crista. She wasn't where he'd left her and Tom didn't spot her among the dancers. Musta gone to the O, he thought.

He ordered another shot and went over what he thought he'd seen in the parking lot. Can't be. No way.

"Hey, man." A middle-aged man stood up next to Tom.

"Hey," he returned, and noticed the guy was sporting a crew cut, like he'd just gotten out of the military and hadn't had time to grow his hair out.

"You know that woman, the one you've been talking to all night?" the crew cut asked.

"Just met her. We're hooking up . . ." he said in case the crew cut had other ideas.

"If I were you, I'd be careful. You never know what's going to show up."

"What do you mean 'what's going to show up'?"

"Miss me?" Crista's voice suddenly came from behind, and the crew cut left.

"Hell yeah," he answered.

"So what path are you on?" she asked, poking the *a* on his T-shirt.

"The path of finding a fine woman like you."

"Shhhit, I'll bet you say that to all the women who come across your path," she laughed, and twirled his hair on her index finger in a teasing way.

Tom pulled her close and smelled a scent unfamiliar to him.

"Hey, is your car parked outside?" he asked.

"Yeah."

"I just saw the weirdest fucking thing out there."

"Oh yeah?"

"Yeah, I mean . . . people used to talk about them when I worked at the Indian Center. One day I was driving on the 101 over by Salt River and I looked up on the embankment and there was a fucking coyote! I didn't think they came that far into the city. He was standing there like he was taking it all in, checking it out. A twenty-first-century coyote!"

"It was probably just a dog that looked like a coyote."

"No, no. I'm telling you, it was a fucking coyote."

"Well, maybe it was lost," Crista said.

For the rest of the night Tom couldn't shake what he'd seen in the parking lot. Maybe it was just a dog. Had to be. Coyotes don't come this far into the city. Hell, it was probably some dog that someone brought in from the rez and it got loose. Yeah, that was it.

"Hey, you all right?" Crista asked. "You look like you could use another drink." She ordered them a round.

Crista reminded Tom of his first wife, who knew what to do. In a time of crisis she was like Captain Kirk, putting out orders and securing the ship.

The fluorescent lights were coming on, signaling closing time. The lights cast a garish glow on the leftovers from the Friday-night crowd and a shadow on Tom's alcohol-soaked brain.

"You look like you need a ride home. My truck's outside, parked near the 99 Cent store. It's a tan Chevy with a feather hanging from the rearview mirror. I'll be out in a few minutes." She handed Tom her keys and left him to fend for himself.

As Tom made his way around the parking lot he wondered where he'd end up with Crista. Probably some Motel 6 in Glendale near I-17, he thought. More like Motel 69, and he laughed at his own joke. Her truck was backed in. A click of the key fob and the door unlocked. The smell that greeted him was the same smell as Crista's. Something odd, something dark. He couldn't put a finger on it. Tom settled into the passenger seat and waited. His head was spinning now, so he rolled down the window. Couples poured into the parking lot and groped at each other; some stopped to make out next to their vehicles. Tom leaned into the soft seat, rested his head against the door, and waited for Crista.

When he came to, he was no longer in the front seat. He was in the backseat and he had the sensation that he was moving at high speed. He sat up and saw pine trees whizzing past him. He'd sobered up enough to know he was no longer in Crista's car. The crew cut was driving.

"Hey! Where's Crista? What're you doing?"

"I had to get you outta there," said the crew cut.

"Where's that woman I was with?"

"I think she's after us."

"After us? Where're you taking me? What's going on here?"

"Hang on. You got your seat belt on? You're gonna need it."

Headlights pierced through the darkness behind them. Tom looked back to see the truck following them. It was gaining on them.

"That woman you were with practices sacrifice to get what she wants." The crew cut pressed on the gas and made the curve past the scenic outlook above Sedona. Something moved outside the window. Whatever it was, it was keeping up with them. It leaped toward the window and Tom saw it. A beast covered with hair, covered with skins. He remembered the stories of the shape-shifters coming out at night to claim their victims. Whatever it was, it shook Tom to the bone, and his heart nearly stopped.

"Jeeezus! Did you see that?" he shouted to the crew cut.

"I know, I know. Bet you wish you hadn't danced with her."

"You mean . . . ?" The pieces were beginning to fall into place. What he'd seen in the parking lot. The smell. Crista.

The tires screeched and he felt the car moving on two wheels before it turned on its side into the shoulder and rolled into the pine trees. The crash broke a trail of pine needles and dust, mixed with the metallic sound of glass and metal breaking.

When Tom opened his eyes he wished he knew a death song, something to make meaning of it all. He saw the tree tops swaying and detected the faint smell of pine. Then the dark shape of the face he'd seen earlier looking down at him.

PART III

A Town without Pity

OTHERS OF MY KIND

BY JAMES SALLIS

Glendale

As I turned into my apartment complex, sack of Chinese takeout from Hong Kong Garden in hand, Szechuan bean curd, Buddhist Delight, a man stood from where he'd been sitting on the low wall by the bank of flowers and ground out his cigarette underfoot. He wore a cheap navy-blue suit that nonetheless fit him perfectly, gray cotton shirt, maroon tie, oxblood loafers. He had the most beautiful eyes I've ever seen.

"Miss Rowan? Jack Collins, violent crimes." With an easy, practiced motion he flipped open his wallet to display a badge. "You give me a minute of your time?"

"Why not. Come on up."

Without asking, I spooned food out onto two plates and handed one to him. For a moment he looked surprised, but only for a moment, then tucked in.

"So what can I do for you, Jack Collins?" I asked between bites. We stood around the kitchen island. Tiles chipped at the edge, grout stained by untold years of spills and seasoned by time to a light brown. The kitchen radio, as always, was on. After 6:00 the station switches from classical to jazz. Lots of tenor sax. California bebop beating its breast.

"Well, first, I guess, you could tell me why you handed me this plate."

"You're not wearing a wedding ring. Your shirt needs pressing, and even with that suit and tie, you have on white socks. A wife or girlfriend would have called you on that. So I figure you live alone. People who live alone are usually up for a meal. Especially at 6:30 in the evening."

"And here I thought *I* was the detective." He forked in the last few mouthfuls of food. "Vegetarian?"

I admitted to it as he went to the sink, rinsed off utensils and plate, and set them in the rack.

"I know what happened to you," he said.

"You mean how I spent my early years."

"Danny and all the rest, yes."

"Those records were sealed by the court."

"Yeah, well . . ."

He came back to collect my dishes and utensils, took them to the sink and rinsed them, added them to the rack. Stood there looking out the window above the sink. Another tell that he's a bachelor, used to living alone. Maybe just a little compulsive.

"Look, I'm just gonna say this. I spent the last few hours up at the county hospital, Maricopa. Young woman by the name of Cheryl got brought in there last night. Twenty years old going on twelve. Way it came about was, the neighbors got a new dog that wouldn't stop barking. They didn't have a clue, tried everything. Then, first chance the dog had, it shot out the door, parked itself outside the adjoining apartment, and wouldn't be drawn away. Finally they called 911. Couple of officers responded, got no answer at the door, had the super key them in. Found Cheryl in a closet, bound and gagged, clothespins on her nipples, handmade dildos taped in place in her vagina and rectum. Guy was a woodworker, apparently—one of the responding officers is a hobbyist himself, says this mook used only the best quality wood, tooled it down to a high shine. Cheryl didn't talk much to begin with. Then about 5 this morning she stopped talking at all. Just started staring at us. Like she was behind thick glass looking out."

"Yeah, that's what happens. You get tired of all the questions, you know they're never going to understand."

"Mook got home from work not long after the officers arrived on the scene. Had some sort of club there by the door, apparently, and came at them with it. Junior officer shot him dead, a single shot to the head. Training officer, twenty-plus years on the job, he'd never once drawn his piece."

Collins opened the refrigerator door and rummaged about, extracting a half-liter bottle of sparkling water. Mostly flat when he shook it, but hey. He poured glasses for both of us and threw in sliced limes from the produce drawer.

"Look, you don't want to go back into all that, I'll understand. But we've got nothing except blind alleys north, south, east, and west. No idea who this girl—this woman—is. Where she's from, how long she's been there."

"Twenty going on twelve, you said."

He shrugged. "Could just be shock. One of the doctors mentioned sensory deprivation, talked about developmental lag. A nurse thought she might be retarded. At any rate . . ." He put a business card on the island between us. "They're keeping her at the hospital overnight, for observation. You see your way clear to visiting her, talking with her, I'd appreciate it."

"I don't think so."

"Fair enough."

"Anyone ever tell you you have beautiful eyes, Officer Collins?"

"My mother used to say that. Funny. I'd forgotten . . ." He smiled. "Thanks for the meal, Ms. Rowan—and for your time. If by some chance you should happen to change your mind, give me a call, I'll drive."

I saw him to the door, tried to listen to music, picked up a Joseph Torra novel and put it back down after reading the same paragraph half a dozen times, found myself in a bath at 2 a.m. wide awake and thinking of things best left behind. Not long after 6, I was on the phone.

"Hope I didn't wake you."

"No problem. Alarm'll be going off soon anyway."

"Your offer still open?"

Nowadays, whenever anyone asks me where I'm from, I tell them Westwood Mall. I love seeing the puzzled look on their faces. Then they laugh.

Everyone here's from somewhere else, so it's doubly a joke.

But I really am from Westwood Mall. That's where I grew up.

I was eight years old when I was taken. I'd had my birthday party the week before, and was wearing the blue sweater my parents gave me, that and the pink jeans I loved, and my first pair of earrings.

His name was Danny. I thought he was old, of course, everybody over four feet tall looked old to me, but he was probably only in his twenties or thirties. He liked Heath bars and his breath often smelled of them. He wasn't much for brushing teeth or bathing. His underarms smelled musty and animal-like, his privates had an acid smell to them, like metal in your mouth. Some days I can still taste that.

I really don't remember much about the first year. Danny kept me in a box under his bed. He'd built it himself. I loved the smell of the fresh pine. He took the jeans and sweater but let me keep my earrings. He'd come home and slide me out, pop the top— two heavy hasps, I remember, two huge padlocks like in photos of Houdini—his own personal sardine. He'd bring me butter pecan sundaes that were always half-melted by the time he got home. I felt safe there in the box, sometimes imagined myself as a kind of genie, summoned into the world to grant my summoner's wishes, to perform magic.

I'm not sure I was much more than a doll for him. Something he took out to play with. But he'd be so eager when he came home, so I don't know. His penis would harden the moment I touched it. Sometimes he'd come then, and afterwards we'd just lie together on his bed. Other times he'd put things up me, cucumbers, shot glasses, bottles, either up my behind or what he called my cooze. He'd always pet my hair and moan quietly to me when he did that.

He worked as a nurse's aide at Good Samaritan and as a corrections officer at the prison out in Florence, pool and swing shifts at both, irregular hours, so I never had much idea what time of day it was when I felt my box being pulled out. Sometimes, from inside, I'd smell the heavy sweetness of the sundae. I was always excited.

Two years after I was taken, we went to Westwood Mall, the first outing we'd ever had. It was our second anniversary, Danny explained, and he wanted to do something special to celebrate. He gave me a pearl necklace, real pearls, he said, and I promised to behave. He'd even bought a pretty blue dress and shoes for me. At Acropolis Greek I stabbed his hand with a plastic knife, kicked off the shoes, and fled. I was surprised at how easily the knife went in, at the way it broke off when I twisted. Flesh should not be that vulnerable, that penetrable.

After that, I lived in the mall. Found safe places to hide from security guards, came out at night or during the rush hours to dine off an abundance of leftover fast food, had my pick of T-shirts, jackets, and all manner of clothing left behind, read abandoned books and newspapers. I had turned from genie to Ms. Tarzan. Periodically I'd watch from various vantage points as Danny prowled the mall hoping to find me. You may remember apocryphal tales of Mall Girl, sightings of which were first reported at Westwood then quickly spread throughout the city's other malls. Eventually everyone came to believe the whole thing was ex nihilo, spun from vapor to whole cloth, no more than a self-serving stunt. The journalist who first reported these tales and devoted weeks of her column to following up on them, Sherry Bayles, was summarily fired. Lack of journalistic integrity, the paper cited. Later, when she was working as a substitute teacher, more or less by simple chance we became friends. She's the only one I ever told about my days in the mall. Endearingly, she did no more than smile and nod.

My Edenic time at Westwood ended after eighteen months. A newly hired security guard gave credence to the stories and lay in wait for me long after his shift was done. I was biting into half a leftover hamburger I'd fished out of one of the trash containers when he came up behind me and said, "I'd be happy to buy you a whole one." His name was Kevin, a really nice man. He bought me that hamburger, complete with fries and shake, on the way to the police station. There, a Mrs. Cabot from Family Services picked me up.

So the second—third? fourth?—act of my life began.

Next morning I woke up in what they call a holding facility. Whatever they called it, it was an animal pen, thirty or forty kids all stuffed in there. One of them came snuffling around my bed like a pig after truffles around 3 a.m. and left with a bloody nose, down one tooth. At 8:00 they gave me a breakfast of underdone, runny eggs with greasy bacon mixed in and carted me off to see a social worker.

She said her name was Miss Taylor. "The report states that you've been living on your own in the mall. Is that right?"

"Yes, ma'am."

"And you're eleven?"

"Almost twelve."

"You told the admitting nurse that before this, you spent two years in a box under someone's bed."

Miss Taylor was sitting behind a desk in an office chair. She rocked back and forth, staring at me. When she rocked back, she went out of sight. There she was. Gone. There she was again.

"The nurse thinks you made that up."

"I don't make things up."

"You also said that during that time he repeatedly abused you."

"That's not what I said."

Ignoring me, she went on: "That he touched you in inappropriate places, put his member in you."

"His penis, you mean."

"Yes. His penis."

"Sometimes he did. More often it was other stuff."

I'd made her out to be just another office zombie, but now she looked up, and her eyes brimmed with concern. You never know when or where these doors will open.

"Poor thing," she said. "I'm so sorry."

"Why?"

"Sweetheart—"

"My name's Jenny."

"Jenny, then. Adults are supposed to care for children, not take advantage of them."

"Danny did take care of me. He brought me sundaes. He fed me, he cleaned my box twice a day. Took me out when he came home."

Tears replaced the concern brimming in her eyes. I had the feeling that they habitually waited back there a long time; and that when they came, they pushed themselves out against her will.

She tried to cover by ducking her head to scribble notes.

Three days later, Mrs. Cabot showed up again to escort me to what everyone kept calling "a juvenile facility," half hospital, half prison. (Daily my vocabulary was being enriched.) The buildings were uniformly ugly, all of them unrelievedly rectangular, painted dull gray and set with double-glass windows that made me think of fish tanks. I was assigned a narrow bed and lockless locker in Residence A—a closed ward, the attendant explained. Everyone started out here, she said, but if all went well, soon enough I'd be transferred to an open ward.

That was the extent of my orientation. The rest I got onto by watching and following along. Each morning at 6 we had ten minutes to shower. Then the water was turned off, though there weren't enough showerheads to go around and even when we doubled up, some girls were left waiting. After that we had ten minutes to use toilets in open stalls before being marched in a line through a maze of covered crosswalks to the dining room. Captives from other residences, boys and girls alike, would just be finishing their breakfasts. We waited outside like ants at a picnic. Once the occupying forces were mustered on the crosswalk opposite, we entered.

School was next, three or four grades and easily twice as many ages lumped into one, with a desperate teacher surfing from desk to desk looking as though this, staying in motion, might be all that kept her from going under. Each hour or so an attendant materialized to cart a roll-call group of us away for group therapy (equal parts self-dramatization, kowtowing by inmates, and surreptitious psychological bullying by therapists), occupational therapy (same old plastic lanyards, decoupage, and ashtrays), weekly one-on-ones with the facility's sole psychiatrist (a sad man whose hopelessly asymmetrical shoulders accepted without protest the dandruff falling like silent, secret snow upon them). Occasionally one of our troop would be led off for shock therapy, only to return with eyes glazed, mother's milk of her synapses curdled to cheese rind, unable to recognize any of us, to recall where she was or remember to get out of bed to pee or, if she did, to locate the bathroom. One or another of us would take her by the hand and lead her, help her clean up afterwards.

I could provide little useful information about my parents or my origin. Scoop the fish from the bowl, which is the whole of what the fish knows, how can the fish possibly describe it to you? Family Services' own searches came to naught as well. Back then few enough possibilities for tracking existed. Children's fingerprints went unrecorded. Enforcement, legal, and support services were not so much islands as archipelagos. I'd been taken more or less at random and kept, first by Danny, then by myself, in seclusion. Four years had passed. Essentially I *had* no identity.

The long and short of it was, I got assigned as a ward of the court and, barring foster placement, which we all knew to be about as likely as universal health care during a Republican administration, was remanded by the court to the juvenile facility "until such time as the aforesaid attains her majority." This majority, I found as I burrowed into outdated law books for impenetrable reasons ensconced in the facility's woeful library, was not fixed. I could petition for it after my sixteenth birthday.

In addition, the court's ruling decreed twice-yearly reviews by the board. For the first couple of reviews I showed up and said my piece, watching women in sober dresses and men in short-sleeve white shirts nod their heads, claiming they understood. Sure they did. As they went home to their families, Barcaloungers, TVs, chicken-and-mashed-potato dinners. I could see why it was called a board. No bending here, just sheer functionality. Nothing came of those first command performances, of course, and after that I stopped caring. Until age sixteen, when indeed I did petition the court—not the mental health, juvenile courts to which I'd been restricted the last few years, but an adult, open court. I'd spent considerable time in the facility's library researching this, doing my best to get my ducks all in a row, even if some quackery were involved.

Mall security guard Kevin, one-time journalist Sherry Bayles, Family Services agent Mrs. Cabot, and social worker Miss Taylor were all there to testify on my behalf. Appropriately demur and deferential, I walked out emancipated. Miss Taylor set up residence for me in a halfway house. "Just until you get on your feet," she assured me.

It was out on Ocotillo around Sixteenth and Glendale, a part of town where, whenever you emerged blinking into sunlight, homeowners on adjacent porches and in neighboring fenced yards stared at you as though you might be a cabbage that had somehow managed to uproot itself and learn to walk. (God knows how the property came to this purpose and at what cost. Some Old Money donation, possibly trying to memorialize an addicted wife or child?) I always smiled my biggest smile, said good morning with eyes steady on these neighbors, and inquired how they were doing on this fine day. By the third week they were calling me over to ask how it was going.

Not spectacularly well, as it happened. Once prospective employers heard I was sixteen, had spent four years in a state facility, and had never before worked, the interview was pretty much over. Never mind court papers certifying me as an adult, or my own composure and comportment at these interviews. Two months in, I began having the terrible feeling that halfway might be as far as I was going to get. I mentioned this when I stopped to chat with old Miss Garrett at the end of the block. She was out in her garden weeding flowers as usual. How those weeds managed to regrow overnight, *every* night, I never understood. But there she was each morning in ancient pink pedal-pushers and sky-blue straw hat, pulling those suckers up with her own rootlike, arthritic hands.

"If you don't mind swing shifts and long hours, honey, I've got a nephew with his own business who's looking for a waitress. Figure you can handle pushy men?"

Cheryl was everything I expected, a plain girl like myself, quiet and superficially ingratiating, with still eyes that reminded me of my friend Bishop from back in the halfway house, or of walls spackled with unreadable graffiti.

Collins took me in and introduced me, then discreetly withdrew.

What can I say? I told her how I had come to pass the middle years of my admittedly short life. I talked about not carrying forward regrets, about simply getting on with things. Halfway through, it occurred to me that what I was saying sounded not at all different from the harangues that hundreds of teenagers suffer daily from parents. We all think we're special, somehow exempt. When the real lesson's how much alike we all are.

I told her I'd check back with her later, that she shouldn't hesitate to call me if she needed to talk, anytime, day or night. Wrote my name and number on the back of a deposit slip, the only piece of paper I could find in my purse.

"Miss Rowan?"

To that point Cheryl had given no indication she was listening, not the least register of recognition, as I spoke.

"Yes?"

"Where are they going to take me next?"

For her, I well knew, the world seemed at this point little more than a congress of *theys*, dozens of theys shoving her about like a pawn on the board, forever testing her survival skills. Pawns were things one sacrificed, things that were captured and went away.

"Some kind of holding center would be my guess. You're over-age for the state juvenile facility. They'll probably try for a shelter of some sort. Depends on what's available. I'll call in later, find out where you are. Maybe we can talk then."

She nodded. For a moment, before they became still again, things struggled to surface in her eyes.

That night after dinner with Collins, upon which he insisted, I came home, poured a final glass of wine, and drank it standing at the front window, looking out at my neighbors' shrouded, brightly lit houses.

As I drew the shower curtain closed, I felt safe in a way I never will outside, and as I washed, I considered how I'd always thought of the scars as something I *put on*, like clothes or a hat, not part of me at all, nothing to do with my essential self, and re-membered the first man in my bed, the first man I'd let see them.

Memories are the history we carry around with us, a history that's mapped out upon our bodies, pressed into the very folds of our minds. So that night I remembered. Just as I go back to the mall at every opportunity, an immigrant returning to the home-land, and feel safe there.

What no one understands is that, lying in the box under

Danny's bed, miraculously I was able to stop being myself and become so much more. I could feel myself liquifying, flowing out into the world. I became numinous. Sometimes, though ever less often as time goes by, I'm able to recapture that.

"Thanks again for touching base with Cheryl," Jack had said as we settled in. The restaurant, Italian, was Mama Ciao's on Mc-Dowell, recently relocated to the abandoned shell of a Mexican establishment and demonstrably in transition.

"I only hope that eventually it may do some good."

"What we all hope. You never know." He sipped a couple ounces of draft. "Have to tell you this one thing."

"Okay."

"I have an ex-wife—not really *ex*, I guess, since all we are is separated. Divorce's been in the works awhile. We have a daughter."

I waited.

"Just wondered how you felt about it," he said, "that's all."

"What's your daughter's name?"

"Deanna."

"You see her often?"

"I used to, when she was young. Had her for weekends, half the summer. As she grew up, less and less."

"Just how long has this divorce been in the works?"

"Little over ten years."

"You check with Ripley, see if that's some kind of record?"

"Think I should?"

"Probably."

His eyes were bright with good humor.

"We all have to decide what's important to us and fight for it, Jack. Sometimes the best way to fight is to do nothing."

"Friends I have left say I'm living in the past, trying to hold onto something that's no longer there."

"The past is what we are, even as we're constantly leaving it."

"You know what? I have no idea what that means."

"Neither do I," I said, laughing. "But it sounded good."

"What's important to you?" Jack had asked as we walked out. Night was settling in, last tatters of daylight become pink banners riding low in the sky. When he took my arm to gently guide me left, our eyes met.

"Everything," I told him.

VALERIE

BY KURT REICHENBAUGH

Grand Avenue

A ll I had left was that look on Valerie's face as she watched Cooper bleed out onto the stained motel carpet. That's the last picture of her.

My mind worked like that when it came to Valerie. A mental slide show of her. Snapshots that I'd arrange in ways that pleased me differently each time. And this was the last one. The one of her standing above Cooper, legs apart, that cut across her right cheekbone, a teardrop line of blood trickling from it.

My arms and legs were cold.

I couldn't move.

It hurt to breathe.

I never thought much about how I'd go out. I wanted another turn at things. Another go-round to see if I could make things different.

Instead, I just had this picture of Valerie and the sad knowledge of just how stupid I'd been.

"Dude, they got a vending machine that sells pussy shots in the men's room!"

I remember looking back over my shoulder at the guy bragging about his find in the john. That was my first sight of Cooper. Healthy, early thirties, a tad overweight, cheeks showing the first blush of hypertension. Wardrobe from Abercrombie & Fitch, with attitude from Scottsdale.

Valerie told me she'd be meeting him at the Bikini Lounge. Said I should come also and get a look at him before the job, you know, get a feel for the target. Her words: *a feel for the target.*

Well, I'd gotten my look. I wasn't impressed.

"Two PBRs," Cooper told Sally, pressing up to the bar next to me.

Sally eyed him with tired patience. "I'll need to see some ID."

I watched as Cooper dug out his wallet and slid an Arizona license and credit card across the rutted wood bar. Johnny Cash began singing on the juke. Always Johnny Cash. I liked Johnny Cash enough, but sometimes it would be nice to hear someone like Duane Eddy for a change.

"Cash only," Sally said, setting the bottles down in front of him. "No cards."

"No cards?" Cooper looked at her like she was crazy. "Shit, hold on a sec." He went back over to the table where I knew Valerie was waiting for him.

Sally looked at me and rolled her eyes.

Cooper returned with his money and took the bottles of beer. He gave me a dose of stink-eye as he did.

I hate guys like him. Too many phony pricks like him all over Phoenix. And he had to come here, my turf, and turn Valerie's head.

The Bikini Lounge had been on Grand since late 1947. It would have remained a forgotten dive until hipsters like Cooper discovered it. I liked it anyway. It was close to where I lived. Started coming here after the Emerald Lounge closed down. Either here or the Alaskan Bush Company, just a piece further down Grand.

Grand Avenue slashed diagonally through Phoenix's grid-lined streets. Certain streets in the city are sunburnt. This stretch of Grand had gone on to skin cancer. But lately the neighborhood had seen something of a revival. Artists found the rents affordable and the setting appropriately retro-beat and moved in, luring adventurous suburbanites in with them, pushing the hustlers, vagrants, and addicts deeper into the shadows just off the main drag.

I'd been to most of the galleries: Red Door, Perihelion Arts,

Art One. I didn't know art from Shinola but I'd gotten used to the boho scene. I figured galleries were better than payday stores.

I once saw a hell of a good Rockabilly band from Tucson in one of the galleries. Can't remember their name anymore. But that's what I liked about Grand. It wasn't lined with phony bullshit you'd find in Scottsdale. Now *that* was a city made for the Coopers of the world.

Phoenix had grown on me. I liked the cowboy skies as the sun exploded against the western clouds, the pomegranate sunsets. The dead streets at night downtown. The lingering mid-century postcard architecture, motel dives, and plazas. I wished the rest of the world would just leave Phoenix alone.

I lived on McDowell, near Seventh Avenue, in a bungalow apartment. I moved there after the Air Force. I'd been stationed at Luke and when my time was up I decided to stay.

Back when I moved into my apartment one of my favorite places was the Emerald Lounge on Seventh Avenue. I'd seen the Hypno-Twists play there a handful of times. Great place to see a band.

The Emerald Lounge was gone now.

Replaced by a Starbucks.

Nothing good ever stayed.

Then I met Valerie.

The earliest snapshots of Valerie are the ones from the Bush Company. The ones that kept me company on those long hot nights when I couldn't sleep. I'd seen her dancing to "Thunder Kiss '65" and I knew she'd be my favorite. I'd only stay there on the nights she worked. I'd sit patiently, nodding the other girls by, taking their dirty looks with them, until she'd finally come over to me. Skin like milk, hair black as coffee, and eyes to match.

"My name's Karl," I told her one night during a private dance.

"Valerie."

"Okay if I ask where you're from, Valerie?"

"Tucson." Red lips against my throat. "What about you, Karl?"

"Right here."

"No one is from here. So, where're you from, really?"

I noticed the accent then. Not Spanish like you'd expect in Phoenix. Something else, Eastern European, maybe.

"Okay," I said. "Nowhere. Then here."

But she wasn't listening anymore, her back against my lap, sliding down between my legs.

I swallowed my beer and looked at my watch.

"Thinking of heading over to the Paper Heart later. They're showing *Faster, Pussycat! Kill! Kill!* tonight," I said to Sally. "What about you?"

"Seen it."

"Come on, Cooper," I heard Valerie's husky voice behind me. "We should get to the motel already."

I had to look at her. Her face, lined beautifully in the glow of the tiki lamp above the table where she and Cooper sat. I tried telling myself how much she hated being with Cooper. She made it clear to me that she had to act like she was into him. But knowing this didn't make it any easier watching them together.

"Yo, you want something?" Cooper shouted across the floor at me. Valerie pretended to see me for the first time. She put her hand on Cooper's arm, saying something I couldn't hear.

Touching Cooper's arm like that, I bet it was something she did a lot. One of her finest talents, touching guys, prodding them, making them do what she wanted. I hated that about her.

"Easy, friend," I said. "No harm meant."

I turned around and looked down at my beer, its foam sticking to the sides of the glass. "The fuck," I heard Cooper continue. "You hear that shit? Ain't your friend, yo!"

I finished my beer. That's right, Cooper, listen to your girlfriend there. Forget about me and think about all that swag you got with you instead. I'm no one. Just another loser in a bar.

My throat burned. I smacked my glass down, feeling Valerie's nails caressing Cooper's arm, his back, other places too.

I couldn't take it anymore. I stood up. "I guess I'm outta here. See ya, Sal."

Outside, the night hadn't cooled any. They rarely did. Not when the days hit above 110 degrees. That's when the heat just soaks into the concrete and glass and waits there until morning. Riding out the hot nights, I'd lay awake in my apartment with the radio on, reading a Luke Short or Louis L'Amour paperback and listening to the whistle of the trains off Grand slide with the hum of traffic on I-10.

A Chevy truck rolled by on Grand, Ranchero music trailing as it passed me.

I could hear singing from the church around the corner. White globe lights hung from its trellises, glinting off the cars and pickups that lined the street in front of it.

My car, a fourth-generation Impala rolling out its last miles, sat parked around the corner on Fifteenth Avenue, across from the boxing club. I could see two Latino boys sparring in the ring. Another worked the bag while a woman, his girlfriend maybe, jiggled an infant on her knee as she watched him pounding the bag, working it, working it.

"He always brags about his jewelry business. How he's a big entrepreneur," Valerie had told me. We were in Mel's Diner on Grand, after her shift. She stirred sugar into her coffee. She put lots of sugar into her coffee, I noticed. She sipped it quickly as she spoke. I wished she'd finish it and we could go back to my place.

"He's just another guy full of shit," I said. I was sick of hearing about Cooper already. "Phoenix is full of guys like Cooper. Forget about him."

"Is Karl jealous?" She put her mug down, smiling on one side of her mouth.

"Karl's tired," I answered. "Karl would like to take you home."

"And do what?"

"You're a smart girl, Valerie. I'm sure you can figure that out."

"Dance for you maybe?" That crooked smile again. "You'd like Valerie to dance for you again tonight?"

"Sure."

"Maybe dance, maybe more than dance?"

I wanted more than the dance. She knew it. "Like I said."

She sipped from her mug. That's the snapshot of her when I first compared her hair to the color of coffee. "I like dancing for you, Karl."

"Yeah?"

She got up from her side of the booth and slid over next to me, her short denim skirt high up her thighs.

"Do you wonder why I tell you about Cooper?"

"You already said it. To make me jealous."

"He wants me to quit dancing. Work for him instead. I can make more money working for him, he says, selling his jewelry designs."

"Why are you telling me this?"

"He carries jewels around with him. He wants to get into the jewelry-design business. He buys from designers and sells them as his own. I asked him once where he gets his jewels. He tells me people who owe him money sometimes pay in jewels. I think he buys jewels with his father's money. Maybe you've seen his father's commercials on TV. His father is that car dealer from California. He marries beauty queens from Texas."

"Again, why are you telling me this?"

"Cooper carries around jewels with him. He shows them to me. I tell him I know people he can sell jewels to maybe. Clients with money. I meet them doing escort jobs. Cooper wants to fuck me like a big shot. He is like a fucking teenager. But a teenager with too much money." I could hear the Eastern venom in her voice.

The door opened and a pair of Phoenix PD came in. Young and athletic looking; ASU Sun Devils material. They both threw brief glances at us before taking a booth near the corner. I heard a cough of static from one of their radios.

Valerie smiled at them.

I looked out the window, at the fenced-in used car lot across Grand. I waited for her to get on with it.

It came with a flicker of hot tongue against my ear. A voice so low, hypnotic; a razor blade coated with the scent of coffee and cigarettes.

"Maybe Karl and Valerie teach the big shot a lesson."

More snapshots of her for the slideshow then. Ones of her dancing for me at my place, swaying to the Roy Orbison tape on my cassette player, wearing nothing by the end of the third song. Then, only in my apartment, would she let me touch her as she danced.

But touching only, nothing else.

That would come later, she promised me.

Until then, she would do other things for me.

Sometimes, afterward, sitting in the chair by the window, she'd talk about her escort jobs, the blue smoke from her cigarettes drifting out into the night. But mostly she talked about Cooper. How he was growing impatient with her. When would she quit dancing and work for him. And when was she going to let Cooper meet with her people. He had big plans and wouldn't wait on her and her people for long.

Then she stopped coming over to my place.

No reason why.

After the last night there, I found her spangled thong under my pillow. It glittered in the light from the window like dreams from the Emerald City. I didn't notice when she left it, but knew she'd left it for me as a souvenir, a promise from her to add to the pictures in my head.

At work, she acted like I was just another creep.

I'd watch as she danced for the other men, waiting for her to come back to me. She wouldn't even look my way.

I'd stay up late after coming home from work, eating chili or tamales from a can that I'd heat over a hot plate. I played my tapes low as I ate. Roy Orbison sang "Mystery Girl" and I would mouth the words along with the song, running the slideshow of Valerie real slow, timing it to the music. She had once danced to "Mystery Girl" for me, before, when she used to come over. I always thought of it as her song.

Of course, it worked.

I had one of the other dancers give her my message.

I was in. I would help her teach Big Shot Cooper a lesson.

I waited in the Desert Sun Motel's parking lot. Cooper and Valerie had a ground-level room, across from the empty swimming pool. The doors to the rooms were painted blue. Arizona-sky blue. Highway blue when the clouds are the only things that break and fall into infinity. Cooper's Lexus sat in front of their door. I'd seen them park there, having followed them from the Bikini Lounge.

No one had meetings in a dump like this, unless it was with a hooker or a dealer. Cooper had to be naïve, stupid, or both to come here with Valerie to do business. This was going to be too easy, I thought.

"Wait for me," she'd told me. "I'll leave the room to get ice and leave the door open. You will come back to the room with me and take the jewels. No problem. Got it?"

It seemed simple enough. That was all I had to do. Go back with her and take his swag.

I waited in the darkness of my car, thinking about how she and I would celebrate later. Thinking about the way she danced for me—until I saw her open the door to their room.

I got out of my car. She looked at me and nodded, an empty ice bucket in her hand.

I went up to the door and waited for her to return with the ice.

"It's about time." Cooper stood up from the bed. A gym bag sat on the corner of it, next to him. He looked at me for a moment, confused. "Hold on a sec. He's that guy from the bar. What the hell is this?"

I heard the door close behind me, the chain sliding on the lock.

"Take it easy, Cooper," Valerie said.

"No, *you* take it easy." Cooper's voice cracked with fear. "What the hell is he doing here? You set me up!"

"Take it easy, Cooper," I repeated.

"Screw you, man!" Cooper dove to the bag and wrenched a small gun from it. He pointed it at me. I don't know shit about guns. I just know that you don't want to get shot by one, no matter how big or small they are. They fuck you up. His gun soaked up the wan light from the lamp. It was small and black in his fist. A woman's gun, I thought, a chick's gun. I could see the barrel tremble.

"You think I'm going to just sit here and let someone rob me? You think I'm stupid or something?"

"Cooper, put the gun away. You're not going to use it." Valerie reached out, as if to calm him. "You said yourself the jewels were insured. Put the gun away."

"Forget it. I'm not a fucking chump! And I'm not letting no cheap whore and her goon-boy rip me off!"

Cooper pointed the gun at her.

I jumped him then, hitting him just as the gun went off. The gun sounded simultaneously with the shattering of the lamp. The room went dark. My ears rang from the shot.

I held onto Cooper's wrist, twisting it, punching him with my free arm as we rolled off the side of the bed. Cooper landed beneath me, the bag spilling beside us.

Cooper yelled then, unintelligible words in the darkness between the bed and the wall where we struggled. I grabbed a loose pillow and crammed it against his face, stifling the noise and trying to keep the gun away.

Valerie pounced on us, pulling at the gun in Cooper's fist. It happened before I knew it. Cooper's muffled screaming ended the instant she fired the gun into the pillow.

Cooper's body collapsed beneath me. My vision tunneled. The small room filled with the smell of shit, gun powder, and burnt pillow foam.

The light from above the sink came on. Valerie stood above us, the gun in her hand.

I saw a cut across her right cheekbone. A thin line of blood trickled from it, leaving a teardrop's path.

That's the one I told you about before. The last one of her.

"Karl." I could barely hear over the dull ringing from the gun. "Karl, we have to get our asses out of here, now!"

The phone started to ring.

"Don't answer it," she said.

Valerie above me. Yeah, that shiny streak of blood on her cheek. I could crawl to her to lick it off . . .

I scrambled away from Cooper's body.

She kicked his legs to the side and searched his pockets, pulling out a set of keys and his wallet. She ripped the wallet open and pulled out the cash, stuffing it into her jeans. She threw the wallet back against his chest.

The ringing stopped.

The pillow remained over Cooper's face.

A dark stain spread on the cheap carpet beneath him.

She went to her knees and grabbed the bag. She threw the gun into it along with the items that had spilled from it in the struggle.

"Karl, we gotta go now!" she said, getting to her feet.

Valerie pulled at me.

"You're hurt," I said.

"I'll live." She shoved me toward the door. "Move!"

Her fingers fumbled with the chain, finally pulling it off. She pulled the *Do Not Disturb* tag off the inside knob and looped it over the outside knob. I slammed the door shut behind us and pushed against it once. The day's heat still soaked into it, warm against my back.

"Worst thing, I figured, is maybe we'd have to smack him around a little, you know. That's it."

Her in the car next to me. The light at Fifteenth Avenue and Grand had turned red. Through the windows of the boxing club, I could still see the kids working out in the ring.

"Stupid fucker. Why'd he have to bring a gun?"

"All the jewels are in the bag?" I asked.

"What do you think?"

She ran her fingers down my shoulder. I reached a hand up toward her face to touch her, stroke her hair.

She leaned back and lit a cigarette, using the dash lighter.

"You got another one of those?"

She pulled another butt from the pack and handed it to me. I used hers to light it.

I sucked in deeply and exhaled. It'd been a long time since I'd smoked. I'd forgotten how good it felt.

"No one saw you? The desk clerk, anyone like that?" I asked her.

"No one. He got the room. I waited in the car."

"You're sure of that?"

"I'm sure. No one saw me. I stayed in the car."

"Okay then," I said at last. "Where do we go now?"

I tried not to think about what she'd done to Cooper back at the hotel. She'd pulled me into this mess and I didn't know how to get out. I felt no closer to her for it. She sat there smoking, thinking about what, I had no idea. About me? About where we'd go next? I was half tempted to just drive her to the bus depot and leave her there.

Be done with it.

No tail was worth it.

Then she put her hand on my leg.

I could smell her body, closer to mine now.

"Your place?" she asked.

I drove, imagining how she'd look in my bed. It had been too long since I'd had a woman in my bed. Okay, she'd just killed a guy and didn't seem to give a rat's ass about it, but Cooper had it coming to him. He should have stayed in Scottsdale, with his television dad, rich girlfriends, and phony so-called business associates.

She had no choice.

I told myself this as I imagined the feel of her dark body beneath mine, the coffee hair spilling across my chest.

We stopped for a bottle on the way.

Vodka.

That's what she wanted.

She took the vodka from me as soon as I got back into the car.

"You sure you don't want to wait until we get to my place?"

She took a pull from the bottle, sighed, and leaned her head back on the seat. "I need this now."

"I've got clean glasses at home."

"Here." She handed me the bottle. I put it to my lips and drank. It burned. I didn't like vodka, but I wanted to make her happy. And I had done everything she asked me to do. What difference did it make what kind of bottle we should get?

I sat down behind the wheel and passed the bottle back to her. She put the cap back on it and set it down on the floor between her feet.

The vodka didn't make much of a dent against the jangling of my nerves. It would take more than a few shots for that.

My hand shook as I turned the key in the ignition.

She put her hand over mine. "You'll be fine now, Karl. It's over."

"I didn't think anyone was supposed to get killed, that's all."

"No one did."

"How much you think we got? In the bag, I mean."

"We count it at your place. We count it, then we go to bed. It will be good for both of us, Karl. I promise. Soon, you'll not worry anymore about Cooper. Valerie will worry for both of us."

"No," I said. I reached for her and pulled her next to me. "We're in it together, Valerie. I said I'd do this with you."

But I didn't really mean it anymore.

I kissed her. I closed my eyes and kissed her in the darkness of the car, tasting the vodka and cigarettes. I tried to put it out of my mind but I could only see her now above Cooper, the gun in her hand, the look of triumph in her eyes.

We parted.

I started the Impala and backed out onto Grand.

Once we got back to my place we would split the goods. I would let her stay the night, if that's what she wanted, but after that I was gone. I needed to get a story. If anyone connected me to her I'd just tell them she was a pickup and that's all. I didn't know shit about Cooper, the money, any of it. It was better that way. I'd let her go. I would miss her, a lot, but I didn't have any choice.

I had driven about half a mile when she told me to pull over, that she was going to be sick.

I steered the car off Grand, beneath the eastbound lanes of I-10. She lurched out of the car and stumbled to one of the pillars that held the freeway above us. I could see her hunched over in the shadows of the overpass, shoulders hitching.

I waited.

The bag was on the floor of the passenger seat next to the bottle.

The jewels were all there in it.

All I had to do was shut the door and drive. Get on I-10 and drive west and don't stop until I hit the Pacific.

She'd have to go back to the stripper pole and escort jobs. Too bad about that, but I didn't ask to be part of a murder.

Her door remained open, leaving the interior light on. I reached over to pull the door shut when I heard her cry out. I wasn't sure. The cars were so loud above us. I called out to her.

No answer.

I got out of the car and went around to her side. Her door was still open. Before shutting it, I looked down at the bag.

I had to see them. Seeing them all there would make it easier leaving her.

I leaned down and reached for the bag. That's the moment I felt the punch of the bullet hit me from behind. Right under my rib cage. It knocked me down against the seat of the car. I could smell her there on the vinyl, and the hot odor of the dirt and tires beneath me.

I slid down from the seat and onto the hard, dry ground.

I could see her above me, gun in her hand, pointing it at me. I tried reaching up to the door handle. Then something slammed into my chest and this time I heard the pop of the gun against the rushing of cars above us.

I couldn't breathe. My mouth worked but nothing came.

She leaned over me.

She kissed me then. The last one.

You ever think about the last kiss you'll get? Who will give it to you? If perhaps it's someone like Valerie out there waiting to do it?

Maybe there are worse things than that.

"I'm sorry, Karl. You don't have to worry now."

I tried to speak, spitting blood at her instead.

The train's whistle brought me back.

Valerie was gone.

So was the Impala.

I could see the ribbon of the overpass above me. It seemed so high. I'd never noticed that before. How high above Grand the interstate was. I couldn't hear the cars on it anymore. They had all gone away.

Everyone had gone away.

I'd reviewed the pictures of Valerie enough. I was tired of it all. There was just the last one of her left anyway.

I could see the moon between the lanes above me. Just a fingernail, really, that was all.

Paint it red and claw my fucking heart out.

The train off Grand cried out again. Maybe it was heading west. It didn't matter. I would be riding that whistle into the black, bringing that last picture of Valerie along with me.

BLAZIN' ON BROADWAY

BY GARY PHILLIPS

South Phoenix

Somebody Told Me" by the Killers pumped from the overhead speakers as Ivan Monk entered the busy fitness club. The facility took up the fourth floor of a new high-rise offering a pool, sauna, and a large expanse of machines and free weights.

Passing by the spin class, he heard the instructor joke into her hands-free set, "My friend told me, looking at the mess of clothes on my bed, 'Girl, you need to get you some new gear.'" The woman, a bronze-hued Latina in a form-fitting outfit, laughed gleefully. She would have been at home on the cover of *Maxim*. "And I realize that light blue sports bras against dark skin can be distracting, but I can get them three for a good price at Big 5. I guess I kind of had it hanging out in some of my outfits, but you know, really, I hadn't noticed." She chuckled again.

Monk noticed. Every man in the class and a couple of the women noticed too. He regretted he couldn't linger and hear more about her choice of workout clothes. He asked a trainer, "Excuse me, where can I find Nazeen Loveless?" The guy pointed a veined finger at a door, and continued his count as a sweating hausfrau completed a series of crunches.

Monk went to the door and knocked lightly. Built into the nearby wall was an aquaterrarium—half gravel and the other side a miniature pond. Various plants he didn't recognize populated the tank, as did several reptiles. A dark green toad sat on a rock, croaking and glaring at him between blinks. Monk glared back.

"Come in," a throaty voice announced.

He entered and shook the proffered hand. From his research Monk knew that Nazeen Loveless was past fifty, but she was still a striking woman with a toned body encased in a silk shirt tucked into a mid-length skirt with a slit. A heavy silver bracelet slid up and down her right wrist.

"So, old Ardmore sent you out here," she said affectionately. She sat back down and he took a seat opposite. Behind her a window overlooked the morphing landscape of Phoenix's south side.

"He's putting out this compilation CD package, as he told you, and asked me to run down some leads to make sure everything was cool rights-wise."

The handsome woman tilted her head, her chandelier earrings tinkling. "And you're Ardmore's coproducer?"

"I've got a private ticket," he said.

"Pardon?"

Monk explained he made his living as a PI. "Ardmore asked me to do his legwork because we've known each other awhile and—"

"Antony never did like lawyers," she finished.

He nodded agreement and removed a PDA from the inner pocket of his sport coat. It was hot as a mother outside but he'd put the jacket on in the comfort of the air-conditioned building to look professional.

"There's a couple of people Ardmore hoped you could help me locate."

"It's been a long time," Loveless said.

"I know," he said sympathetically. "When I was a teenager, I remember KDAY playing the hell out of 'Blazin' on Broadway.' I still have the LP it was on, *Double-Barreled Funk*."

"You weren't into disco then?"

"I got into my share of clubs with my fake ID, sitting around playing Pong and backgammon," he admitted, "learning the Hustle and trying not to sweat all over some girl. But I have to credit my sister Odessa with being the keeper of the flame when it came to R&B and Soul. She predicted disco would die, though not the numbers like what Hayzell and the Sugar Kings performed."

Loveless seemed distracted for a moment, then asked, "Who are the ones you're trying to find?"

He consulted his handheld's screen. He'd initially argued strenuously with his old lady about how his steno pad was trustworthy, how words on paper had proven satisfactory for hundreds of years. But she'd prevailed.

"Believe me, you'll get hooked," Superior Court Judge Jill Kodama had said. Damned if he now didn't find his CrackBerry indispensable.

"How about Minnie Thaxton?" Monk asked. "Also, what about Burris Parchman?" He looked up expectantly.

"When Ardmore called last week I figured Minnie'd be one of the people you'd want to talk to. In fact, her set's closing tonight at the Raven's Mill. I can call over there to let her know you'll be coming."

"Thanks." He noted this using his stylus. "And Parchman?"

She folded her arms, shaking her head, a morose cast to her features. "You know he was a slave to that 'caine."

"Ardmore understood he'd been clean and sober," Monk suggested.

"Last I knew, and this was maybe '97 or '98, he was back in Baltimore living in a shelter. But," and she held her hands apart, "that's the last I heard."

Parchman had been a session man, keyboardist and organist on several later Hayzell and the Sugar Kings numbers. It was believed that Parchman had come up with an instrumental called "Do Your Thing" on one of the tracks. There had been several conflicting publishing credits for the tune and Monk hoped to settle the matter. But Parchman was most known as the man who'd killed Hayzell Mumford, the Sugar Kings' lead singer.

"Well, I'll talk with Minnie and see how that goes."

"She's going to like you," Loveless observed. "She must be

pushing back seventy, hard, but she appreciates her some younger sturdy mens, as she would say."

"I ain't that young no more," Monk averred.

Her eyes brightened. "You're upright and got those shoulders. That's good enough."

They both chuckled and he asked, "Is there anyone else around from then who I should talk to? I believe Hayzell's mother is alive."

She bristled. "You said you only wanted the ones who wrote some of the numbers."

Monk hunched a shoulder. "I like to be thorough."

"You're nosy," she declared.

He grinned, hoping to defuse the tension. "That too."

"What is it that you're really after?" she hissed, an edge in her voice. "About how Hayzell was killed over drugs?"

Monk was going to offer a denial but she leaned forward, her hands splayed on her desktop. "I know goddamn well that he was, now don't I? I've had plenty of offers to tell my story, from *Rolling Stone* to a couple of white boys over at ASU doing a book on the Phoenix rhythm-and-blues scene. I haven't said anything to them about then, and won't to you either . . . Look, I need to get back to work."

Monk rose and put out his hand. "Thanks for seeing me."

She pretended to be reading some paperwork and mumbled, "Uh-huh," and didn't proffer her hand again.

At the Raven's Mill that night, Minerva "Minnie" Thaxton tore up a rendition of T-Bone Walker's "Cold, Cold Feeling." The club had been closed for years but several enterprising types, including a skateboarding champion turned brand name, had cleared up the title, then refurbished and reopened the place. There was money to be made on the nostalgia angle, and there were the loft dwellers trickling into the south side who knew all about the blues from public television.

The audience was more white and young than black and

old, but the applause was genuine and the vibe mellow. She finished her first set with one of her own numbers, "The Heat of My Heart," which showcased her searing riffs on guitar. Monk was allowed backstage as had been arranged, and after announcing himself, he entered Minnie Thaxton's dressing room.

"Sheeeittt," the big woman said, sipping more of the Stoli-over-ice Monk had been advised to bring. After introductions, she'd asked him to pour one for her and one for himself from the short dog he'd brought along. "That chick always did have her ways. Even back then when Nazeen and Hayzell were going around together, she was whispering in his ear about how he should go solo and whatnot."

She took another dainty sip. Monk figured she could drink like that all night and not be affected.

"You know she was my manager for a while?"

"No, I didn't know that."

"Oh, yeah, Nazeen may be high-toned, but she can TCB, honey. She handles that fitness club hustle but puts on a few doo-wop concerts each year too. I play 'em, it's good money."

"She was your manager after Hayzell was killed?"

"Yeah," she said, swirling the contents of her plastic cup. She tilted her head back. "That was some time around here. You from L.A. and I know about Watts in '65 and all that, but black folks here in Phoenix, child, we caught double hell when it came time for us trying to get ours." She shook her head. "Then, as now, this is Goldwater Country. It don't matter he was part Jewish, that didn't temper a goddamn thing. Don't let them fancy golf courses over in Scottsdale or what they building round here fool you," she shook a ringed finger at the wall, "there's plenty of redneck cowboys left to remind you in case you get giddy."

She cracked herself up and had another taste.

"I understand Hayzell died in his mother's arms and you two were there. Is that why Nazeen Loveless is so sensitive about it? Watching him die?"

She put her feet up on a hassock and kicked off her heels. "I guess," she sighed. "It messed her up bad when it happened. We all knew he was snorting up enough snow to coat the Rockies, but she wanted to believe she could help him. Well, she did for a time." She licked her bottom lip. "Too bad he loved that shit more than her."

"Burris Parchman was a replacement band member, wasn't he?" Monk's other task from Ardmore Antony was to clear up inconsistencies in the liner notes he was assembling. The producer also knew the eye couldn't resist a juicy murder. The misguided and misunderstood fascinated Monk, for wasn't he one of them? In understanding them, wasn't this a method to better understand himself? He was as hooked on probing the psyche as Hayzell or any other cokehead was on his drug.

"Yeah, that Jheri Curl–head fool Burris sure could burn up that Hammond B-3. Jimmy Smith and Jack McDuff didn't shame him, I'll tell you that. Coke wasted Hayzell, but it was tonic to Burris . . . Speaking of vices," she jiggled the lonely ice in her cup at Monk, "hit me one more time 'fore my next set, dark and lovely."

He did but refrained from refilling his supply. "So he and Hayzell were arguing in the recording studio?"

"That's right." She drank and chewed a piece of ice. "Used to be there was only Audio Recorders here in town when I got here in the early '60s. But by then, nineteen and seventy-six, we had a couple of others, including Express Tracks. There was a break in taping and people, you know how they do, drift off, go outside and have a smoke, be it a regular cigarette or a border special." She winked. "But these two go into this little room in the back and snort up. Seems Hayzell then accused Burris of stealing from his stash."

"Did he?"

She made a face. "Sheee. Who knows with those two? But like I said, this is AZ and they don't play around here. Sure, by then the Black Power thing was played out, but you gotta remember that the Sugar Kings had stepped out there after Hayzell heard Marvin Gaye's "What's Going On" and got his head bent. Not to mention being high and getting inspired listening to Funkadelic and Sly Stone. Him and Burris even got into a little acid like them white boys cause they heard Hendrix and George Clinton had dropped some. So toward the end of '71 we started experimenting. Doing some protest songs, for lack of a better word, in our concert mix. Songs about getting over. Sheeee." She gulped what was left of her vodka. "We almost got shot in Flagstaff."

"Hayzell carried the gun for protection?" Monk asked.

"Partly for the peckerwoods," she allowed, "but he also dealt with bad folk on the road since he was always on the hunt for nose candy. Whatever the reason, way Burris tells it, their argument got out of hand and Hayzell pulls his roscoe. They wrestle and the gun gets knocked to the floor. Burris dives for it as Hayzell picks up a mike stand to brain him. Even when he wasn't loaded, Hayzell did have something of a temper. I certainly remember several times when he'd go off on us after a gig for messing up the beat or coming in too slow or too fast on the bridge. He couldn't read music, but goddamn his eyes if he didn't have the most natural sense of timing I've ever witnessed."

Thaxton had been one of the few women in that era making a living playing guitar. She gathered herself and added, "Burris had the gun. One shot and Hayzell went down, a fatal wound to his chest. We come rushing in, and at that precise moment his mother arrived to surprise him and take him to lunch. It had been weeks since he'd been back in Phoenix, you see."

She finished her drink and plopped the cup down noisily on the dressing table.

"Parchman is tried for second-degree voluntary manslaughter. He does five years and some change at Safford." She slipped her shoes back on and straightened her stylish wig. "It almost killed him, but Hayzell's daddy did a magnificent service for his only son." A quaver went through her voice but she remained clear-eyed.

"You know where I could find Burris?"

A mirthless laugh rumbled in her chest. "You gotta understand, when he got out he tried coming back on the scene. But it was strange, follow me?"

"Him being the killer of Hayzell Mumford, the south side's own. Whatever the circumstances."

"Exactly. He was off the blow but hit rock bottom with the booze. He'd get gigs but it didn't take long for some fool or another to bring up the incident and he'd be getting more attention than he wanted."

"Like a regulator in the Old West who could never outrun his rep," Monk observed.

"Now, could be I heard he was up Oakland way last I notioned on it. But," she sighed, "that's been a long damn time too. At least ten years." She held out her hand. "Help me up, baby. I need to get back out there and entertain."

There was a knock on the door and a trim bespectacled man in his early forties leaned his head in. "Five minutes, Minnie," he said, grinning at her and frowning at Monk. He wore a houndstooth sport coat.

"Okay, honey," she replied, blowing him a kiss. He withdrew but left the door slightly ajar.

Thaxton stretched and said, "I'll have my man go over these papers and we'll be in touch with Ardmore."

"Great, I appreciate your time."

"Not a problem."

Monk departed and was at the side exit door when the man with the glasses stopped him.

"What'd you want with Minnie?"

Monk told him, assessing him as a protective younger boyfriend.

"Hey, that sounds like a winner," the guy enthused when Monk got to the part about the proposed agreement for Thaxton's songs. "Let me give you my card. I'm Minnie's manager."

Monk guessed there'd been a succession of "sturdy mens" in his age range as her managers. He glanced at Charles Estes's card while handing the man one of his own. "Good to meet you."

"You know, my uncle wrote a couple of songs when he was a Sugar King. But maybe you're not going to include him because of what happened. Really, it's messed up what they laid on him."

"Your uncle is Burris Parchman?" Monk said.

"He's not really blood, but our families have known each other a long time. My dad and him went to the same grade school."

"Charles, get over here," Minnie Thaxton called out, standing before her dressing room door.

Estes grinned sheepishly at Monk. "Her majesty needs me."

"What about your uncle?"

"Holler at me tomorrow, man. My celly's on the card."

He rushed away and Monk returned to the Ramada Inn on First. After all these years chasing chuckleheads, from the common street thug to the truly flagitious, and getting socked in the head or worse for his trouble, he was still on a budget. It was hard being the People's Detective, he lamented.

Early the next day, Charles Estes called Monk, who was drinking coffee at a local café. "Hey, man, sorry I kind of misrepresented matters last night. Truth is, I haven't seen Burris in a long time. I don't know where he could be."

"Maybe somebody in your family might know."

"I'll see what I can do," and the line went dead.

That was a kiss-off. Thaxton must have told Estes to get the party line right. Why didn't she want him talking to Burris Parchman? It must have something to do with the shooting. Phoenix was unknown territory to him. But he had a day left on the room that Antony was paying for, and figured he'd use the time productively.

At the main library on Central, an imposing five-story rectangular structure seemingly modeled on a space-age toaster, he went through collected bound hard copy and microfiche newspaper accounts of the shooting. He studied the coverage in the black newspaper, the *Arizona Sun*, and the white press too, including the *Herald Examiner* in L.A. The pieces contained various mentions of the pioneering civil rights work of Hayzell Mumford's parents, the Reverend Asa Fairchild Mumford and Dr. Justine Mumford, PhD in social anthropology. From World War Two and Jim Crow–divided Fort Huachuca, where the reverend was an officer not inclined to bow and scrape to whites, to the early '90s, the Mumfords were a driving force in various struggles for social justice. From job equality in the public sphere, school betterment for minority students, and housing integration in the greater Phoenix area, they'd been at the center of many pivotal moments of change in the state.

On July 4, 1976, during the nation's bicentennial, Phoenix, like a lot of cities, put on a large parade and celebration. The Mumfords were to be honored, and, Monk noted in one account, the Sugar Kings were slated to perform. But it had been the week before that the fight had taken place at the studio, so naturally that segment of the festivities had been canceled.

From what Monk could gather, the reverend was not a fan of his son's avocation. "I cannot be reconciled with Hayzell's pursuit of these most temporal and tempting of concerns," Mumford was quoted. Another article contained, "I can only continue to pray that the Lord will guide him out of this episode of his life and return him to the fold."

More recent online searches showed that the father had died in 1998. The partisans who attended the funeral included Harry Belafonte, Oliver Stone, who at that time was trying to get a film made about the Mumfords, and former Congressman Gus Hawkins, the first black man elected to the California legislature. Monk then read a quote from Nazeen Loveless in the *Examiner*:

One shot and Hayzell goes down, a fatal wound to his chest.
We came rushing in, and at that moment, precisely, his mother
arrived to surprise him because she wanted to take him to
lunch. It had been weeks since he'd been back in Phoenix.

Monk did an eyebrow raise worthy of Spock. He then searched for references to Parchman. There were no articles about him online except for the time during the shooting. But looking back at the bound hard copies of the black newspaper, he spotted several ads for local clubs where Burris was listed as a headliner. The last one was from 2004. That was just a few years back, indicating he was still active, at least then, in the Phoenix area. Loveless and Thaxton had said Parchman had disappeared before that. Maybe he snuck into town and left promptly. Or maybe not.

Burris Parchman wasn't listed in the white pages, and though Monk called several music booking agents, he got nada. He did find a listing for the Mumfords' church, Greater First Congregational Methodist on East Jefferson, once the heart of the black community's south side.

"Yes, you see," Monk told the helpful woman over the phone, "I'm wondering for the purposes of this documentary we're putting together if we could interview Mrs. Mumford. I realize she retired some time ago. Is there a way you can get her a message?"

"I would like to help you," she said. "Justine would love to participate, only . . ."

"Yes?" Monk said in a solicitous tone. What sort of bad ju-ju was he racking up lying to a good woman like this?

"She's been under the weather," the woman said in a way that suggested Mrs. Mumford wasn't simply suffering from a cold. She was in her eighties, after all. "Let me see what I can do. Give me a number to reach you at, would you?"

He gave her his cell number and the one to his office in Los Angeles, then hung up.

Monk walked about downtown, came upon a barbecue rib and chicken joint, and had a late lunch. It was past 2 and still over a hundred degrees of dry heat. His cell chimed as he swallowed a bite of tri-tip sandwich. After his hello, a quiet voice said, "My name's Burris Parchman. I hear you've been looking for me."

"Oh, yes, sir. Who told you?"

"Charley did. Course, he also convinced me to let him resurrect my so-called career. Once the Sugar Kings compilation comes out, he said he'd be able to get me some new gigs." He had a rumble of a laugh like the organ he played. "Well, one thing at a time, I guess."

"Where are you?" The number and area code hadn't come up on Monk's screen.

"Sure, let me give you this address. I'm staying with a friend."

The house was a neat little Craftsman not unlike those Monk was familiar with in the older parts of L.A. It was east of downtown in a mostly Latino section judging from the *Llantas* Goodyear and mini-mercado signs.

"Come on in," a pleasant voice said on the other side of a screen door.

"Thanks," Monk said, stepping into a freshly painted room with little furniture and no TV. The hardwood floors looked like they'd been recently refinished. The walls were bare.

"She's getting some work done," Burris Parchman remarked. The musician was a thin, medium-complexioned black man in his mid-sixties with a trim mustache and receding hairline. He wore wrinkled khakis, a short-sleeved shirt, and raggedy tennis shoes. "As you can see," he continued, pointing at the open windows, "the air-conditioning hasn't been put back in. But I have some iced tea. I was just about to have a glass. You?"

"Sure, that'd be great," Monk said.

"Cop a squat," Parchman said as he stepped into the kitchen. He soon returned with two glasses and put one before Monk on a side table. The coaster was already in place and was from the Raven's Mill.

"So tell me about this project."

Monk sipped his drink and began to speak, half rising from his chair to hand over the paperwork. His head suddenly felt light and he sat back down quickly, his mouth dry despite the liquid. Coltrane's sax was moaning "Naima," but he knew there was no music on. He drained his drink, his throat closing up. He stared at the residue in the bottom of the glass. Were those scales?

"Say," Monk began, dropping the glass, his fingers telling him to do so. "Why would Minnie and Nazeen Love . . . Lovenobody." He giggled but it sounded like one of those demon clowns in a low-budget horror movie. "Why would they lie to me about where to find you?" Why was it so hard to get a sentence out?

"This is the West, Mr. Monk. We protect our legends around here." Parchman seemed to be talking to him underwater. It was as if Monk were floating up to the moon and watching the earth recede beneath him. He stood but his shoes had ballooned way out of proportion like in a cartoon. He fell over and was quite content to lie there on his side, his ear to the floor listening for the *woo woo* of the Underground Railroad. He smacked his lips, tasting purple while he counted the infinite swirls and whirls within the wood floor. His heart beat rapidly and sweat doused his face and shirt front.

"How long will he be like that?"

"I don't know but we need to get him out of here. Then wipe the house down for his prints and put the *For Sale* sign back up."

Monk rolled over and glared hazily at the green Martians with their elongated heads discussing his fate. Through a window he could see a giant ant from *Them* looking at him too. He decided this was a party. Especially since Lee Dorsey was singing, "*Everything I do gohn be funky from now on.*" He sang along, trying to snap his fingers.

Hands lifted him off the undulating floor. The Martian with

the fancy silver bracelet was talking again. "Check outside and we'll put him in his car. Get his wallet."

"We driving him away from here?"

"That's too risky. It's better to get him behind the wheel," the silver bracelet said. Clearly, Monk cogitated, this one was the H.N.I.C., ah, the H.M.I.C. He giggled again. Kurt Vonnegut, the size of a fly with insect wings, landed on his arm. He said in a tiny voice, "Three to get ready and two to go, bro." Kurt the Fly-Man flitted away. Monk was sad to see him go.

"He could hurt somebody," one of them said.

"We're in this too far now. We can't have him hurt *her*," one of the Martians said.

In a blue haze, they walked him to his car. Or was it a stage-coach? He squinted at the giant ants hitched and ready.

"Giddy-up!" he yelled. He went all rubber and, jerking his arms free, flopped to the ground. Time for a sit-down on these mufus, he reasoned. He had to catch his rocket to the moon. His honey would be waiting for him. "I got to call Jill," he added, rolling around on the ground like a temperamental child.

"Get his ass up before somebody sees us."

He was snatched upright and hauled to his car. Keys were plucked out of his pocket and he grabbed at them.

"Cut it out," a nearsighted Martian said, hitting him in the face.

"We can't leave marks or it won't look right," the H.M.I.C. warned.

"Good advice," Monk said, trying to get out of the diving bell but forgetting how his legs worked. A jackrabbit with the head of a strawberry hopped onto the hood and quoted Wole Soyinka.

"The human factor, alas, is a ponderous and imponderable factor of history."

"You got that right," Monk mumbled. Transfixed by the literate rabbit, he became gradually aware that he was in motion. He had a hold of the steering wheel. The radio speaker fuzzed and

Henry Ford spoke. No, Monk listened closer and realized it was Ann Sothern as *My Mother the Car.* She was trying to tell him something about pedestrians and traffic lights, but the horizon flipped over and everything came to a thundering halt.

Propelled forward, Monk cracked his head open on the windshield. Blood dripped into his eyes and he blinked them clear as he stumbled from the wrecked vehicle. The car had jumped the curb, plowed over a mailbox, and finally came to a stop when it smashed halfway through the side of a building. Martians and creatures with tentacles for arms lunged at him and he ran, so happy he remembered how to make his legs work. He knew what they really were beneath their disguises.

Canadians. Canadians terrified him. Sneaky infiltrating bastards. On he ran through the jungle and into the desert, his heart thudding in his ears, drowning out the sirens and the yelling and the cursing. He ran and ran and stared crying. Suddenly, he stumbled across an arid landscape where the snouts of crocodiles stuck out of the sand like cacti, their fearsome crooked teeth snapping expectantly.

Monk stepped tippy-toe around them and came upon the squatting marble statue of the Great Aztec Toad. Only it wasn't a statue but the living toad god Tlaltecuhtli. The Earth Mother toad opened her maw, and after hesitating for a moment, the Canadians getting closer with their monkey sirens, he dove into the black. He swam and crawled through the murk, panicked that he'd never find his way out. It was then, at his lowest, that he saw his dead father, Sergeant Monk, Mechanic Monk, Husband Monk, stepping out of a door from nowhere.

Monk's dad held out his big calloused hand. "Come on, Ivan, you can do it. Come on, son. Just a little further and you'll be safe."

"Wait for me, Pop." Crying and bleeding, he ran and leapt through the doorway.

* * *

Dr. Justine Mumford's private room at the Northcross Manor rest home smelled faintly of gardenias and hyacinths, her favorites. The flowers commanded the room in various baskets and vases, and her attendant had already filled three paper shopping bags with *Get Well* cards. There was to be no recovery for the civil rights icon, but just as she had confronted adversity, threats, and violence in her life, she faced death with bravery and aplomb.

"It's going to be fine," Mrs. Mumford said, her voice barely audible above the humming of the respirator.

Nazeen Loveless cried softly, holding onto the old woman's hand. Age and illness had diminished the elderly woman's physical shell but her voice yet reflected her power of conviction.

"It's been three days and the cops are still looking for him," Charles Estes whispered. He stood further back from the bed, where Loveless and Minnie Thaxton hovered. He switched off the radio he'd tuned to local news.

"Soon it won't matter," Thaxton said.

"What won't matter?"

The three turned and stared mutely at Monk, who stood in the doorway. He had crashed his Galaxy 500 into some boarded-up storefronts, just down the block from the long-defunct Express Tracks recording studio. The police had been called but he'd run away howling before they arrived. He'd spent several hours hidden in a Port-a-Potty at a strip-mall construction site. At some point he pissed himself as the hallucinogen in his system wore off. Assuming the cops were looking for him, he'd waited until nightfall to sneak away. Monk had collect-called L.A. and asked Jill Kodama to wire him money for toiletries and a room at a hot-sheet motel, since it wouldn't be safe to return to the Ramada Inn.

Estes started forward and Monk said calmly, "I'm not high now, Charles. You want to jump bad, I'll be swinging back this time." Estes paused. "We don't want to disturb Mrs. Mumford, but you three need to do some 'fessin'." There was complete silence other than the old woman's breathing. "I do have a guess." He pointed at her. "She killed her son, didn't she? And you got Parchman to take the fall."

The other three gaped.

"As I came down from my trip," Monk continued sardonically, "a lot of clarity percolated up. I became fixated on comments from you two," he indicated Thaxton and Loveless, "about when Mrs. Mumford had entered the studio that day."

Loveless blurted, "We were exact."

Monk replied, "That's the point. Given the excitement of the moment, witnesses routinely don't recall events in the same sequence. If it's too tight, too rote, something's up. And in both your accounts, to me and to the newspapers, you used identical phrasing."

Loveless and Thaxton looked at each other.

Monk rubbed his lower jaw. "By the way, was that a Colorado River Frog at the gym? Used the toad skin as a chaser in the Timothy Leary cocktail you slipped me?" Not only had he reread the news accounts, but he'd also studied up on toads, frogs, and bufotenine, a hallucinogen the croakers and some plants produced, at the library. Monk found that if you were quiet, off in a corner doing your own thing, the library made for a nice hideout.

He came further into the room. "You must have also used some substance to get your witch's brew into my bloodstream quicker. Now, you could have given me a heart attack or psychotic breakdown . . . But I ain't mad at you," he added sarcastically, suppressing his anger. "I suppose you brainiacs discussed my outright kidnapping first, huh? Anything to get me out of the way long enough for the lady here to pass on and any questions I raised to be discounted."

Loveless deflated.

Mrs. Mumford moved and said, "Help me sit up."

"Justine . . ." Minnie Thaxton started.

"No, no, please." She held out a hand and Thaxton used

the control to raise the top portion of the bed. "Come over here, young man."

"Yes, ma'am." He stood by the side of her bed, hands clasped before him.

"I did it," Justine Mumford said, looking beyond the walls, then back at Monk. "I came down to the studio to talk with Hayzell that day. The drugs, the sex, those things of course disappointed me. But I knew at the bicentennial celebration, where his father and I were to be honored, he was going to sing that song."

Monk frowned. "'Blazin' on Broadway?'"

She closed her eyes. "Yes, the damned hit of his. Part of the lyrics talk about a certain woman the singer meets and falls for. He was referring to a real woman. Someone his father knew . . ."

"Someone he had an affair with?" Monk hedged.

"It had happened in the early '60s," Minnie Thaxton said hoarsely. "She was a member of the church and a young widow. Her son and Hayzell went to Sunday school together, and the son had spied the reverend tippin' in one night."

Loveless glared at her for being so coarse in front of the dying widow.

"I forgave him," Justine Mumford said, "but Hayzell never did. As he grew up and they grew more apart about everything from baseball teams to the Vietnam War, he wrote that section of the song to get back at the man he considered to be a hypocrite."

"Justine hushed the affair up around the church," Loveless said. "The woman and boy left town."

"But the band knew, cause Hayzell made a point of telling us," Thaxton added. "It was a big joke to him."

"So it was you two arguing in the backroom of the studio?" Monk asked the old woman.

She gave a brief nod. "The church was the landlord of that property. Gospel used to be recorded there. Imagine. I had a key and came in the back way to try and talk to him away from the others. As we argued, Burris heard us and rushed in, trying to get him to calm down. Hayzell was medicated, as was usual then, and pulled his gun on Burris. They fought and the gun dropped to the ground.

"I picked that pistol up," the old woman proclaimed. "I suppose I thought to scare him." Her eyes got wet. "But he taunted me, belittled his father and spat on all that we'd worked so hard for. He said he was going to enjoy singing that song to all those who'd be there for his father, and he threatened to tell everyone how he came to write it . . . How could my own son be so hateful?" Thaxton handed her tissue paper. She sighed and said, "Yes, I killed him, murdered the flesh of my flesh. I committed the greatest sin there is." She turned her head away to the wall.

"We covered it up. We had no choice," Minnie Thaxton explained. "It was one thing for one dope-fiend musician to shoot another. But the woman who was the symbol of Arizona civil rights? We just couldn't give that kind of ammunition to the crackers." She looked pleadingly at Monk. "We just couldn't."

Dr. Justine Mumford passed away peacefully two weeks later. Luminaries such as Jesse Jackson and former president Bill Clinton attended her august funeral. Several legal entanglements were hanging over Monk in Phoenix, but the prestigious law firm that represented Greater First Congregational was providing its services pro bono.

Ardmore Antony had a lot of unanswered questions, but the rights to his compilation were secured. The CD was eventually released, with extra tracks and updated liner notes, including recent remorseful quotes from Burris Parchman. The tragic story of Hayzell Mumford's demise remained unaltered.

Nearly forty years after its original release, "Blazin' on Broadway" by Hayzell and the Sugar Kings enjoyed a renewed run on the R&B charts.

IT'S LIKE A WHISPER

BY MEGAN ABBOTT

Scottsdale

T he thing about Bob," she said, and her fingers snapped the ties on Julie's cocktail apron, "he's so American. He's so American."

Julie nodded. It was good to see Brenda again, and she liked looking at her. She had a Clairol-girl face and silver-blond hair washed twice a day, but things were happening behind those glinting blue eyes and you could feel her winking at you all the time.

Julie looked across the lounge at the man in the beige denim shirt and slacks sitting on one of the low chairs and it was Bob Crane, just like switching a television channel.

"Look at his face," Brenda was saying, and she slid her fingers under the sash on Julie's apron and pulled her close, so she could hear her. "It's so blank. It's like a billboard."

Julie didn't know what Brenda meant, but this was how she always talked. Brenda liked to dance and she made the scene in Phoenix at Bogart's, B.B. Singer's, Chez Nous, Ivanhoe's, where she'd introduced herself to Bob. She was always meeting people and she said it was her special energy. You could like it or not, but Julie liked it.

"So let's make it happen," she was saying and she took Julie's arm and they walked toward Bob Crane, their heads nearly bobbing together, matching blond locks to their waists and smiles popping. Bob was watching them, watching them and smiling, and what man in the Registry lounge wasn't?

"Who's the tomato?" Bob said as he rose. He was handsome and, old as he was, almost as old as someone's dad, he didn't look like a dad. The way he turned toward her, so casual, so knowing, like he'd been waiting for her.

When he looked at her, something sharpened in his eyes, sharpened into a spark, and then his face lit, like a camera flashing, and there he was, Bob Crane. He was giving her Bob.

"This is Julie Sue, Bob," Brenda was saying. "She's got tits you'd serve soft at Dairy Queen."

Bob looked down at Julie's chest in a funny, sly way, and she felt like Fräulein Helga. "Well, nothing wrong about that," he said. "So, Julie Sue," and he bent forward just slightly so she would know she was the only one he wanted to talk to, "are you going to be my friend?"

"Yeah, Bob," Julie replied, and she could feel a tickle in her knees. This would be something. "I'm going to be your friend."

She told them she had to work until close and Bob said she could meet up with them later. They'd be at the Safari coffee shop and then back to Bob's place. He wrote his address on a napkin and gave it to her.

Brenda leaned toward her and whispered in her ear, "Do you think he can handle us?" Bob was looking at them and he folded his arms across his chest, just like on the show. Just like Colonel Bob Hogan. "He does that on purpose," Brenda added, "it's a gas."

"What a picture you two make," Bob said, grinning. "My blond babies."

And she and Brenda leaned into each other, necks bent, heads touching, smiling tangerine lipsticked smiles.

"Like Siamese blondes," he said, and he made a sound like laughing.

Carl came by an hour before close, a little high. He was drinking a screwdriver at the bar.

"Baby," Julie said, "I have to break our date. Brenda came by. I'm meeting her for breakfast."

Carl gave her a long look. "Brenda's back," he said, smiling a little. "Hey, that's your scene, babe."

"I'll see you later," Julie said, and Carl's face looked so shiny. His mustache was slightly wet. She remembered it was the suit he wore when they met about seven months ago, at the Bombay Club. He sold synthesizers and wore those woven sandals, huaraches.

She watched him stir his drink with his finger and flick it dry. "Go with God, Julie Sue," he said. "That chick is bad news."

He turned and faced the bar. They'd partied at Brenda's once and Brenda had read the tarot and told Carl that he was letting his hang-ups hold him back and that secrets were being kept from him. Later she told this story of how Linda Kasabian, the Manson girl, was her old babysitter. She said Linda read her cards once and told her she would die young, stabbed against a white wall. Everyone at the party freaked out a little and Carl said she was bad news.

"I like Brenda and I haven't seen her in a while," Julie said. Brenda was so much fun. And there was Bob Crane.

"Keep your head," Carl advised, looking in the mirror above the bar. "You know what I'm saying."

The Safari was one of her favorite places. Once she saw Angie Dickinson walk through the lobby in a white bikini. But the coffee shop was quiet that night and she didn't see Brenda and Bob. "They were here, but they left," the waitress said. "He'll probably be back later."

Julie looked at the napkin for Bob's address, then decided to drive over to the Winfield Apartments.

On the way, she tried to remember the *Hogan's Heroes* theme song. It kind of made you want to march. What was that thing the fat guy in the helmet always said on the show, "I hear nothing, I see nothing, I know nothing . . ."? She wondered if Bob was still friends with the *Family Feud* guy. Maybe he'd come to town too.

Brenda really knew how to make a scene. Julie'd met her by the pool at the Camelback Inn awhile back. Brenda was stomach-down on a deck chair, barelegged, wearing a Mott the Hoople T-shirt and sunglasses. Purple eye shadow smeared across one temple.

"Hey," she'd said, twisting around to talk to Julie, cross-legged on a beach towel. "I know you."

"I don't think so," Julie answered.

"No, no, man, I *know* you," she said, propping herself up on her elbows. "You have freckles behind both knees."

Julie smiled. "You just saw that when I was doing my back." But she knew she hadn't turned over yet.

"It was awhile ago," Brenda said, grinning. "You had the sharpest tan lines. You had the swimsuit with the keyhole in the front."

Julie didn't say anything.

"You shouldn't have let him do that," Brenda said, and she shook her head.

"What?" Julie started, feeling dizzy, wondering if she had sunstroke. "What are you talking about?"

Brenda shrugged. "Maybe it wasn't you."

They'd gone swimming and then to one of the rooms where Brenda was staying with two musicians. They were high and they had a bottle of rum and Julie drank some. They told the girls to get in the shower together and they did. It was fun and Brenda was beautiful with that long twisting hair, and it'd been a good time. They got free tickets to the concert at Feyline Field.

The air conditioner was going. It was cool in the apartment and there was one floor lamp on and the television set.

"Join the party, Julie," Brenda said. She was naked and her white dress was on the floor. Julie felt overdressed in her uniform, though it was so short she couldn't bend over, even to reach behind the bar.

"Welcome to Casa Bob," Bob said, standing up in his under-shorts.

There was a buzzing sound. She thought it was the air unit, but it wasn't. It was the camera running in the corner, on a big tripod.

"Look," Brenda said, pointing to the television. "Bob's on TV again."

"I never left," Bob said.

Julie glanced over at the television and it was Bob and Brenda having sex on the sofa. Brenda's head was in Bob's lap, her blond hair white on the screen and spread in all directions.

"Julie," Brenda said, "Bob can help so you too can make it on the big screen. Or small screen."

"Baby, I can make you a star," Bob said, smiling at Julie.

"Can I have a drink?" Julie asked. She thought a drink would be a good idea.

"She likes Southern Comfort," Brenda said, tucking her legs beneath her on the striped sofa.

"I'm sorry," Bob said. "I just moved in and I don't drink. But I want to make Julie happy. Someone brought me some Scotch at the theater. Do you like Scotch, Julie?"

"I like Scotch, Bob."

He smiled again and said he was glad. "I like that place," he added, talking about the Safari. "Did you ever roast cocktail weenies in that big charcoal fireplace?"

Julie grinned and drank her Scotch. Brenda was tugging at the back of her uniform, trying to drag the zipper down. Julie tried not to giggle. "Carl sure couldn't handle this," she said.

"I go there every night," Bob said. "I like the coffee shop."

Julie felt the cold air hit her shoulders and breasts. Brenda ran her hands down Julie's stockings and hooked her fingers underneath to pull them off.

Julie peered at Bob, who was sitting on the arm of the sofa, wearing his glasses so he could look back and forth between the television and her.

She wondered why he wasn't on TV anymore, and why he was here, like this. She hadn't been to his play at the Windmill, but she bet it was terrific.

"You seem like a good person, Julie," Bob said. And there was something in his eyes and it made Julie feel funny, even sad, and it must've been the Scotch, which sometimes brought her down.

"I am," Julie said, as Brenda pulled the stockings from her feet. "I am a good person."

"Bob," Brenda asked, "would you like to see how good she is? Would you like to watch me? I can make her beautiful." Brenda wrapped her arms around Julie's stomach and nuzzled her neck.

"She's already beautiful," Bob said.

"I can make her more."

"You can try."

In the living room, when it was going down, Julie couldn't stop looking around, couldn't stop thinking, This is happening, wow, isn't this a trip, Colonel Hogan himself, and she looked at the camera on its big tripod and the stack of cassettes in the corner, and she saw a leather jacket on the floor in the corner and she wondered if that was the jacket he wore on the show and wouldn't she like to get into that, and her eyes caught her reflection on the TV screen and there she was and she saw herself and Bob Crane and she saw her eyes and they were startled. And she saw Brenda and Brenda was looking too. Brenda was staring and her dark eyes looked so big Julie thought they might swallow the screen.

They ended up in the bedroom. Bob walked behind her, putting his hand in her hair. They had sex on the bed. The buzzing in Julie's ears was making her head hurt and the Scotch was making her dizzy. It seemed liked everything in the apartment was plugged in and running.

The room was dark and at one point it was just her and Bob and the light from the living room flashed on his face, above her. And it was that face, and she thought, it's like getting it on with the slick cover of a *TV Guide*. But it wasn't really like that. It wasn't like that and she couldn't name it, but looking in his eyes, it was doing things to her. It felt like something had passed over between them. She was seeing something and it made her so sad, all of a sudden. She felt her face wet and she thought, I'm crying. I'm crying. Why am I crying?

Later she couldn't be sure if it had happened.

After, she and Brenda went back into the living room. Brenda put her dress on and helped Julie zip her uniform back up.

They were giggling at first, and talking. It was like a slumber party, curled upon the sofa.

"I'm getting back into music," Brenda was saying. "Steve bought me a keyboard. Maybe Bob can help me. He used to be a big deejay in L.A. He knows people in the biz."

"Maybe," Julie said, and she felt a little sick. She thought she should lie down.

She leaned into the corner of the sofa and Brenda kept talking, on and on, and Julie fell asleep.

"Do you hear that?"

Julie's eyes flew open and Brenda's face was big in front of hers, her hand grabbing Julie's wrist.

"What?" Julie said, trying to prop herself up. "What?"

"Do you hear voices?" Brenda whispered, loudly.

Julie couldn't hear anything.

"Someone's trying to get into the apartment," she said, and they both looked over at the front door. "They're trying to break in."

"No," Julie said. "You had a bad dream."

"I'm worried about my house." Brenda jumped to her feet. "I need to get home."

"That doesn't make any sense. Just relax, Brenda."

Brenda's body was shaking and Julie stood too, head groggy,

and tried to speak slowly and firmly, like you're supposed to do when someone's having a bad reaction to dope.

"Brenda, you're fine. You're fine."

"It's like the dream," she said, her voice pitching up and down. "It's like the dream."

"See? You were just having a bad dream. Don't be scared, Brenda." Julie put her hand to her own head, fighting off the dizziness. That buzzing noise was back. It had been gone while she slept and now it was back and it seemed louder.

"I'm sensitive that way," Brenda said, gravely. "When the moon is a certain way, I can get these vibrations. It's like a whisper. When I met Bob, I had this picture. It came to me. I blacked out for a second and it was like I could see something was in his way. It was a darkness, on his bed. A darkness there on the bed with him."

"Brenda . . ." Julie said, starting to feel something prickly in the back of her head, like touching a hot wire.

"And when I got here, it was like I was hearing an atmospheric disturbance in the place."

"No. No," Julie said, but her voice quavered. "It's the air conditioner. It's the equipment.

Brenda, you—"

"And now I can see it. I can see it on the wall like a shadow." She pointed at the wall by the front door.

Julie couldn't see anything, or thought she couldn't. There were lots of shadows, more than she could count. The prickling in her temples was worse and worse and she felt so hot, even with the air blasting behind her.

"I know you see it," Brenda said. Then her voice rushed up fast and she pointed at the wall. "It's behind you, Julie. It's behind you!"

Julie felt her heart rush up her chest and she turned around so fast she nearly fell. The minute she did, she felt silly. "Brenda," she started, but she couldn't make her voice calm. "Did you drop a tab? Did you drop a tab?"

"You know I don't use that. I don't use anything," Brenda replied, and her eyes were so wide and she kept putting her hand to her forehead and she started pacing back and forth in front of Julie.

"There's nothing there, Brenda. Are we . . . are we still sleeping?" She knew it didn't make sense but she felt it, she felt it looking all around the room, which was like the TV screen, everything either black or white, black cassettes and equipment and the tripod and shadows and white walls and Brenda, who was standing stock-still in front of the coffee table.

Suddenly, Brenda's hand flew to her mouth. "The thing in the corner," she said. "The thing in the corner."

"What thing? What thing?"

"It sees you, Julie."

And Julie felt her heart thundering and she wanted Brenda to stop and she wanted to leave. She wanted to leave but couldn't imagine how to make her body move to the door.

"Stop it, Brenda," she said, her voice jangling. She wondered how Bob did not wake up.

"It's here. It's here. Silent. Waiting. Voices, or a rush. Julie, don't let it see you. Don't let it . . ."

Julie felt her hands dart out and cover her ears. There was the buzzing and behind the buzzing it was like there were whispers and in the whispers was Brenda's voice, urgent and throbbing, beating like a drum. "Julie, Julie, watch out. Watch out."

She felt her arms fling out and shove Brenda, who staggered backward and curled into herself, and Julie ran to the bedroom door and saw Bob was sleeping still and the sounds of his breathing were so peaceful. But there was Brenda behind her.

An awful feeling came to her as she watched Bob. She felt like this was something Brenda was doing to Bob. She felt like Brenda might be the dark thing.

"Don't, Julie," Brenda was whispering. "Don't go in. You'll bring it in there."

Julie backed up and turned around and her hand swung out and cracked against Brenda's face and Brenda's eyes stuttered shut and open and something broke and Brenda paused and Julie stood still, her hand shaking, and the pause stretched and the hurtling look in Brenda's eyes was gone.

"Julie," Brenda said. And she didn't say anything else. There was a coolness in her face, a sudden calm. And there was a knowingness to it, like she could look at Julie and see everything.

"I have to go," Julie said. "I have to go home now. Don't I. I have to go home now."

Brenda stared at her and nodded.

"Do you want to come with me, Brenda? I think you should come with me."

But Brenda gave a half-smile and turned and walked toward the bedroom. She could see the flash of white sheets as Brenda slipped into bed beside Bob, who let out a forlorn sigh.

Julie grabbed her handbag and walked over, stopping at the bedroom door. "It wasn't me, Brenda." She wasn't even sure what she meant. "I didn't bring it . . ." Her voice trailed off.

Brenda, hair falling over her face, lying there, looked at her but didn't say anything.

It was two weeks later, the day after the murder, when she called the police. Everyone in town was talking about it. Everyone had seen Bob, at all his places. Bob and his friend John, the one the police knew did it. Everyone was getting called in or getting visits. Carl told her to make the call or it could be worse. This was right before Carl started up with the hostess at Bobbie McGee's and before she got into that new scene, the crowd that hung out at that dance place in Phoenix. The detectives came by and asked a lot of questions. They showed her pictures and it was terrible seeing them. Why do you have to show me these? she said, and seeing him lying there, nearly as she'd left him the week before, lying on his bed, eyes closed, but with that dark mass streaking from him, across the sheets.

For weeks and weeks she replayed it all in her head. It usually started with a dream, and the dream was always the same and it always began with her walking toward him in the Registry lounge, and that look in his eyes, like he was expecting her.

It wasn't long after that she drove by Brenda's place and saw new people living there. She asked around at the Safari, the Camelback, Chez Nous, Bogart's, the modeling agency in Phoenix. One night, a regular at the Registry told her that she'd heard Brenda went to Mexico to make a film and was killed in the desert.

It was his face she remembered, long after. Brenda had said it was so blank, vacant, or transparent, like glass, knocking light and shadows off everyone. Or maybe it was a mirror. But that wasn't how it was to her. In her head now, he was right before her, his eyes filled with things, cluttered with them, with desperation and darkness and loss and, now she saw it, surrender. It was as if he was waiting for it, for her. She knew that somehow he was.

Author's note: This story is a fictionalized account of a real-life incident, as reported in Robert Graysmith's Auto Focus: The Murder of Bob Crane *(Berkley, 2002).*

PART IV

THE CRY OF THE CITY

DEAD BY CHRISTMAS

BY DAVID CORBETT

Tempe

I'll tell you what ruined my marriage, and it wasn't gambling or drink or chasing skirt. Our son, Donny, was walking home from a friend's house when a LeSabre blew the stop sign, ran the poor kid down in the street and dragged him twenty yards, then fled the scene.

Seven years old, Donny was. And he fought, or his body fought, half the night, until the ER surgeon came out with that look on his face, to talk with Barb and me.

All I remember of the next two weeks is I went on a mission—horning my way into the loop as every department in the valley tracked down the driver, even tagging along when the arrest came down in Apache Junction. They put two men on me, to make sure I didn't take my shot as they dragged the guy out. His name was Phil Packer, an insurance adjustor with a DWI sheet ten years long, bench warrants in four counties—he'd been hiding in his girlfriend's trailer.

After that, every time Packer shuffled into court from lockup for a hearing, I was right there, front row, eye-fucking him and his wash'n'wear lawyer. None of which made a difference, of course, nor was it anything close to what Barb or our baby girl needed from me. That wasn't part of the mission.

My wife called me out on all that one night—it was late, she'd had a few, her face streaked with mascara from sitting in the dark with a bottomless cocktail and her son's ghost. Melodie, the baby, lay asleep in her room. I'd been out in the car, driving around, something I did a lot.

Seeing me there, Barb stood up and tottered closer, into the light. Her eyes were puffy and raw. "I'm sorry. Do I know you?" She had that tone.

I said, "I had to finish up some work."

"No. I called. You left hours ago."

I had a lie ready. "A CI called, he wanted to meet. They didn't tell you?"

She laughed acidly, inches from my face now. "You're such a coward."

Looking back, I think of the things I might've done, might've said, but all I could come up with in the moment was, "How many have you had?"

"Not nearly enough." She shoved the glass into my hand, a dare. "You know, Nick, disappearing isn't the same as dying."

I remember feeling cold all over. "You're not talking sense."

"You're jealous of Donny." Her eyes, glistening in the light, turned hard. "Somehow you think staying away is going to make me miss you. The way I miss him. Christ. Are you honestly that pathetic?"

Some scientist should measure the speed at which shame turns into hate. I'll never forget that sound, never forget the feel of the glass shattering in my hand or the sight of her crumbling in front of me, no matter how much I try. There's some things "sorry" won't cure, no matter how many times you say the word, or even how much you mean it.

It's said that only one in five marriages survives the death of a child, and maybe I should take comfort in the numbers. Regardless, it was my divorce that turned me into a workhorse, not the other way around.

This was the early '90s and I'd rotated into robbery, great place to get lost, the numbing paperwork, sixteen hour days if you want them. There were four of us from different departments—Phoenix, Tempe, Scottsdale, Mesa—meeting once a week to share intel. We'd had twenty restaurant take-downs around the valley the previous six months, all the same guy. He came in at closing, when the back door was propped open by the kitchen crew—that's when they dragged the rubber mats out to the parking lot for the nightly hose-down. Meanwhile, inside, the money was getting counted and bagged for deposit.

The robber wore dark coveralls, gloves, a ski mask, and he always slipped in and out within minutes, which meant he knew the business. Brandishing a snubnose, he'd prone out the manager, tie him up with plastic cuffs, the kind they use for riot control, then snatch the night deposit. Right before leaving, he'd grab the manager's wallet, dig out the driver's license. "You're gonna say some wetback did this," he'd whisper. "I know your name. I know where you live." Even after we found out the guy was white, we still had vics swearing to our faces he was Mexican.

Finally, luck stepped in, as it does more times than most cops care to admit.

Two cars responded to a domestic here in Tempe—how's that for poetic? One cop grabbed the husband, the other took the wife, separated them, different rooms. The wife—eye swollen shut, cracked lip—she bawls to the cop there with her, "You know all the restaurant jobs around here the past few months? That asshole in the next room, he's the one you're after."

The woman wouldn't swear out a statement, though, so the uniform tracks me down in robbery at the end of his shift to give me a verbal. I'm Tempe's case agent on the restaurant spree. You can imagine, he lays out the scenario, I'm cringing a little. Everybody on the force knew my business. Even so, I should've been thrilled, right? Finally, a suspect.

The guy was Mike Gallardi, his wife's name was Rhonda. Together, they ran a hole-in-the-wall called Mike's Place out on Baseline Road in South Phoenix. You could get a coronary just reading the menu but the place was clean, with a small counter and maybe a half dozen booths.

Here's the thing: They catered to cops. You walked in, one whole wall was dedicated to fallen officers. Flash a badge, your kids got free sodas with their meals. Come in on duty and no one's around? Boom, wink, you ate free.

I'd been at their place just once, a couple years before, taken there by a buddy of mine in traffic division. Rhonda worked the register and counter, a shy, chesty, bleached-out woman in her thirties. Mike was the talker and he came out from behind the grill to toady up, all shucks and gee-whiz.

How to say this—I don't trust people who backslap cops. They always want something. Not that I made much headway on that point when I broke my news to the robbery roundtable.

"No way Mike's the suspect." This from Cavanaugh, the detective from Phoenix. "I can name fifty guys right now, this minute, who'll vouch for him."

"His own old lady handed him up."

"After he batted her around, yeah. Go back, now that she's cooled off. I'll bet she admits it's crap."

He had a point, of course, domestics being what they are. But something about the way he said it made me think what he meant was: *What would your wife say about you, Boghossian, if we gave her the chance?*

Thankfully, the four commanders overseeing the roundtable agreed with me and ordered surveillance. The teams worked in rotation, each department on for three days then making way for the next detail. But Mike was smart. He made our guys early and burned them in heat runs, crazy Ivans, every kind of stunt you can imagine to flush them out. Once he just stopped in traffic, walked back to the unmarked car, and said, "Why are you following me? I haven't done anything."

I could just picture him, over one of those free burgers or shrimp baskets he doled out, pumping guys for information on tail jobs: *C'mon, tell me, I'm just so doggone curious.* And cops—hated by damn near everybody, grateful for someone who actually gives a rat's ass—I'll bet they couldn't tell him their stories fast enough.

It got to me, sure. We were the ones who'd trained this guy—inadvertently, granted, but he was smarter than he should've been because of us. He was pulling out our wallets, whispering our names and addresses. And yeah, like everybody else he'd chumped, I felt ashamed.

Two weeks later, I got a call from surveillance: "Boghossian, get this. Gallardi and his wife locked up their place as usual but didn't head home. They checked into a hotel on the frontage road along I-10."

I knew the strip, we all did: a line of restaurants flanked that part of the freeway.

As I drove on over I thought about Rhonda's tagging along. It surprised me, I'll be honest. Maybe Cavanaugh had been right—I should've gone up to her early, asked her to confirm what she'd said that night Mike trashed her. And even though I knew that would've tipped our hand, now she wasn't just keeping mum, she was joining in. I felt responsible, like there'd been a point in time when I could have saved her. No surprise, I felt like that a lot back then.

I met the team at the hotel and, sure enough, after 11:00, Mike came out of the room in dark coveralls, a day pack around his waist. He walked down a side street to the parking lot of an Applebee's, then hunkered down in a patch of oleander to watch the kitchen crew do its thing. The radios started to buzz—we had our man, no more doubts. After a half hour, Mike eased out of the bushes, retraced his steps, and slipped back into his and Rhonda's hotel room.

The next day, when I called the robbery roundtable together to report, Cavanaugh went from looking like he'd lost his dog to acting like he meant to kill somebody.

"Okay," he said finally, "I'm in. If Mike Gallardi's our guy, he'll get no favors from me."

I volunteered for surveillance at Applebee's, even though it meant staying alert for hours on end with the windows rolled up in hundred-degree heat, drinking warm Coke and pissing it all back into the empty cup.

At 9, our eyes at Mike's Place reported that Rhonda had left, heading toward home. An hour later, Mike locked up and followed suit. A collective moan went out over the radio. He'd called it off. Then, not long after, we heard that Mike and Rhonda were on the move again, leaving the house together. They were on their way toward us.

The voices on the radio perked back up—this was the night, we could feel it. And we knew we'd have to watch the whole thing play out, let him go in, rob the place, or it'd come apart in court. But what if he sniffed us out? What if he took a hostage?

Rhonda drove down one of the side streets and parked, then Mike hopped out, headed for the parking lot. I slouched in my seat, a drunk snoring off a bender. Through slit eyelids I watched him saunter toward the back of Applebee's, and for an instant he looked straight at me. It was dark, some serious distance separated us. Even so, I sat stock-still, wondering if I'd been made.

He turned away and ducked inside the concrete dumpster enclosure. Two other men with eyes on the door reported they had visual, and we had a man out front too, in case Mike tried to run that way. Surveillance units got in position to take down Rhonda when the time came.

At half past 11, the kitchen crew trooped out, propped the back door open, and dragged out their slimy black mats, sudsing them up, hosing them down. I kept up my ruse, dripping with sweat but not moving, sipping air through the window crack. Mike stayed put too, even after the kitchen crew vanished again, leaving the door open as they mopped the floors. After midnight they humped on out again, collected their mats, and dragged them back inside.

A whisper crackled on the radio, *"What's he waiting for?"* Another whisper snapped back, *"Off the air."* We were all raw from the heat, testy from sitting still so long. Over the next hour, the employees came out in ones or twos, lingering for at most a smoke before driving away. Finally, the manager trudged out, locked up, not carrying a deposit bag—he'd left it in the safe—then got in his car and left.

Mike waited another fifteen minutes before sliding out of the dumpster enclosure. Hands in his pockets, he meandered across the parking lot, shooting one last glance in my direction. Minutes later, surveillance confirmed that he and Rhonda were headed back home.

We waited in place another two hours. Mike might come back, I thought, try to burglarize the place, clip the trunk line on the alarm, pop the safe. Finally, I called in to Rooney, the grave-yard sergeant, to report. "I want everybody to stay put, Roon. The money's all there, he's coming back in the morning when they open up."

"I'm calling it off," Rooney said. "Your guys have been stuck in their cars for six hours now. It's still what, ninety-five degrees outside? Besides, from the sound of it, you got made."

"The sound of what? You're not sitting here."

"I need a team to report to the rail yards. Call just came in. Somebody made off with two dozen cases of Heineken."

I almost spit. "You're pulling my guys off because a pack of kids rifled a boxcar?"

"We've got a squeaky victim."

"Meaning who?"

"Meaning the Westbrook family."

The Westbrooks, wholesale distributors throughout the state, in-laws at the statehouse, a cousin in Congress. Somebody asks you what it's like to be a cop, I thought, tell them this story.

I got home to my apartment about 3, showered the sticky grit off my skin, and crawled into bed. I still wasn't used to sleeping by myself back then and I lay awake awhile, puzzling the whole thing through. Get a cop alone, find him on a day he wants to be honest, he'll tell you the cases that bothered him most always involved a suspect who someway, somehow, reminded him of himself. And I knew Mike Gallardi pretty well, I thought. Down deep, where it mattered, he was weak. That's why he liked power, not just over Rhonda but the people he robbed—gunpoint, the terror in their eyes. *Do what I tell you.* Like a cop, or his bent idea of one: a guy who gets what he wants, even hammers his wife, and never pays. I was going to change that. I'd be the one who finally made sure he suffered, if only for the chance to tell myself I was different. I was better.

Eventually, I drifted off and dreamed I stood in the doorway of a house off in the desert somewhere. A wounded dog limped toward me through the moonlit chaparral. As it drew close, I looked into its eyes, and saw my son looking back at me.

The next thing, the phone was ringing.

It was Rooney. "I don't know what to say, Nick. Applebee's got hit this morning, 8 o'clock." Some throat-clearing. "Just like you said."

I rubbed my face, checked my watch. 8:30. "How much?"

"Twelve grand."

Hardly a take worth risking your freedom for, I thought. But this wasn't just about money. I wondered if Mike had driven back alone, or if he'd dragged Rhonda along with him again. And maybe she didn't feel bullied at all. Maybe, for the first time in a long, long while, she felt married.

"We're never gonna catch this guy without a wire." I was laying out my case to John Tally, the county attorney. "He's getting cocky—cocky crooks get sloppy and that's when people get hurt."

Tally tented his hands, rocking in his chair, sunlight flaring in the windows behind him. An ASU man, politician to the bone, he was tan and fit, pompous, cutthroat. "I'll approve a wire," he said finally. "And a task force, but I want hard numbers on bodies."

"Phoenix and Tempe'll pony up ten men apiece," I said, guessing. "Scottsdale and Mesa half that each, an even thirty."

"You're lead agent," he said pointedly. "Team up with Tom Kolchek for the wire affidavit. And don't be fooled by his looks. He's the smartest guy I've got."

I stood up to leave. "I want to call off the surveillance, make the target think he's in the clear."

Tally glanced up, like I'd already become a bother. "I told you," he said. "You're lead agent."

Tally was right, Kolchek looked like your Uncle Monty—thick all over with thinning hair and sad-sack eyes—but he was one of the sharpest cops I ever worked with. The affidavit came to a hundred pages and was airtight, detailing every job, how Mike came to be our suspect, the ensuing surveillance, the continuing robberies, everything. We argued that, given Rhonda's new accomplice role, phone communications between the house and the restaurant could prove fruitful. The judge granted us thirty days for the wire, with a re-up possible for another thirty if the need arose, which would carry us through the holidays. But if we didn't have results by then, tough. We'd have to bag up and go home.

We notified the phone company of our target lines and anticipated start date, so they could build the parallel circuits for the wiretap. Two days later, they called back to tell us Mike had disconnected his home phone. He'd done it the same day we submitted the affidavit.

Kolchek hung up and sat there, thinking it through. Finally, in an oddly sunny voice, he said, "We'll bug his house."

"You don't get it," I told him.

"I get it," Kolchek said. "So? We tighten the circle of who knows what, rewrite the affidavit, wire up his house. Maybe we'll get lucky. You get any better ideas, let me know."

I didn't get any better ideas, of course. And every time I tried to imagine who might be tipping Mike off, I could never convince myself I had the right man. Cavanaugh was the first and obvious choice, given how long he'd stuck up for Mike, but he was a hard cop and I'd seen the betrayal in his face before the Applebee's job. Besides, like he'd said, fifty cops would vouch for Mike in a heartbeat—any one of them could be our leak.

Kolchek and I reworked the affidavit, kept the wire on the restaurant phone, and asked for three transmitters for the residence—one in the living room, one in the dining room, one in the bedroom—sensitive enough, at ten thousand dollars a pop, to catch voices throughout the house. The judge signed off and Kolchek introduced me to a tech for the county attorney's office named Pritchard, who'd go in and actually set things up.

"I'll go with," I told Kolchek.

"No, I will," he said. "I'm a pretty good lock pick and we only need two men inside."

"What about the dog?"

Kolchek cocked his head. "Dog?"

"A white shepherd," I said. "It's in the surveillance reports."

"Right. I remember. What's your point?"

"I used to work canine. The white ones are unpredictable, you don't want to go in there alone." That was mostly crap, but there was no way I wasn't going with them. I wanted a look inside that house.

The next day, when Mike and Rhonda were at the restaurant, Kolchek headed up their front walk and took a Polaroid, then went to the hardware store, bought an identical door, and set it up in his office, practicing till it took only forty-five seconds to pop both locks.

Meanwhile, I scoped the neighborhood for the best spot to place the undercover van. Mike and Rhonda lived in a mazelike community of town houses grouped in quads, and the geometry of the place was all wrong; there was nowhere within a hundred yards of their unit to park the van and not stand out. Then I saw there was a unit for rent one quad over. We could set up the wire room in there, as long as we kept a low profile.

I hit up Tally's office for the rent and two days later, when Mike and Rhonda and most of the neighbors were off to work, we moved our guys in. Me, Kolchek, and Pritchard headed over for our entry to plant the bugs, while a ram car took up position on the street to force a fender bender, stall for time, if Mike or Rhonda came back while we were still inside the house.

When we got to the front porch, though, we found a brand-new security gate with two additional locks, barring access to the door. Kolchek just stood there, staring, holding his lockpick tools. "This isn't happening." He glanced at his watch and swallowed hard. Inside, the dog was barking like the place was on fire.

I started heading for the back of the house. "Bet you're glad you brought me along now."

There was a privacy wall around the patio in back and I scaled it, dropping down onto the pavers. A sliding Arcadia door led inside, with an insert for a doggy door. I got down on the ground, reached through, and flicked aside the dowel lodging the door in place. The dog realized what was happening then, and as I slipped inside he turned a corner and charged toward me, hackles raised, fangs bared.

I reached frantically in my pocket for the syringe of Isoforane I'd brought along to knock him out, only to sink my thumb into the needle. "Goddamnmother*fuck*!" I played air banjo with my hand for a second, then, glancing up, saw I wasn't the only one to miscalculate. As his paws hit linoleum, the dog lost traction, sliding toward me helplessly. Stepping forward, I caught him under the jaw with a kick so fierce he cartwheeled backwards.

"Get in the goddamn bathroom!"

The dog sulked off, mewling, as I checked my thumb, hoping adrenalin would ward off any grogginess. Suddenly, I remembered my dream from weeks before—the lonely house, the wounded dog. A chirp from my radio broke the spell.

I clicked on. "Yeah?"

"*We heard that, detective.*" It was one of my guys in the wire room. In the background, laughter. "*Punt the pooch—that what they teach you in canine?*"

I switched off my radio and searched out the front door. When I got there I found out the security gate was locked from inside, requiring a key. "This nails it," I told Kolchek through the grating. "Somebody's tipping this guy off."

"We'll talk about it later," Kolchek whispered, standing exposed with Pritchard on the porch. "Get us inside."

Kolchek lacked the physique to scale the privacy wall, so I found a window in a small utility room near the back for the two men to crawl through. Once everybody was inside, we headed to the living room to set up shop. Kolchek got busy taking Polaroids of the room so we could put it back the same way we found it.

"Look at this," I said, pointing to the couch. There were sheets, blankets, a pillow. "Christ, she's kicked him out of bed. They're in the middle of another fight."

"Get to work," Kolchek said. He was testy and pouring sweat. It dawned on me then that, despite a first-rate mind, Kolchek lacked any serious operational experience. The glitch with the locks had rattled him.

Pritchard hooked up his transmitters to the phone lines. Even though the service had been cut off, the wires still held voltage. We set them up in the three different rooms as planned, and Pritchard asked me to contact the wire room to see if we were live. Only then did I realize I hadn't switched my radio back on after that crack about my canine prowess. When I flipped the button, a voice came through almost screaming. "*Jesus, Boghossian, where'd you go? We've been trying to contact you for ten minutes. The wife's on her way, just west of Pepperwood. You're lucky she stopped for smokes. Move!*"

We rushed to test the transmitters through the wire room and got an all-clear. Kolchek's hands shook so bad from nerves he couldn't screw the plates back on the phone plugs, so I took the screwdriver from him, told him to pack with Pritchard, I'd close up.

They scrambled out the utility room window and I locked it behind them. Turning back to finish up, something caught my eye, something I'd overlooked before.

On a shelf near the door, a small day pack rested among some other odds and ends.

We had no warrant to search the house or its contents, but I took the day pack down regardless and opened it up: A ski mask. A pair of black garden gloves. A .38 snubnose and a dozen plastic cuffs.

There was a desk in the room and I laid the contents out, retrieved the Polaroid from the dining room, and took a picture. This was a trophy, not evidence—I wouldn't even tell anybody about it, let alone show them the picture. The whole investigation might vanish down a hole if guys started jabbering. I packed everything up again and put the day pack back where I'd found it, but then my curiosity got the best of me and I searched the desk. In the bottommost drawer, I found a snapshot—Mike with Cavanaugh, up in the mountains somewhere. They were hunting together, carrying shotguns, the best of friends from their smiles. Rhonda, I guess, had snapped the picture. I took another Polaroid. This too, of course, wasn't evidence, and I told myself it didn't really prove anything. It was just a reminder—my reminder—of what I might be up against.

I ran back to the dining room and was just about finished putting things back in place when the voice came through my radio again: "*Boghossian, she's at the corner.*"

I barked into the mouthpiece, "Ram her!"

I was making one last check, comparing where everything was with the Polaroids, when I heard the collision outside. It was about fifty yards from the house, some undercover cop plowing into Rhonda's back end at the stop sign. I opened the bathroom door and told the dog to stay, then headed toward the patio, fit the doggy door insert into place, and reached through to slip the dowel back onto the runner.

Beyond the glass of the sliding door, I saw the large white dog slink into view. Our eyes met. He flinched a little, tail lodged between his legs. Ashamed, like everybody else.

It was up to the boys in the wire room now. I checked in as often as I could, but the days went by, nothing. Mike knew we'd been in there—tipped off by Cavanaugh, I supposed, something I had to keep to myself. Besides which, just like I'd thought, Mike and Rhonda were in a tiff, the two of them seldom speaking.

As time passed, though, I felt strangely encouraged. I knew the dynamics of the simmering fight. I heard the cues—the caustic one-liners, the icy silences. Somehow, some night, something would set them off. And the words would come boiling out, things they'd regret forever.

As it turned out, that night came right before Thanksgiving. And the somehow and something of it proved, to my way of thinking anyway, too apropos.

The surveillance team trailed Mike to a porno arcade near the airport. We'd watched him visit smut shops and strip clubs all over the valley, not sure if he was casing the places or had just grown tired of not getting any at home. This time, though, according to the cop watching from the parking lot, Mike came out wobbly.

"I may be wrong," the radio voice reported, "but I think our boy just had himself a little love."

When Mike got home he wasn't inside five minutes before he launched into Rhonda—a fight over nothing, but so blistering that everybody in the wire room shuddered. When one of the cops reached out to turn off the recorder, though, honoring the minimization guidelines, I told him, "Wait." We'd gotten our first lead in this case after a brawl between these two. I could justify listening on the grounds there was a reasonable expectation that, in their fury, one of them would say something useful. Accusing.

The voices kept rising, more and more shrill and cruel. And sexual. One Mormon on the wire crew blushed, but everybody kept listening, each of us wondering what we should do if, at some point, one of them tried to kill the other. And yes, finally, we heard scuffling. I reached for the phone to dial dispatch as I heard Rhonda stammer oddly, "M-Mike, n-no. No!" The yelling turned to muffled cries, then rhythmic, whimpering moans. Gradually it dawned on us that Mike had decided on a little show'n'tell, to demonstrate for Rhonda what had happened earlier that night, during his encounter at the porn hole.

"One good pipe-cleaning deserves another," somebody cracked.

"Turn off the machine," I said, knowing we'd get nothing of any use now. Adding insult to injury, Mike moved back into the bedroom that night. So that's how you make your marriage work, I thought, hating him even more.

The first thirty days played out, no results. We got an extension but none of the departments would pony up the manpower like before. They put rookies on the line-of-sight details. Once, after letting a tail car pass him, Mike chased the cop all the way down Central Avenue, flashing his brights, just to embarrass the kid.

Meanwhile, the wire crew was going batty listening to nothing and more of nothing. We were back where we'd started—we'd never catch Mike Gallardi except red-handed, coming out the back of a restaurant. And everything we knew about him said that if that happened, he'd make us kill him.

"The man's gonna be dead by Christmas," someone quipped, and it became the unofficial slogan of the whole operation, until I told everybody to knock it off. "If you're right, and we take him out, you don't want to have to explain that little mantra to Internal Affairs."

Given where we stood, though, I decided it was time to tickle the wire. I went to Tally again, told him we needed to put some pressure on the couple, inflict a little fear.

I showed up at Rhonda's front door when surveillance confirmed Mike was at the restaurant alone. I came in a marked unit, the strobe spinning out at the curb, and the uniform who'd driven stood with me on the porch. No more avoiding the neighbors—we wanted their attention now. Inside, the dog went off when the doorbell rang, then went still, dropping his tail, when he saw me beyond the grating.

Rhonda deadpanned, "Gee, if I didn't know better, I'd think you and the dog knew each other."

I pulled the subpoena from my jacket pocket and gestured for her to open the security gate. "Rhonda Gallardi, you're to appear before the grand jury on December 5th. You're not to discuss your scheduled appearance or the subject matter of your testimony with anyone except your lawyer—not even your husband. Understood?"

She looked taken aback but hardly stunned—some fright in her eyes, but a baiting grin too. I wondered if that was how she looked right before Mike hit her.

"What if I don't open the door?"

"I'll just set it down on the porch here. Either way, you're served."

The grin faded a bit, her fear quickening into anger as her eyes checked the cop behind me, then slid back. "This is harassment."

"Guess how many times a day I hear that."

"Because you're a prick?"

I nodded for the cop to head back to the car. Once he was out of earshot, I said, "Know what I think? You've been trying hard for a long time to make things work—your restaurant, your marriage. I admire that. But the point where things were gonna change is gone for good." I stuck my hands in my pockets, to look harmless. "You want to turn that around, now's the time."

Women who've been hit more than once have a look—sad and yet defiant, almost mocking, but defeated all the same. Come on, I thought, invite me in, talk to me. I knew, given the chance, I could open her up, end this thing. But her eyes turned hard and far away again. "Leave your papers on the porch," she said, then shut the door.

In the wire room, we listened when Mike came home that night. Apparently, what I'd said registered, at least a little, because the good wife unloaded.

"No more! I'm done."

"Shut up, Rhonda."

"I'm not gonna lie under oath for you! I never wanted—"

"I said shut the fuck up, Rhonda!"

The sound of scuffling came again. I grabbed the phone to dial dispatch. But a minute later, they were outside the house, walking the dog. The perfect couple—Mike with his arm around Rhonda's shoulder, holding her close, loving, protective, whispering into her hair.

Rhonda got coached well for her grand jury appearance. All her answers reduced to: I don't remember. I'm not sure. *I don't think so. I don't know.*

"He beat us," I told my guys afterward, like I was confessing to some crime of my own.

A week later we went in to pull the wires, and I was hardly shocked to see they'd put a three-piece console in front of the wall socket where we'd planted the living room transmitter. They'd been a step ahead of us the whole time. Took us an hour, though, to take the knickknacks down, drag the big thing away, claim our bug, then push the monster back and make sure all the junk was in the right place again, even smoothing the carpet so you couldn't tell anything had moved.

The operation got bagged, departments couldn't justify the

manpower anymore. We went around to restaurants, schooling them on smarter ways to close up at night—it was all we could do at that point. Maybe Mike would decide his luck had played out. Or maybe he'd get reckless, hurt somebody, and the whole thing would heat up all over again.

On Christmas Eve, I visited Barb and our daughter for the annual holiday torture—unwanted presents, forced smiles. And no talk of Donny, as though the only thing that could keep the pain at bay was a punishing silence.

But then, walking to my car, I heard the front door click open behind me. Turning, I saw my daughter—she was five then— running toward me in her red velvet dress and green tights. Behind her, Barb waited in the doorway, a silhouette.

Melodie scooted up, gripped my hand, and pulled so I'd bend down. In a solemn whisper, she said, "Don't be sad, okay? It's Christmas."

"I'm not sad," I lied, but she'd already dropped my hand, spun around, and fled back toward her mother who let her back in, then closed the door.

Later, at my own place, drinking Scotch as I flipped through the channels, I got the call from dispatch. A steak house up in Paradise Valley got hit right at closing. I was on my way to the scene when the second call came in. Shots fired. The address made my stomach drop.

By the time I got to the condo the place was alive with cops, strobes spinning around the complex, mingling eerily with the Christmas lights. I got out of my car and pushed through the crowd of neighbors outside. The cop with the entry/exit log took my name and badge number, then waved me in.

Techs and detectives ambled about. A spindly tree stood in the living room, sagging with ornaments and tinsel. One of the guys from homicide pointed me back to the kitchen.

In the breakfast nook, I found a uniformed cop standing guard over Cavanaugh, who sat gripping his head. He glanced up just long enough to catch my eye, his gaze frantic with calculation.

To the uniform, I said, "Do everybody a favor and stand back a little. He makes a grab for your gun, you may both wind up dead."

From the kitchen I made way toward the utility room. A body sheet covered a sprawling form on the floor, a pool of drying blood trailing out from underneath. Spray patterns hazed the walls. A handprint smeared the doorframe.

In the bedroom, wearing an undershirt and cargo shorts, Rhonda sat with hollow eyes, stroking the shepherd who lay at her feet whimpering. A female officer stood guard, one hand on her sidearm, as though she intended to shoot the dog if it so much as moved.

It took a second for Rhonda to sense I was there in the doorway. Glancing up, she blinked, took me in. Her hair was a mess. She looked ashen and lost.

Cavanaugh would take the fall, pleading out to manslaughter. His story—I can't say whether it's true or not, though I tend to believe more than I doubt—was that he and Rhonda, his cop-crazy buddy's wife, were lovers. The night Mike found out, he knocked Rhonda around awhile, then went out, got coked up, and took down his first restaurant. He'd been pumping Cavanaugh for information on robberies for ages, claiming he just wanted to know how to protect his own place.

Mike came back from that first job in an odd heat, feeling invincible—the man he was meant to be—and told Rhonda that, if he ever went down, he'd hand up her lover as the man who'd taught him everything. Cavanaugh had to protect him then, to protect himself, protect Rhonda. He began tipping Mike off on the robbery investigations, staying away from Rhonda once the surveillance began but getting messages through by using the guy who washed dishes at their restaurant as a go-between. That went on until Rhonda's grand jury appearance, after which she told Mike she'd dime him out herself if he didn't stop, she didn't care who got hurt. And Mike obliged her—until Christmas Eve.

He missed it, that nervy heat when he slipped in, pointing the gun. The fear. The begging.

As soon as he left the house for Paradise Valley, Rhonda picked up the phone, dialed Cavanaugh, told him she was leaving for good, she'd had it. He told her to wait, he'd be right over. They meant to be gone by the time Mike got back but—here again I'm not sure what to believe—he surprised them, slipping into the house unnoticed. It was self-defense, if you looked at it right, though Cavanaugh knew better than to take that to trial.

But all of that was yet in the telling as I stood there in the bedroom doorway. The dog ignored me for once, still whimpering, its ears pricked up. It was Rhonda who stared right at me.

"You're the one whose wife walked out," she said finally. She left the rest hanging, but her voice was accusing. She wouldn't be gloated over, not by the likes of me.

I don't know how to explain it. Despite her contempt, despite everything, I felt for her. And I could afford to be gracious, not because I was different or better or even because it was Christmas. I remembered my daughter's words, whispered in my ear: *Don't be sad, okay?* I had a piece of something back I'd thought was lost for good. It felt a little like being forgiven.

"My wife had good reason to leave," I said, thinking: *Why lie?*

But Rhonda just turned away. With a soft, miserable laugh, she said, "Like that's all it takes."

I lingered awhile, waiting her out, but she said nothing more, just leaning down now and then to console the dog.

With profound thanks to Detective Jay Pirouznia, Tempe PD (Retired).

WHITEOUT ON VAN BUREN

BY DON WINSLOW

Van Buren Strip

W hat it is is it's hot.

Beads of sweat pop onto Jerry's forehead the second he steps out the door of his motel room. Do Not Pass Go, Do Not Collect $200, Go Directly to Jail, my man. Like there is no transition period between the air-conditioned chill of the room and the outside world of Phoenix—it's just like *wham*, the heat hits you like a punch in the chest.

Last night the noisy old air conditioner in the cheap motel had forced him to choose between not sleeping because of the banging of the machinery and not sleeping because of the stifling heat. He'd chosen not sleeping because of the noise.

August in Phoenix, Jerry decides as he walks out onto Van Buren, is a bitch.

Who comes to Phoenix in August?

Well, me, he thinks.

And Benny Rosavich.

And what's Rosavich doing here in the summer, anyway? God knows the slick prick has money, he could be anywhere, why did he have to pick the freaking desert? Aren't Russians supposed to like snow, and sleighs and ice hockey and shit like that? Go after an Israeli, you expect to find him in the desert, not a Russian.

Maybe he's a Russian Jew.

Jerry forgot to ask.

Like it matters.

This stretch of Van Buren is empty at noon. A ghost town. Nobody is out there who doesn't have to be. One or two meth whores with shriveled chins like crones on the slow stroll, trying to stay on the shady side of the street. Ain't no shady side at noon, ladies, Jerry thinks. The sun is straight above and burning down on our heads like the glare of an angry God. Burn right through you.

The pro he picked up last night wasn't bad. Skinny with no tits, but the price was right for a half-and-half. Guys who'd been down here before had told him Van Buren was thick with working girls, you couldn't swing a dead cat without hitting one in the ass, but there hadn't been so many. She was all right, though, she did the dirty deed. Strictly speaking, it was against established procedure, picking up a girl, especially a pro, but he has a hard time sleeping the night before a piece of work and it helps to get the snake charmed.

He walks down the street toward the motel they told him Rosavich is at. He's at a motel on Van Buren, you can't miss it. Hate to tell you, boys, but there ain't nothing but motels on Van Buren, a lot of them closed and boarded up, though. This was supposed to be a happening place back in the day, but that must have been a lot of days ago. He's been on the street, what, two minutes, and the back of his one-size-too-large baby-blue polo shirt is already soaked. Nice. He takes off his ball cap and wipes his brow with the back of it. A Yankees cap, because it's distinctive, people remember it. Let them go chasing around New Yaaawk for him. He'll toss it in the nearest dumpster on his way out. He has uncles would beat him half to death they saw him with a Yankees cap on, but this is a do-what-you-gotta-do-to-get-by world.

Long freaking walk to the Tahiti Inn. The freaking Tahiti Inn. Tahiti?! Ain't that like an island with swaying palm trees and cool ocean breezes? Brown-skinned women with small firm breasts and coconut drinks in their hands? What is it, like a joke or something?

He guesses he could have taken a cab but that just leaves one more witness. Cops always talk to cabbies and he already had one who brought him in from the airport. Better than renting a car, though, that just leaves a paper trail and more people who've seen you. So better to walk, even in this heat.

Couldn't have done this in the wintertime, right? When the snow is blowing sideways into your eyes, your toes feel like they're going to snap off, and a flight to fun in the sun is just what the doctor ordered? Sit out by the pool with a piña colada in your mitt and pity the poor bastards scraping frost off their windshields back home? Noooo, you have to come in freaking August.

They say it's a dry heat, but so is an oven. He reaches around and feels the handle of the pistol tucked into the back of his jeans. It's still there, nice and snug. Last night he'd stopped by the pawn shop they'd told him to go to, and the counter guy slipped him the gun, no problem. A nice clean work piece that won't hold a print.

He walks for another minute and then stops in his tracks.

Jerry feels dizzy for a second. The sun is so bright and hot it drains the color out of the world. Like the whole world goes white.

A whiteout, he thinks.

Abe likes the sun.

He goes out onto the little balcony—just big enough for a lawn chair—at the motel where he has a permanent room on the second floor. He's bare-chested with faded lemon-yellow Bermuda shorts, white socks, and sandals. He likes to feel the sun on his chest. The docs have lectured him about skin cancer but for crying out loud he's eighty-three years old and the prostate is going to kill him before the cancer will.

Old men get cold, and the sun feels good.

Abe feels like he's always cold these days, what with his bum circulation. His feet are always chilled, and his chest is like an old icebox. Death itself. He sits down with his grapefruit juice and vodka and looks out at the street. Nothing much to look at now, but it was something back then. It's still beautiful in the movie that rolls through his head in bright old Technicolor.

Back then, when you drove into Phoenix from the east, this was the main street, the highway, and the motor hotels lined it on both sides. Beautiful places too. He remembers the names—the Rose Bowl, the Winter Garden, the H&R, Camp Joy. Pretty places with free ice water and swimming pools. One of them—which one was it? he asks himself, cursing his memory—had a big-screen outdoor movie you could sit and watch at night. Those soft desert winter nights.

They were good times. Him and a few of the boys would come to relax, get away from it all, and you could do that in those days because Phoenix was an open city, no funny business allowed, no blood spilled. It was good to come down from Detroit, especially when they were fighting it out back then, the Jews and the guineas. Good to come down and soak up some sun, have a few drinks, a few laughs, eat Mexican food you couldn't get back then in Detroit. Get laid.

The women in those days, Abe thinks as he watches the two sad whores across the street. Secretaries, receptionists, and nurses would come down on the train from Detroit, Chicago, Omaha, and they were here to let their hair down and have a good time too. You'd loosen them up with a few drinks and take them to eat at Bill Johnson's Big Apple where there was a chance at seeing a movie star or two who would maybe recognize you from Las Vegas and come over and say hello and that would cinch the deal with the girl, all right. You could bring her back to your room at the Deserama and in the morning lie in bed and watch her roll her stockings back up her long legs and you'd say, "See you, kid," and there would be no complications.

Now he remembers bringing Estelle here on their honeymoon, on the way to the Grand Canyon. That was just down the street at the old Sands. He remembers her perfume, the way her black hair touched her shoulders, how she took her slip off and hurried under the sheets. But she was game in bed, Estelle—bucked like a champion. That was a long time ago, he thinks, when a breeze would give you a hard-on, and now Estelle is gone and the Sands is a homeless shelter.

A homeless shelter.

He leans back in his chair, closes his eyes, and feels the sun on his face.

Her feet sweat in the tight shoes.

What's bothering Evie more than anything right now. Her feet are swollen from the heat and the damn shoes are too tight anyway. Red FMs and skintight jeans that grab her harder than a fourteen-year-old boy in the back of a car. Sunlight glistens off the sequins on the body shirt that shows her stomach, not as tight as it used to be after two kids.

What she's doing out on VB at noon, two kids, a pimp, and an ice jones to support, you put in the hours. Got popped by vice just two nights before too—her third bust so she's headed for a stretch and needs to make some before she goes. They gonna take her kids too, 'less she can get her auntie to take 'em first. Except auntie ain't gonna take no kids unless they come with a little cash attached. She got troubles of her own, her own rent to pay, and the liquor store don't give the vodka away.

Evie keeps an eye out for the cops. They're everywhere these days—"cleaning up Van Buren." They already closed three of the motels where she took johns. The rest are closing on their own, anyway. Won't be nothing left of VB soon, it's just fading away.

Van Buren, Van Buren.

Used to be a girl could make a living here, you call it living. She looks down the street and sees the guy coming. Black ball cap, big old blue polo shirt hanging loose over new jeans. One more middle-aged white guy trying to hide his thinning hair and spare tire. She's looking for a john to jack and he could be the one. Take him in the alley behind the dumpster and while he's busy thinking about her mouth on his thing and all those sweet noises she'll be making that wallet will pop out his back pocket like that button on the turkey when it's ready at Thanksgiving. Even if he wakes up, what's he going to do? She has a blade in her back pocket and can fillet him like a fish. Johns don't go to the cops neither, because what they gonna say? Cops will put in about one second flat, worrying about that wallet. What you deserve, you go looking to nut on Van Buren. Take that back to New York. "You wanna date, honey?"

Man keeps walking, like he can't see her, like she's invisible. She walks alongside him.

"Honey, you wanna date?"

"Not today."

"I'll show you a *good* time."

"I'm sure you would."

"You can be sure."

"Another time, baby. I'm busy."

I ain't your baby, baby. I ain't nobody's baby, baby baby baby. "What other time, baby? I'm out here all day."

The man just keeps walking. Walking and sweating. Maybe she'll see him on the way back from wherever he's going, he's so busy.

Her feet hurt.

Itching in the heat.

Jerry finds the Tahiti Inn.

Just in time too, because another two minutes he might have passed out. Last freaking job I take in the desert, he thinks, in the summer anyway. They want some guy taken off the roster in Phoenix in August, they can call somebody else.

The money is good, anyway. Do the job, hit the airport, fly back to Providence, and take Marcy on a little weekend to Block Island, like she's been bugging him. Not much to ask, and she's a good baby, Marcy, she don't make too much trouble.

He walks past the big sign with the goofy tiki mask. The main office is shaped like a Tahitian hut, or what they think it looks like, anyway. Jerry doesn't know—he's never been to Tahiti or even Hawaii. Maybe he should spend a dollar and take Marcy to Hawaii, might not be a bad idea to get a little distance after this. Sit on the beach, watch the girls do the hula, maybe get Marcy fired up a little to lose those last five pounds.

Room 134.

They told him Rosavich is in 134.

Good. No stairs to go up or down.

He finds 134, pulls out the gun and holds it behind his back, then knocks on the door.

Abe dances with Estelle.

In his waking dream, the sun having lulled him into semisleep. In this dream that is not a dream, he's in the old El Capri Ballroom, whirling her around, little dots of perspiration on her neck as she looks up at him and smiles. She wears a cornflower-blue dress and a string of pearls.

They had come down to Phoenix after the thing with Sol Hirsch went bad. Poor, stupid Sollie, hanging from the rafter in that loft while they took baseball bats to him. He finally told them what they wanted to know, but Abe had felt sick after that, and tired, so he'd said to Estelle, "Let's take the new Buick down to Phoenix, stay on Van Buren. Do some dining, some dancing, get a tan." She wouldn't sit out in the sun, though, she said she liked her skin white and so did he. The few minutes she would sit out with him she'd wear that big floppy sun hat, even in the pool; she did the breast stroke and kept her head above the water. Then she'd go into the room, into the cool dark, and read paperback books and nap until he was ready to go to dinner.

That night at the El Capri she was so pretty.

He was young and handsome.

Van Buren was beautiful.

He sees Sollie Hirsch, his hand jerks, knocks the glass of grapefruit juice over, and he wakes up. Wonders where he is and then sees he's on Van Buren under a white hot sun.

* * *

She don't find nobody.

Cars go by but don't even slow down to take a look. No one walks by—everybody has found a cool, dark place to be.

Everybody except me, she thinks.

Ain't no cool, dark place for me in this bleached-out world.

The door opens and Jerry steps into a world of darkness.

So dark after the bright sun that he can't see Benny Rosavich spring cat-quick with the knife.

Rosavich plunges the blade into Jerry's leg and then slices sideways, severing the femoral artery. Jerry screams and backs out the door, which slams shut in front of him. The pistol falls from his hand and clatters on the baked concrete. He grabs his leg, trying to hold the blood in, but it pours around his fingers as he staggers out past the goofy sign and the Tahitian hut, onto Van Buren Street.

Abe looks down from his balcony and sees the man stumble up the sidewalk. A disgrace for a man to be drunk this early in the day. A disgrace and a shame. The man stops as if he's lost and Abe wonders for a moment if he has sunstroke, then he sees the trail of blood and the man pirouette in an almost graceful dance before he staggers on.

Evie sees him come back.

Walking all goofy, like he's messed up on glue or paint or something. She looks for the gold ring around his lips but doesn't see any and then she realizes that he's *really* messed up, his pant leg all bloody. He looks at her and this time he doesn't call her "baby," he just says, "Help me, please," and topples at her red shoes.

Evie looks around, don't see nobody but some old man trying to stand up on the motel balcony. She reaches down and slips the wallet from the man's back jeans pocket where it was all snug and tight against the new fabric.

Then she walks up the alley into a thin slice of shadow.

Jerry rolls over.

Toward the sun.

Feels it in his face. It's warm, and good now, because the rest of him is cold and he's shivering.

He looks up at the sweet sun and smiles. Then the world goes white.

BY THE TIME HE GOT TO PHOENIX

BY DOGO BARRY GRAHAM
Christown

for Larry Fondation

Luis wanted to go and get Catboy, but he knew he couldn't. The cops might be watching the apartment, and even if they weren't, they would certainly have forced their way in by now. They would either have taken Catboy to the pound or just ignored him, in which case he would be on the street. Luis fought a temptation to drive around and look for him.

He knew he'd better get out of town right away. At first he thought that the cops would think he'd left by now, so it might be safer to stay put and hide. But where would he hide? Too many people knew what he looked like and might call the cops as soon as they saw him. He knew there would be many *vatos* getting pulled in for questioning and fingerprinting on the off-chance that they might be him. Once he was far from Santa Fe he'd be safer, and safer still when he was out of the state. They'd be looking for him to head for Mexico, but that was okay with him because he wasn't going to Mexico . . .

The place Vanjii moved into was in an apartment complex on Phoenix's west side. There was a public phone out front with a sign that said, in Spanish, *YOU CAN CALL MEXICO FROM HERE.* Someone was always using it. Most of the people in the complex had jobs, some had phones and some didn't, and none of them had any money.

Vanjii shared the apartment with two other people. Carlos, who'd been introduced to her by an old high school friend, had come to Phoenix from Santa Fe to learn to be an auto mechanic. He was hardly ever home. School and work kept him busy during the days and evenings, and he spent many of his nights at his girlfriend's place.

The other roommate was Jaimie. She was a native of the city, and had been doing well in her life until she'd suffered a head injury when a stranger stomped her for no reason that anybody knew of. Now she was frightened all the time, and never left the apartment unless she had to. She would often forget what she was talking about in the middle of a sentence. She worked part-time as what she called a "telephone actress," talking dirty to men who called a phone sex company which patched the calls to her home number.

After paying her rent in advance, Vanjii had less than forty dollars. Her father had given her the money for the rent and the bus trip to Phoenix. She knew it wouldn't be hard to find a job, but she didn't have a car, and the bus service was a joke.

The apartment was on Seventeenth Avenue and Highland, about a mile away from the Spectrum Mall. On her third day in Phoenix, Vanjii walked to the mall and talked a clothing store into hiring her.

The walk to work was dreamlike. Some of the streets had no sidewalks, so she walked in the gutter. Everything seemed too huge, fast, and loud to be real. The cars blasted by, the drivers sometimes yelling at her just because she was walking. She felt so tiny. The only other people she saw walking were homeless, and they always came up to her, and they always said the same thing. *Hey. Hey, I ain't panhandling. It's just that my car ran out of gas a couple miles away, and I lost my wallet, and my wife and kids are in the car, and . . .* Vanjii had nothing she could give them.

The heat didn't seem too bad while she was walking. But when she headed into the mall, with its air-conditioned chill, and sat down, the sweat came out so fast she felt like it was spurting out of her pores. She'd go into the restroom, take off her shirt, and wipe herself down with paper towels, then put on some deodorant. She'd work all day, stopping only to eat the lunch she'd packed. When she walked back home, it would be getting dark and she'd be nervous, but she knew it wouldn't be long until she'd have saved a few hundred dollars and could buy a car.

Vanjii wondered about Luis, but it all seemed so far away that it didn't hurt as much as she'd thought it would.

Luis had been in a bar on Cerrillos Road in Santa Fe when it all started to go to shit. He was talking to a guy about selling a little pot, something to make some quick money, to keep eating and maybe pay next month's rent. It was about 7 in the evening, happy hour in the bar. The place was crowded, and the parking lot was full, so Luis had parked in a small lot across the street.

Luis crossed the street in the darkness and walked into the lot. When he reached his car, he saw that it had been wheel-clamped.

He stood and looked at it. Then he got in the car and sat there. "Fuck!" The word came out on a breath of laughter, but his face was wet with tears. He wiped his face with his hands and sat breathing quietly, trying to get ahold of himself. Then he stepped out of the car and walked around the building, hoping it was still open. It wasn't.

As he moved back to his car, a white man approached him. "Is this your car?"

"Yeah." Luis pointed to the clamp. "I don't get this."

"I did it. I'm Dan Ward, I'm a partner in this company—"

"What company?"

He pointed at the building. "This company. We're a security company. This parking lot's private property."

"I didn't know . . . Sorry. I didn't see no sign."

"It should be obvious that this isn't public parking."

"Yeah. Sorry. I had to meet a guy in the bar over there, I

couldn't find a place to park. I didn't see nobody here, so I thought it'd be okay."

"Well, you can see that it's not."

"Can you take that thing off my car and I'll go?"

Dan Ward nodded. "Sure. If you want to pay me your fine now."

"What?"

"There's a forty-dollar fine for parking here."

"Bullshit. You can't do that. You can't just decide to fine somebody. You can tell me to get out of your parking lot, that's all."

"I'm not interested in a legal debate. I'm telling you there's a clamp on your car, and it's not coming off until you give me forty dollars."

"I don't have forty dollars."

"Uh-huh."

"Honest to God, I got about twenty, and I need that. It's all the money I got."

Ward looked at him and said nothing.

"Look, how about if I give you my address and you can—"

"Yeah, sure." Ward laughed. "How about if you come back here when you've got the money, and you can have your car back."

"Okay," said Luis. "Okay. I'll give it to you now. Here . . ." He reached inside a pocket of his jacket.

When he had the knife out, Luis swung it in a big circle, holding it with both hands, like someone swinging a baseball bat. It went into Ward's body with such force that Luis felt the impact like a car hitting a wall. The momentum threw Luis to the ground and he held onto the knife and tore it across Ward's lower abdomen and then slid it out. Luis jumped back up, still holding the knife, and saw that Ward was running away from him, letting out a noise that sounded like a mule braying. Ward made it a few steps, trying to ignore the things that were spilling out of him. But some of his intestines were trailing on the ground, and when he stepped on them his head seemed to shatter in a scream that never made it past his lips as he fell and the pain swallowed him.

Luis stood over Ward, raised the knife, hammered it into his spine, and left it there. Then he walked to the car, unlocked the door, got in. Blood was dripping from his hands. His body was shaking but he felt calm. He opened the glove box and removed a few things—sunglasses, the break-up letter from Vanjii, the Bulldog .44 she had hated. He put the sunglasses and letter in his jacket pocket and stowed the gun in the waistband of his jeans.

He walked out of the parking lot into the street. As he moved, he felt his wet shirt chafe his skin. There was a 7-Eleven a couple blocks away. It had a phone outside. Luis dropped two quarters into the phone and dialed Miguel's number.

He got voice mail. "Hey, it's me. Something just happened . . . you'll probably hear about it. If you can, come and meet me tomorrow morning at the place where you hurt your ankle that time. Bring me some clothes. Come at around 9 o'clock. If you don't want to, that's okay. Later."

He hung up the phone and walked away. After a few minutes he stopped, turned around, and walked back to the 7-Eleven.

The guy behind the counter was named Randy. He was twenty-two. There were no other customers in the store when Luis walked in, trembling, clothes bloody, blood in his hair, head swiveling, glancing around the place.

"Hey, man, you okay?" Randy asked. "You need an ambulance or something?"

Luis pulled the Bulldog and pointed it at him. "Open the register. Give me the money. Don't touch an alarm or I'll fucking kill you."

"Please don't fucking kill me." Randy opened the register, started taking the cash from it and putting it on the counter.

"Hey! What the hell!"

The voice came from behind Luis. He turned, saw a young woman who had come in the door and was now on her way back out. Her name was Laura, and her two-year-old daughter was outside in her car, fastened into the child seat. Luis pointed and fired. The sound of it concussed the air in the room. The bullet propelled Laura out the door—went in through her lower back, tore through her bladder, and exited through her side. She lay on the asphalt and cried for her child as the life leaked out of her.

"Please don't fucking kill me," Randy said again, but he was leaning over the counter, terrified, pawing at the gun in Luis's hand. Luis fired again, and most of Randy's face came apart.

Luis pocketed all the bills from the register and left the store. He knew where he was walking to, but he didn't know if he would get there before a cop grabbed him. It would depend on how long it took before somebody found the bodies at the 7-Eleven, or the body at the parking lot. Even if that happened soon, he might still make it. He would have to elude the patrol cars, but there was a strong wind blowing, so there would probably be no police helicopters cruising tonight. It was out of his control, so there was no use in worrying about it. Better just to keep walking, stick to the dark residential streets wherever he could, just keep walking, and either he would make it to Hyde Park or he wouldn't.

The stew was bubbling on the stove. Vanjii stirred it with a wooden spoon. It contained beef, carrots, tomatoes, and potatoes, and was seasoned with pepper, garlic, and cumin. Luis had shown her how to make it.

Carlos was out with his girlfriend. Vanjii was going to share the stew with Jaimie, who was in the living room taking a phone call that had been forwarded by the sex line. Vanjii could hear her talking in a put-on, lisping, little girl voice. *"Yeah, honey . . . Feel me contracting my ass around your cock . . . Oh, yeah . . ."*

Vanjii stuck her head in the living room, looked at Jaimie, and mouthed, *Contracting?* Jaimie grinned and shrugged. She had been watching TV when the call came, and she was still watching it, though she had muted the sound. The show was *Beavis and Butt-Head.*

* * *

Curled under a bush in Hyde Park, Luis thought it would be funny if he froze to death during the night.

The place was a preserve of mountain and forest right there in the city. Luis made it there without seeing a cop, and had spent an hour hiking up the mountain in the dark. He stopped near a spot where Miguel had sprained his ankle while walking with Luis about a year earlier. He hoped Miguel would understand his message and show up there in the morning.

It was now around 11. Luis's intentions were simple. He was going to try to rest, and hope he didn't die in his sleep. When he woke, he was going to talk to Miguel, if Miguel showed. If Miguel didn't show, he would have to make another plan, but that was all he had right now.

He was shivering, huddled in his jacket, arms wrapped around himself. Coyotes howled off in the darkness somewhere, and Luis wondered if they would eat him if he died here. He didn't know if he would be able to sleep in such cold, but he soon felt the shivering stop and the drowsiness come. That should frighten him, he thought; Luis had read that people who freeze to death feel like they're pleasantly falling asleep. He knew it should frighten him but it didn't. If this was a taste of the grave, it wasn't bad, it wasn't bad at all.

When he woke up he was cold, but he was alive. He looked at his watch. It was 7 in the morning. He stood up, stretched, took a piss. He wished he had a book to read, something to pass the time. He was still tired, but not tired enough to sleep anymore. He walked around in the woods, sometimes jogging a little, until he was warm. He wasn't hungry, but he was very thirsty.

He wondered if Miguel would come. He wondered why he had told him 9 o'clock, rather than earlier or later. It had just come out of his mouth like that. Several minutes before 9, he headed back to the spot where Miguel had fallen. He wondered if Miguel would remember exactly where it had happened.

Then he heard his friend calling his name.

"Hey," he yelled back. A moment later, Miguel came in sight.

They stood there in the grass among the trees and looked at each other, Miguel in his suit and tie, Luis in his bloody jeans and jacket.

"Jesus Christ, man," Miguel said.

"You hear what happened?"

"Yeah. I didn't know what the fuck you were talking about when I got your message, but it was on the news this morning. Three people, shit . . . Did you really do it?"

"Yeah."

"What *for*, bro?"

"I don't know."

"You don't know. You kill three people but you don't know."

"One guy clamped my car . . ."

"Yeah, it said so on the news."

"And then I robbed the 7-Eleven. But I really don't know."

"I don't even know what to say."

"Thanks for coming here."

"Fuck you. What am I supposed to do, just forget about you?"

"I didn't know if you would."

"That's because you don't know shit." Miguel started to cry.

"I need clothes," Luis said.

"I brought you some, like you asked. They're in my car. Wait here and I'll get them." Miguel walked to the road, got a backpack from his car, headed back into the woods. Luis was now sitting on the ground. Miguel dropped the backpack in front of him.

"Thanks," Luis said.

"You better head for Mexico. There's no way you can beat this. They got you on video at the 7-Eleven, and they got a body laying next to your car. White people. You're looking at death row for sure."

Luis didn't say anything.

"Get to Mexico. You can just disappear there, they'll never

find you. The narcos'll cover your ass if you work for them. But go. You gotta go."

"I know. I'm gonna go."

"How?"

"I'll steal a car."

"You know how to hot-wire?"

"No."

"You gonna kill somebody to get a car?"

"I don't know. Maybe."

Miguel was crying hard. He took out his car keys and threw them at Luis. "Asshole. Asshole. Take my fucking car."

"Miguel . . ."

"Shut up. Take the fucking car. I'm still paying it off, so I guess insurance'll cover it, maybe. I'll wait a couple days before I report it stolen. At least you won't get pulled over driving a hot car."

"Thanks. You know the cops'll probably figure it out that you helped me."

"Fuck them. They got to prove it." Miguel sat down on the ground beside Luis. "Asshole. What happened? I thought I was gonna be best man at your wedding for sure."

"You would've been."

"I know. And you would've been *my* best man. Oh my God. My God."

They sat there together for a few minutes, not looking at each other and not saying anything. Miguel stopped crying, wiped his face with his tie. Then Luis said, "Hey, Miguel?"

"What?"

"Listen, it's gonna be all right. I'm gonna be all right."

"Sure you are."

"No, I mean it. I don't want you to be worried. I don't want you to worry about anything. It'll be all right."

Miguel stood up, and then Luis did the same. Luis held out a dirty, bloodstained hand, and Miguel squeezed it. "You gonna be in touch sometime?" Miguel asked. "At least let me know you made it?"

"Don't worry about anything."

"You got money?"

"Yeah."

"Shit. You got it from the 7-Eleven."

Miguel walked away. He didn't look back.

Luis opened the backpack and searched inside it. There were two pairs of jeans, two T-shirts, a thick shirt, a wool jacket, boxer shorts, socks, a pair of running shoes. He stripped off his own clothes, the cold making his teeth chatter, and put on Miguel's. The shoes were a little bit too big, but they would do. He spat several times on the shirt he had taken off, and used it to wipe his hands and face. He bundled his discarded clothes together and hid them under a bush. Then he picked up the backpack and walked to the road.

Miguel's car was a white Camaro. Luis got in and looked at himself in the rearview. There was still some dried blood on his face and in his hair. He licked his fingers and rubbed it off his face, then ran his fingers through his hair, brushing the red flakes away. Then he put on his sunglasses and started the car.

As he drove down the road into Santa Fe, he saw Miguel walking quickly. He honked the car horn, and Miguel waved a little. Luis watched him in the rearview until he couldn't see him anymore.

He drove at the speed limit to Albuquerque. The car had a quarter tank of gas left. He wondered whether it would be safer to stop at a busy gas station there in town where he might be recognized but probably wouldn't be noticed, or in a quiet one outside of town where he was less likely to be recognized but more likely to be noticed and remembered. Somehow it felt as though a gas station in town would be safer, but he just didn't want to get out of the car, so he pulled onto the I-40 going west and filled up with gas at a place about ten miles out of the city.

He kept thinking about his apartment, about the things it

contained, his plates and cups and skillets, Catboy. His life with
Vanjii. He wished he had asked Miguel to take care of Catboy.

In the early evening, he crossed the Arizona state line. When
he reached Flagstaff, he got on I-17 and headed south, until the
pines gave way to cacti.

When Vanjii got home from work, Jaimie told her that her dad
had called twice. She called him back, and he told her what he
had seen on TV. Vanjii yelled at him, then said she was sorry. She
hung up. Then she found Miguel's number and called it. Miguel
didn't want to talk because he was afraid his phone might be
tapped. He didn't tell Vanjii that, he just said he had to go out
somewhere. She was angry with him, but he called her from a
public phone about ten minutes later and they talked for a long
time.

By the time he got to Phoenix, it was around 8 in the evening.
Luis exited on Seventh Street, turned onto Roosevelt, and followed it to Grand. When he saw the Bikini Lounge, he wanted to
stop there just because it was someplace he had heard of.

The place wasn't busy, even though you could get some
brands of beer for a dollar a bottle, and a pitcher for three dollars.
A guy was deejaying, playing soul standards from the 1970s. Luis
ordered a beer and sat at the bar and listened.

At the beginning of a Curtis Mayfield song, a woman and a
man got up and started to dance, standing right in front of the
deejay's booth. They danced slowly, holding each other close.
The man was balding and the woman had gray in her hair and
Luis somehow knew they had been together for years. It felt like
a knife in his spine.

Jaimie was in the living room working the phone, talking to men
as they jacked off. Carlos, as usual, wasn't home. Vanjii was in the
kitchen drinking coffee and staring at the table. She hadn't told

Jaimie anything, and didn't think she was going to. She didn't even know how to tell it to herself.

A fly landed on the table. It sat there, eyes sending images to the brain, lungs receiving oxygen, heart beating with certainty. Vanjii didn't think, she just slapped with her hand, coming from behind so the fly saw nothing, and then the fly was crushed flat, just a stain on the wood. Vanjii washed her hands and made more coffee. She wondered when she'd be able to cry.

When Luis left the bar, he walked around for a few minutes. At 1 in the morning, it felt hardly less warm than a summer afternoon in Santa Fe. A person slept in every other doorway. Luis wanted to walk farther, but he could find nowhere to head to, so he went to his car.

He was almost out of gas. He stopped at a Circle K on First Avenue and Van Buren. As he was pumping the gas, a guy came up to him. "Hey. Excuse me . . ."

Luis looked at him and didn't say anything.

"Listen," the guy said. "I need a favor. My little girl's sick, and she's on East Fillmore, and I need to go there and see her tonight, but I got no car. If you can just give me a ride up there, I'll give you five bucks for the gas."

Luis didn't question the guy's story, because he could see right through it. The reason the story wasn't more credible or better explained was because the guy was junk sick, and he wanted to go visit his dealer.

"I been asking lots of people, and they all said no. I really need to see her, man."

"Okay," said Luis. "I'll take you there, but I ain't got time to wait for you and bring you back."

"That's okay, that's no problem. I just need you to take me there. Thank you."

The drive took about five minutes. The guy clumsily tried to make conversation, and Luis went along with it. "Okay, right here," the guy said, pointing to an apartment complex. Luis slowed down and the guy got out. "Thanks a lot, man. Really."

"Sure," said Luis. The guy tried to pay him for the gas, but Luis shook his head and drove away.

The neighborhood was nicknamed Gangs R Us, and the cops were going there more and more often, trying to show a presence. Luis passed a police car waiting at a corner. When the cop saw the New Mexico plates, he thought Luis might be either a visitor who'd gotten lost or a drug dealer doing some interstate networking. Either way, he fell in behind him and turned on his lights.

When Luis saw the lights, the panic rose up inside him like vomit, and he fought to control it. He knew Miguel hadn't reported the car stolen yet, but even if it was just that he had a light out or something, the cop would ask to see a driver's license.

Luis pulled over and turned off the engine. He watched the officer get out of the car and walk toward him. When the cop was almost to his window, Luis started the car and took off.

He turned a corner, hit the brakes, jumped out of the car, and ran. He heard the cop car approach behind him. Luis ran harder, shrieking air into his lungs, looking for cover, a place to hide. There wasn't any.

"Hey, asshole! Stop right now or I'll shoot!"

Luis stopped. Raised his hands. Turned around.

The cop had gotten out of his car and was pointing a gun at him. "Lie down and put your hands behind your back."

The concrete warm against his cheek. The handcuffs closing around his wrists.

Madison Street Jail was only a short distance from the bar where he'd spent the evening. He was booked in and fingerprinted and put in a cell.

It was known as the Horseshoe, and it was like no jail Luis had ever heard of. People would be rotated from cell to cell so that they lost track of time. The cells they put him in were completely covered with men. There were men sleeping curled around the toilet that had shit dripping off the sides and piss all around the floor. Men were sleeping on top of other men. Some were using toilet rolls as pillows. They lay on the trash that was scattered everywhere from the sack lunches that were provided. The smell was like a kick in the face by a dirty foot.

No one is sure how long Luis stayed there, but it wasn't very long.

Jeremy Ruvin should have been a cop. He loved cops, and cops loved him. Like many veteran cops, he was a legend in his own lunchtime. But Ruvin wasn't a cop. He was a reporter.

He had spent twenty years at the *Phoenix Weekly*, a free sheet that was distributed throughout the city. It was part of a national chain of weekly papers, and it regarded itself as the only real news outlet in the valley. This wasn't much of a boast; Phoenix was a city without a real newspaper. The main daily, the *Arizona Republic*, was almost devoid of news and existed to further the interests of the corporations that were developing the city. Its rival, the *Tribune*, had a publisher who openly supported the banning of reporters—including the paper's own—from government meetings to discuss whether public money should be given to aid corporate development. A famous local swindler once observed that in Phoenix, when you try to sell people out, they take the first offer.

The *Phoenix Weekly* was a tabloid full of long, turgid stories that few people read. But Ruvin's stories won Arizona Press Club awards every year, and had been doing so for as long as anyone could remember. Although his stories were as slanted as those of his peers, they were packed with lurid detail. The cops gave him access that they gave to no one else. Because, no matter what the facts might be, Ruvin would always make them look good.

This was something they needed. Phoenix was among the leaders of the country when it came to unjustified police shootings. The city had to pay out millions in lawsuits, and more were pending. But in the world of Ruvin, every cop on the force was a heroic figure who only shot or beat up unarmed civilians when it was strictly necessary. He never actually lied in print—he just stayed away from stories that might show the police department as it really was.

Ruvin had few hobbies. The only thing he cared about was his identity as a reporter, and the only people he hung out with were the cops and prosecutors he wrote about. In his mind he was famous, his world a black-and-white movie in which he wore a raincoat and fedora with a tag that read *PRESS*, and talked out of the side of his mouth. He imagined the raincoat and fedora so vividly that when you were in his presence you felt like you could almost see them.

When the cops realized that they had Luis, then realized that they didn't have him anymore, the first reporter they called was Ruvin.

Ruvin and Detective Zack Blantyre had been friends for years. Blantyre had asked Ruvin to write a biography of him, and Ruvin had been sporadically working on it. Now they sat in Durant's restaurant on Central Avenue, and Ruvin asked Blantyre what had gone down.

"We don't know what happened," Blantyre said.

"Zack. You find out you have a triple murderer in your jail. Then you find out he's not in your jail anymore. And you're telling me nobody knows what happened?"

"Okay, off the record—for now, okay . . ."

Ruvin nodded.

"We do know. He just walked out of there, him and four others. Somebody forgot to lock a door, and five of them just walked. We know it happened, we just don't know *how* it happened."

"No matter how I write it, you know that's not going to look good."

"No shit. No shit. I mean, it's not like it's the first time this kind of crap's happened at the jail . . . but a fucking three-time killer? You know as well as I do, most of the guys in the jail are in there because they're fucked in the head and got no money . . . but you get guys like this sometimes. I've been saying for a long time that something like this was gonna happen down there someday if they didn't start hiring people who know which way is up."

"He's from New Mexico?"

"Yeah."

"So what did he come here for?"

"How should I know, Jer? While we're asking stuff, what did he kill three people for?"

"I'll sit on this," Ruvin said. "But I can't for long."

"I'm not asking you to. I just wanted to let you know about it first."

"Appreciated. Look, I'm not gonna wait and eat lunch. I'll get something on the run. I'm gonna head out to New Mexico today."

Luis didn't expect it to work, but when the other guys started to walk out, he simply followed them. And when nobody stopped them, they kept walking. And when they were outside on Madison Street in the sunshine, and the cops who were entering the building ignored them, they split up and kept walking.

Miguel was in his pajamas eating toast for breakfast when the cops knocked on his door. He let them in, they asked him about Luis, and he lied. Then they asked him where his car was, and he knew he was fucked. They let him get dressed before they put the handcuffs on him.

Luis knocked on the door. Vanjii opened it. She was wearing shorts and a T-shirt with the name of the store she worked for on it. She had been getting ready to head out to work.

Her first impulse was to close the door, but Luis pushed it open with his foot and stepped into the apartment. They stood there in the living room looking at each other.

"You gonna kill me?" Vanjii said, her voice breaking.

"What?"

She began to sob. "I don't want to die . . ."

"What would I kill you for? Why would I do that?"

"You killed those other people . . . I don't know . . ."

"You think I would hurt you? You're scared of me?"

". . . Yeah." She looked so small, her face crumpled, tears and snot everywhere.

"You said you knew I loved you and you'd take that where you could get it . . ."

He reached out to touch her. She was too frightened to pull away, so she closed her eyes and cringed violently when he put his hand on her shoulder.

Jaimie came out of her bedroom "Vanj? What's wrong? You okay?"

Luis turned like an animal and ran.

He walked, not trying to hide himself, not trying to stop the sun from burning him. He walked along Camelback until he reached Seventh Avenue, and then he headed south to Encanto Park. It was only a few miles, a distance that would have meant nothing to him in Santa Fe, but the heat of Phoenix made it seem like he was wading through hot water. When he reached the park, his head was spinning and his mouth was as dry as the ground.

He lay down in the shade of a tree and kept still until his vision came into focus. Then he moved around, looking for someplace to get water. The cops had taken all his money. He went up to people and asked them if they'd buy him some water; one guy gave him a couple dollars and told him there was a vendor at the children's play area, Encanto Kiddie Land. He went there and bought a bottle of water and then lay down under another tree and drank it all.

He remembered how Vanjii had looked when she'd cried. He didn't know it, but his own face now looked like hers had, twisted like it might come apart, bawling, snorting, so frightened. He couldn't believe he hadn't known she would be afraid of him. Who wouldn't be afraid of him? He thought about the life he always pretended to himself that he had: cooking, listening to music, driving his car, reading books, talking to his friends, falling in love with Vanjii, taking care of his cat. And he thought about the life he really had: people scared, people hurt, people dead.

Vanjii was sitting on the couch and Jaimie was holding her while she cried. She kept trying to explain what had happened, but Jaimie's head condition made it hard for her to follow because she couldn't remember things. She just kept stroking Vanjii's hair and saying, "It's okay. Nobody's gonna hurt you."

Ruvin didn't have to spend long in Santa Fe. He talked to the cops and asked if they'd let him talk to Miguel, but they weren't Phoenix cops so they wouldn't. Then he walked around the barrio, knocking on doors. Some people told him Luis didn't exist, that he was just a ghost, a legend, a scary story for late at night. Other people gave him names and addresses. He was soon talking to Luis's mother. She didn't have much to tell him in terms of facts, but she gave him plenty of color he could use in his story. About an hour later, he was sitting in a living room talking to Vanjii's father.

As soon as Ruvin left that apartment, he pulled out his cell phone and called Blantyre. He got voice mail. "Zack, it's Jerry. I'm in Santa Fe. Listen up, I've got an address for you . . ." He recited it twice. "It's the address of the kid's girlfriend. They used to live together, and she moved to Phoenix a few weeks ago. He must have gone there to see her. I'm just gonna head to Albuquerque and fly home, so do me a favor—don't do anything until I get there, okay?"

He put the phone away and got in his rental car.

Luis lay on the ground for most of the day, sleeping on and off. He stayed there after the park closed and it got dark. Then he got up and started to walk. It was hard to move. Each step hurt. He knew he needed more water, but he wasn't going to ask anyone for money, and he wasn't going to hurt anyone for it. He walked for two hours, falling a few times, always getting up and walking on.

The apartment door seemed to explode as the cops forced it open. Vanjii, Jaimie, and Carlos were sitting in the living room, and when the cops saw Carlos they pointed their guns at him and screamed at him to get down on the floor. Vanjii and Jaimie screamed back at them. From a safe distance, Ruvin took notes.

Luis couldn't walk any further, and he'd never known where he was heading to anyway. He saw a public phone outside a liquor store, went to it, fumbled in his pocket for the change he had left after buying the water in the park. The call would cost fifty-five cents, and he knew he had a little more than that. He found it and fed it into the machine and dialed.

"Hello?" said Vanjii.

"It's me. Listen, I'm sorry I scared you. I don't want you to be scared . . ."

"Okay," she said, and he heard it in her voice.

"The cops are there, huh?"

"Yeah."

"I'm so sorry, honey."

"I know. I am too." Pause. "You don't sound good."

"Don't worry. Can I talk to the cops?"

"What're you gonna do?"

"I'm just gonna keep on loving you, that's what. That's the only thing I can do. And nobody's gonna get hurt no more. You don't need to be scared no more."

She said something to someone else. He couldn't hear what it was. Then a voice said, "This is Detective Blantyre."

"Yeah, hey, bitch. Fucking listen. Here's where I'm at—Eleventh Avenue and Roosevelt. There's a lot across the street from the liquor store. I'll be waiting for you there."

"What are—"

"Shut your fucking hole. Come on down here so I can kill your white ass." Luis hung up, walked slowly across the street to the empty lot, and sat on the ground.

Vanjii. Vanjii. Vanjii. I'm so scared. I love you and love you and I'm so scared.

A homeless guy wandered into the lot. He came over and tried to talk. "You better get out of here," Luis said. "The cops are coming. It's gonna be bad."

The guy didn't believe him, thinking he just wanted the lot to himself. But then he heard the sirens and knew it was true, and he ran.

There were six cars. Luis was sitting with his back to the wall; the cops stood behind the cars, forming a semicircle around him. They all had guns aimed at him.

Vanjii. Vanjii. He kept bringing her face into his mind, remembered how she looked when she was smiling in the bathtub in candlelight and loving him.

"LIE DOWN ON THE GROUND AND PUT YOUR HANDS ON TOP OF YOUR HEAD! DO IT RIGHT NOW!"

He stood up, flipped them off with one hand, and reached in his pocket with the other, pretending he was grabbing for a gun. He didn't get his hand out of the pocket before the bullets hit him, turning him weightless and throwing him against the wall. It hurt and it didn't hurt and then it hurt again. The cops kept on firing until there were bullet holes even in the soles of his feet, but he didn't know that. He thought about Catboy, and hoped that nobody would be mean to him.

CONFESSION

BY STELLA POPE DUARTE

Harmon Park

Big Boy's real name was Edward Ornelas, but nobody ever called him Edward, because by the time he was ten he weighed in at over 150 pounds. He lived east of Nineteenth Avenue, in the Central Projects, close to the neighborhood where the girl disappeared last October. Big Boy lost twenty pounds once he was put in juvie at age eleven, for shoplifting at Woolworth's, taking things you could buy for nickels and dimes, Batman and Robin plastic figures and a Batman car. The reason he got a term at juvie was because one of the clerks said he had seen him several times lifting things, but couldn't prove it, so due to suspicious behavior, and to teach him a lesson, he was given six months at Boys Town.

His mother Luz, who subscribed to the *Catholic Monitor* and attended meetings of the Sodality of Mary at St. Anthony's, was so ashamed of him, she wouldn't visit him. She had the entire church pray rosaries for the salvation of his soul, and kept a photo of her son on her dresser with a candle burning in front of pictures of saints including one of St. Michael the Archangel with his foot planted on the Devil's neck. Luz's sister, Nena, who didn't subscribe to the *Catholic Monitor*, and could have cared less about sodalities or saints, went to see him with her daughter Atalia, who was a sophomore at Phoenix Central High. Atalia insisted that Big Boy was innocent of stealing the Batman and Robin figures and had been mistaken for another boy, a huge Indian kid nicknamed Squirt.

"He didn't steal anything!" Atalia told her mother as they

drove to see Big Boy. "All he had in his pockets were toothpicks and bubble gum. That guy at the store had it in for him . . . he's always watching the Mexican and black kids. I tell you, this time it was an Indian kid . . . I saw him. Big Boy's nothing but a cry baby. He's probably crying every night in juvie. We should talk to the judge."

"Never mind," Nena said. "Nobody will believe you, just leave it alone, he'll be out soon."

Big Boy was freed from the detention center exactly six months later; thinner, sullen, and reinvested in his life, as his PO, Howard Franco, described it. "Done his time," Franco said at the court hearing. "Now he's ready to take his place in the community, finish eighth grade and move on to high school. Right, Ornelas?" Franco never called him Big Boy, as he didn't think the kids should be identified by anything except a number or their last names.

Luz was there, sitting next to Franco, watching her son one chair away from her. Her eyes filled with tears as she thought of how thin Big Boy had gotten. Maybe she had been too hard on him. After all, he had always been close to her, maybe too close. She worried he didn't like girls, and now she worried maybe he had a boyfriend in juvie. She worried that other boys his age wouldn't be stealing Batman and Robin plastic figures, and maybe his cousin Atalia had been right in the first place—the store clerk had it in for him. She cursed the day Big Boy's father, Edward Sr., had walked out on her to get together with an older woman, a barmaid from the American Legion Hall, the place that boasted a dark, musty bar where Edward Sr. drank himself into a stupor every Friday night. Her boy needed a male figure in his life, she reasoned, and decided to call up Father Leo at St. Anthony's, the most saintly man she knew, to stand guard over her son's life.

Father Leo had a huge bald head, and a smile that went from ear to ear when he was in a good mood. When he was in a bad mood, he shook his fist at whoever happened to stand in his way, assuring them they were all headed for Hell if they didn't take their religion seriously. He could be seen at night walking up and down the sidewalk in front of the church, reciting litanies to honor saints and supplicating for the souls of his disobedient parishioners. It was rumored he had a crucifix in his room with a Jesus hanging on it with real glass eyes that shone in the dark and kept Father Leo company as he lay on his bed weeping over the sins of the world.

When Luz approached Father Leo about taking Big Boy under his wing, he told her he would hear his confession, then asked her to pay the two-dollar fee so he could join the St. Anthony's Boys Club. Most of the club members were altar boys, and were also part of Father Leo's baseball team. Big Boy wasn't athletic, so he told the priest he'd rather just be an altar boy and not play ball, and the priest told him that confession was the first requirement for becoming an altar boy, as boys with ruined souls were unacceptable.

In the dark box that represented the confessional, Father Leo prepared to hear Big Boy's confession one Saturday afternoon, with two skinny girls and their grandmother waiting in line outside the thick curtain that covered the doorway of the chamber. Big Boy's legs felt like two iron rods glued to the vinyl-covered kneeler with its seam ripped open on one end.

The screened panel opened with a sound that made Big Boy jump, and in the dim light he saw Father Leo's profile leaning up against the wire mesh.

"Bless me, Father, for I have sinned," His mouth went dry as he fumbled for the rest of the words. "Ah . . . this is Big Boy."

"Don't tell me who you are!" said Father Leo impatiently. "You're a sinner, that's the only important thing, God doesn't care about anything else." On the other side of the thick curtain, Big Boy heard one of the skinny girls laugh, and he wondered if they were standing close enough to hear what the priest had said.

"Now tell me the truth, did you shoplift at Woolworth's? As you know, *Thou shalt not steal* is one of the Ten Commandments."

"No, Father, I didn't steal, but I wanted to . . . sometimes."

"Well, wanting to is just as bad as doing it. You have to live clean from your heart. The Devil wants your heart, don't you understand?" Then there was a pause, and Father Leo moved closer to the wire mesh screen. "Never mind about Woolworth's," he whispered. "What about that girl who disappeared last year, what do you know about her? She was one of your friends, wasn't she?"

"Who? Nanda?"

"Yes, Nanda. I know how you boys looked at her . . . and now she's gone."

Big Boy's face got bright red in the dark confessional. He felt hot, and shuffled on the kneeler. He knew who Nanda was, all the boys did. She wasn't afraid to let the boys touch her breasts, two huge mounds that grew on her chest, on summer nights at Harmon Park. Usually one of the older boys would end up taking Nanda around the backside of the bathroom stalls, behind bushes that grew next to the concrete wall, and spend time touching her in the dark and doing things that all the other boys wanted to do. Even Simon the Freak had put his hands on Nanda, and he was a kid who didn't even get a hug from his own mother. The boys didn't have to worry about Nanda's father and mother coming by to get her, as her parents were the neighborhood drug dealers. Both were junkies and most nights they were busy entertaining some thugs who drove a black Oldsmobile with a Nevada license plate.

"Were you one of the boys who touched Nanda?"

"No. But I gave her a gift once . . . a little cross."

"The one you stole from Woolworth's?"

"No! It was my sister's, but she didn't want it anymore."

"Well, you still stole it if it belonged to your sister. And why did you give it to Nanda? What did you want? Did you think nasty things about her?"

Big Boy felt his hands sweating, and his heart thumping against his T-shirt. "Yes, I guess I did. But I gave her the gift because she was my friend."

"All the boys were her friends!" said Father Leo. "Don't get smart. Now say ten Our Fathers, and ten Hail Marys as penance. And don't let me hear that you've been stealing again, or thinking nasty thoughts about girls." He mumbled an absolution, and raised his hand in the dim light, blessing Big Boy. Then, with one quick motion, he shut the screened panel.

The next day, Big Boy walked by Nanda's apartment and noticed the black Oldsmobile with the Nevada license plate parked outside on the street. He peaked inside the car and saw a girl's jacket in the backseat. Through the tinted windows he couldn't tell if it was Nanda's. He thought of the girl, of her soft, fleshy breasts, and felt guilty for lying to Father Leo. He had touched Nanda, and had never forgotten how beautiful her skin had felt under his hand. He had kissed her too, because she had told him he could. He had looked into Nanda's dark eyes, stared deep into the luminous pupils, shiny as if she had just shed tears, and he had seen her sadness. Instinctively, he had looked up at the sky, as it seemed to him that a part of Nanda had suddenly taken flight. She had stood in front of him that Sunday night when he was still in seventh grade and she was already in eighth. Just stood there, watching his hand on her breast, as if she was a mannequin, and he could have done anything he had wanted to do. Big Boy had gently smoothed back her hair and hooked the chain with the tiny silver crucifix around her neck. She had smiled at him then, and it was the first time Big Boy had seen the dimples on her cheeks.

Big Boy dismissed the memory of the silver chain from his mind . . . the one he had stolen at Woolworth's. Another lie he had told Father Leo. The clerk had been right, he had indeed lifted things from Woolworth's, including the silver chain he had given to Nanda. She had been happy wearing it, and Big Boy didn't regret taking it.

Nanda wasn't in school the next day, and nobody gave it a second thought. She had been absent many times, and Monday was one of her favorite days to stay home. There was talk that she wouldn't be able to graduate, and would have to repeat the eighth grade. Big Boy hoped she'd fail, so she could be in his class, then he'd get closer to her, maybe be the one who took her behind the bathroom wall at Harmon Park.

Nanda's parents were unconcerned by her disappearance, saying she had the habit of running away to her sister's in Los Angeles and hiding out. She'd be back soon, they said. The truant officer from school stopped by, but could get nothing more from them. They weren't worried, they said, she'd come back, this was normal for her. But the girl didn't come back. She had simply disappeared and people in the projects talked about it every day for months. The girls were glad she was gone, now they had more control over their boyfriends, and their mothers were glad to be rid of her, now their daughters wouldn't be plagued by Nanda's loose ways.

"She's probably pregnant," Atalia told Big Boy one time when she visited with him at juvie. "She's probably somewhere having a baby, and she'll be back after she has it."

"She never told me she'd be leaving," Big Boy replied.

Atalia frowned at him. "I didn't know you were that close to her. Why should she tell you?"

"We were kind of friends," Big Boy said, squirming in his chair. Across the room he saw one of the boys who had touched Nanda one night, pulling down her underwear and making her cry. He looked away, remembering how she had run away, with the boy holding up her underwear like a flag and laughing.

Nanda didn't come back to school, and Big Boy missed her. She had slipped her hand through his after he had linked

the chain with the cross around her neck, and leaned into him.
"You're my best friend," she had whispered. Big Boy remembered
her voice, distant somehow, and still sensed the pressure of her
hand in his, the palm warm, delicate to his touch. He'd thought
of Nanda every night he spent at juvie, and now that Father Leo
had asked him about her, he had started thinking about her all
over again.

Being one of Father Leo's altar boys meant there would be many
rules to follow. Big Boy had to be sure there were enough hosts for
the masses he served, and that the wine was ready in the chalice
when the priest walked into the sacristy. The door to the priest's
closet containing his vestments was to be unlocked, the candles
on the altar had to be lit, and the Bible Father Leo read from
placed on the altar and opened to the reading of the day.

Big Boy felt as if Father Leo could look right through him. He
sometimes saw the priest kneeling down in front of a picture of
the Sacred Heart of Jesus before mass, his face in his hands. He
seemed like he was praying, maybe listening to the voice of Jesus
in his head. Big Boy felt as if the priest was watching him around
the girls who came up to receive Communion during mass. He
had ordered him not to think nasty thoughts, and since that time,
that was all Big Boy thought about. He remembered Quincy, a
black kid from juvie, who had told him all there was to know about
girls, and that real men did it to them, and didn't ask any questions. Big Boy wasn't sure what "did it to them" meant, but he was
hoping to find out, maybe from Ernestina, one of Nanda's friends.

Big Boy had gotten into the habit of watching Ernestina at
school every chance he got, noticing how her sweater plunged
into a V, showing the smooth skin of her neck, and lower still,
to the outline of her breasts, almost identical to Nanda's. He got
his courage up one day at lunch and talked to her at the drinking
fountain, towering over her, even though she was a year older
than him.

"Have you seen Nanda around?"

"Nah, she's gone. Her mom won't say where. I think she went to California." Ernestina took a drink from the fountain and the water dribbled from her lips to her chin and onto her chest. It took all of Big Boy's strength not to reach over and brush the drops of water from her chin and kiss her. She watched him, suddenly tossing her head and laughing out loud at something somebody said to her, then she walked past Big Boy like he wasn't even there.

"I'm so proud of you," Big Boy's mother said to him one Sunday morning at breakfast. "My own son, serving mass! Maybe someday you'll be a priest . . . Yes, I want you to think about it." She picked up Big Boy's three-year-old sister in her arms. "Lizzie can get married and have kids someday, but I want you to be a priest, a saint, like Father Leo. If it weren't for him, I don't know where we'd be. He brought me a food box the other day and had the sodality help me pay the rent. I tell you he's a saint! Now he's watching over you. Franco called him the other day to see how you were doing, and Father gave him a good report."

"Why did my PO call Father?" Big Boy asked.

"I told him Father Leo was as good as your own dad, and better because he's really taking an interest in you, so he put him down as your mentor. I tell you, God's blessing us!"

Big Boy trudged to St. Anthony's that morning to serve 10 a.m. mass, and thought of Father Leo looking through him, reading his thoughts, and now he was talking to Franco.

Walking home after mass, Big Boy decided to go by Nanda's apartment. He walked past the bakery and El Toro Restaurant to cross Central Avenue and get to Nanda's, all the while watching out for any of the boys who normally hung around that section of the projects. Maybe one of them would want to challenge him for coming into their territory, then he'd need a good excuse, or he'd have to fight to get out. He saw no one. It was a spring day, the weather warm. He saw kids playing a baseball game at Harmon Park in the distance, and caught sight of the park's swings, the old rusty merry-go-round, and the bathrooms, the faded walls marked up by gang signs, and he longed for Nanda. He longed to see her one more time, look into her sad eyes, watch her take flight, then catch her in his arms again and fill her with kisses, slowly caressing each breast.

Big Boy noticed the black Oldsmobile parked in front of Nanda's apartment and peered into the car's window, this time not spotting the girl's jacket. He saw boxes in the backseat, luggage and papers strewn around.

"Hey!" yelled a man coming out of Nanda's apartment. "What do you think you're doing? Get away from there!" The guy was tall, over six feet, wearing a jacket in spite of the warm day. He had sunglasses on, and wore a beret cocked at an angle.

"I'm not doing anything," Big Boy answered, "I was just wondering . . . if you've seen Nanda."

"And who would be wanting to know?" asked the guy, walking leisurely up to Big Boy, lighting a cigarette.

"A friend."

"She ain't got no friends . . . cousins maybe, but friends?"

Big Boy felt his stomach cramp as the guy leaned next to the car, puffing on his cigarette. He stuck the cigarette in his mouth as he rolled up his sleeves to show off his tats, blue webs that climbed up his arms.

Big Boy wanted to walk away, disappear like Nanda had, but now that he was so close to this man who had just walked out of her apartment, he was determined to get some information from him.

"Are you from Las Vegas?"

"Yeah, and who wants to know?"

"Big Boy."

"You ain't that big. Nobody's big, we're all the same size. Ain't nobody can outrun a bullet." Then he laughed as he saw Big Boy's face turn pale. "Want a cigarette?"

"Nah, that's okay."

"Ah, yeah, Nanda. Now, there's a girl, if you know what I mean. Now, she's big in all the right places." He laughed again, gruffly. "Right, Big Boy? Is that what you want? Some action?" The guy sneered, then reached into his pocket to take out his car keys. "I gotta go," he said. "Ain't got no time to be talking to big boys who are full of shit. Is Franco your PO?"

"Yeah. How'd you know?"

"Been on the streets all my life. Tell that son of a bitch he owes me. He owes Chano, and I ain't forgot." Then he climbed into the Olds, and Big Boy stood watching the car creep down the street, thinking how Nanda would have looked sitting next to Chano, smoking a cigarette.

Months went by, the whole summer, and other girls joined the boys at Harmon Park—Ernestina and Yvette and a few others who were loud and bossy and played hard to get, but let themselves be caught in the end. Atalia visited Big Boy and told him to stay away from Harmon unless he wanted to get involved with narcos and floozies who did it with everybody. No matter what she told him, Harmon Park drew Big Boy like a magnet, leering at him with memories of Nanda, soft, fleshy breasts, rich warm places inside her he'd like to get to. Sometimes tears crawled down Big Boy's face late at night as he thought of Nanda disappearing like a puff of smoke, and everybody moving on with their lives, as if it didn't matter at all. Maybe she was living in Las Vegas—dancing at a casino. But she was too young for that . . . or maybe she was dead. When Big Boy said the word *dead* in his mind, he flinched, as if he had been hit in the face. *Dead*, her body lying out somewhere in the desert. Big Boy closed his eyes tight to block out the thought.

On the anniversary of Nanda's disappearance, Father Leo called Big Boy into his office.

"Stop moping around about that girl," he said nonchalantly. "I know you're trying to figure out where she is. If I were you, I'd drop it. Clean heart, remember? I think you need another confession, you're way overdue. Confession on Saturday, at 2 p.m. Be there."

"Yes, Father."

"Oh, by the way, Franco says you're almost ready to be released from probation, and I told him you were totally repented— no more shoplifting at Woolworth's. Right, Big Boy?"

"Right."

"You don't want to follow in the footsteps of Chano—you know, the guy who visits Nanda's family sometimes."

Big Boy looked up at Father Leo, surprised that he knew anything about Chano. Maybe he had visited him in prison, or heard his confession. Then he saw Father Leo smile broadly, as if he had just caught Big Boy sneaking a sip of wine from the chalice. He pulled open the drawer on his desk and reached in, taking out a silver chain with a small cross. He watched Big Boy closely, saw the fear in his eyes as the boy glimpsed the chain he had given Nanda in Father Leo's hand.

"I want you to give this to Ernestina," Father Leo said quietly, leaning close to Big Boy. "You understand, don't you?" He waited, dangling the chain in midair between them.

Then he sat back as Big Boy took the silver chain from his hand and dropped it in his pocket.

"Confession on Saturday, don't forget," Father Leo said.

ABOUT THE CONTRIBUTORS

MEGAN ABBOTT is the Edgar Award–winning author of *Queenpin*, *The Song Is You*, and *Die a Little*, as well as the non-fiction study, *The Street Was Mine: White Masculinity in Hardboiled Fiction and Film Noir*. She is the editor of the collection *A Hell of a Woman: An Anthology of Female Noir*. Her fourth novel, *Bury Me Deep*, is loosely based on the Winnie Ruth Judd "Trunk Murderess" case from 1930s Phoenix.

Sherry Busbee

ROBERT ANGLEN is an investigative reporter for the *Arizona Republic* who has been nominated three times for the Pulitzer Prize; in 2005, the Arizona Press Club named him journalist of the year. Born in Los Angeles, he has worked as a skip tracer, bill collector, cab driver, and process server. His stories have appeared in newspapers, magazines, and several anthologies, including *Night Terrors* and *Diablo*. He and his wife are parents of triplets.

Mary Reagan

LEE CHILD, the author of twelve best-selling novels, has been a television director, union organizer, theater technician, and law student. He was born in England but now lives in New York City, and leaves the island of Manhattan only when required to by forces beyond his control.

DAVID CORBETT is the author of three critically acclaimed novels: *The Devil's Redhead*, *Done for a Dime* (a *New York Times* Notable Book), and *Blood of Paradise*—which was nominated for numerous awards. His short fiction has appeared in numerous anthologies, including *San Francisco Noir* and *Las Vegas Noir*, and he contributed a chapter to the world's first serial audio thriller, *The Chopin Manuscript*. Corbett lives in Vallejo, California.

Stella Pope Duarte

STELLA POPE DUARTE has won two creative writing fellowships from the Arizona Commission on the Arts, for *Fragile Night* and *Let Their Spirits Dance*, her highly acclaimed debut novel. Duarte has won honors and awards nationwide, and her most recent novel, *If I Die in Juárez*, is the story of the over 400 young women brutally murdered in Ciudad Juárez. Currently, she teaches creative writing for an assortment of college, university, and community-based programs. She lives in Phoenix.